# AN OPEN SECRET

CARLOS GAMERRO

# AN OPEN
# SECRET

Translated from the Spanish by
Ian Barnett

PUSHKIN PRESS
LONDON

Original text © Carlos Gamerro
English translation © Ian Barnett 2011

*An Open Secret* first published in Spanish
as *El Secreto y las voces* in 2002

This edition first published in 2011 by
Pushkin Press
12 Chester Terrace
London NW1 4ND

ISBN 978 1 906548 48 3

*Work published within the framework of "Sur" Translation Support
Program of the Ministry of Foreign Affairs, International Trade and
Worship of the Argentine Republic*

Cover Illustration  *Cumulus Clouds above Road Patagonia  Argentina*
© Eastcott Momatiuk

Frontispiece  Carlos Gamerro
© Thomas Langdon

Set in 11 on 14.5 Monotype Baskerville
by Tetragon
and printed in Great Britain on
Munken Premium White 90 gsm
by TJ International Ltd, Padstow, Cornwall

**www.pushkinpress.com**

*The English version of this novel is dedicated to the memory of Anthea Gibson (1941–2010), who made it happen.*

# AN OPEN SECRET

*To speak is to lie—*
*To live is to collaborate.*

William S Burroughs

# Chapter One

"A MURDER IN A SMALL TOWN."

"Why here of all places?" asks Mati.

"It's the only small town I know."

"Is that why you've come back?"

"And to see you all."

"So what's it going to be? A film?" enquires Mati again.

"Or a book. Not sure yet," I reply.

Don Ángel's third call to table spares me from giving any further details:

"Dinner's ready *che*! I know you've got some catching up to do but do it later."

"Fefe I look at you and I swear I can't believe you're really here," blurts Guido, who's so far said next to nothing. "How many years has it been?"

I'm slow to answer because I'm hauling myself up from the sofa, whose springs my body has recognised with consummate ease, as I eye the souvenirs of trips to Europe and the Middle East that the current occupants of the house have never made, and rediscover the roughness of the old tiles under my feet—the furniture, the ornaments, the floors of the house that used to belong to my grandparents until their lifelong neigh- bours, the Tuttolomondos, bought it from them. "I'm back in Malihuel," I say to myself in mild amazement. "Back in Malihuel."

"'Bout twenty isn't it?" I eventually reply.


"So you want to write about Malihuel do you? Someone's already written a hydrographic survey on the lagoon, donkeys' years ago, 'bout roughly … When was it Nene?"

On the corner of the main street and the one variously known as Post Office, Phone Centre, Courts or Yacht Club Street stands the most traditional bar in Malihuel, Los Tocayos, whose current landlord, Don Porfirio Dupuy, is a direct descendent of one of the two Hipólitos that opened the original establishment. Three blue doors on the main street and two on the other provide access to a vast vertical expanse of sea-green walls, barely alleviated by their lining of varnished wood cladding, the framed photos of Don Porfirio's pampered pups, the trophies from the Colón dog track and a Chinese imitation antique clock. The premises are L-shaped, with a billiard table and two Foosball tables at the far end of the long arm, and the bar tables in the short one and the elbow, evidently arranged around the one presided over night in night out by Don León Benoit.

"Nineteen seventy-three," the waiter answers without hesitation.

"Nene's our walking encyclopaedia, there's only Professor Gagliardi knows more than he does. And there isn't much

14

in it mind. Is it something like that you're going to write?"
Don León asks.

"No," I counter.

"He's a real writer," Guido sitting next to me sets him
straight. "He writes stories, novels ... Literature," he adds,
in a nutshell.

"Oh, we've got that here too. If it's literature you're interested in I imagine you'll have read *His Honour's Dream*,
it's set right here in Malihuel, tells the whole story of our
foundation it does. No there's a lot been written about
this town believe you me, don't write us off, the other
towns hereabouts may be bigger but they don't have our
history. We've been here since colonial times you know.
The lagoon's right there on the very oldest maps. The
Northern Frontier ran through here. Indian territory back
then. We suffered several raids, and the civil wars to boot.
There was a fort here razed to the ground by none other
than General Lavalle himself, on his way north. We've
got history to burn here. 'A town of two centenaries,' as
the song goes. So it's literature is it? I was told you were
interested in geography or ecology, goodness knows why.
Who was it told me Nene?"

"Licho."

"See where idle chatter gets you? And there was I finding
out about the chemical composition of the lagoon water,
which as you know is highly medicinal. Is that any use?"

"Careful, he'll try and rope you into the beach-resort business next," Guido chimes in, and Don León smiles.

"The town'll go back to living off the lagoon again one
day, and then they'll have to put up a statue of me right next

to the Comandante's. Now there's a tale to be told, the one about the Comandante's statue."

"Right, sure," I nod. "I had something more recent in mind though from the last I dunno twenty years at the outside," I say, and then, sensing or imagining a buzz of alarm, I explain: "It'll be a work of fiction though, right, not a document? I mean the town in my story'll have lots in common with this one, the setting, the lagoon, that kind of thing, but … "

It wasn't as easy to explain as I'd first thought.

"I'm even going to change the name so there won't be any mix-ups, you know, people coming up to me afterwards saying no it isn't like that, it wasn't like that at all … I'm going to change the name," I repeat.

"Uh-huh," Don León remarks. "And what are you going to call it if you don't mind me asking?"

"Malihuel," I reply. "The town in my story's called Malihuel."

"CRIMES HERE IN MALIHUEL as I can remember … Can you remember any Vicente?" Don Ángel asks his brother.

"There was that one case ages ago now, you weren't even born," Vicente replies. "That business at the Arana Hotel. Remember?"

"Do I. The number of times I must've heard it. You know how it goes don't you Fefe?" Don Ángel asks me.

"Mamá used to make me check under her bed every night to make sure Señora Arana's killer wasn't there. In Buenos Aires as well!" I answer.

"Travelling fabric salesman he was, I met him once," Vicente's voice starts up but is overtaken by his brother's.

"Don't know about under but definitely on top. Most people reckoned the salesman was just the lover and it was the husband who … " He stabs the air with his knife. "Anyway they ended up pinning the dead wife on the guy. Two birds with one stone Arana killed. Closed the hotel not long after that and scarpered. You can still see the walls out in the Colonia opposite the station. You taken him to see it yet Mati?"

Don Ángel is sitting at the head of the table at the welcome dinner the Tuttolomondos have laid on for me. Naturally, I've been accorded one of the places of honour at his side; his elder brother Vicente, the other.

"We could drop by tomorrow afternoon if it dries up a bit," answers my inseparable childhood friend, Mati, sitting next to me. The days I spend in Malihuel I'll be staying at his house, which had belonged to his parents until they bought my grandparents' house.

"The roads in the Colonia are impossible when it rains," Don Ángel confirms. "Is it something like that you're going to write Fefe?"

"Something like that," I lie. "A crime novel I thought. I thought it would be a good idea to set it here in Malihuel. You know … crime committed in Malihuel, population three thousand, everyone knows everyone else, no outsiders in town that night. So the murderer's got to be one of them. Everyone suspects everyone else. Or maybe it's a conspiracy the whole town's in on."

"You're unlikely to get anyone in this town in on anything," quips Guido, philosophically buttering a roll and asking his

17

brother with a nudge of the elbow and a flick of the eyebrows to pass the salt. Mati obliges with a growl.

"'Specially when there are people who can't even get on with their own family don't you reckon?" Don Ángel spears a last mouthful of *pionono* with his fork after speaking. Guido chews his buttered roll and shrugs.

"Can I get you another slice Fefe?" asks Celia, who's been doing the second round of the table with a serving dish and a portion poised between spoon and fork. She smiles at me with her whole face—mouth, eyes and wrinkles—every time she looks at me or talks to me. She's extremely happy to see, me that much is plain. I hadn't noticed she was so fond of me as a boy. Or maybe I'd forgotten.

"Thanks, I'm fine for now." I never was much one for *pionono*. That sickly sweet taste … "I'll save myself for the spaghetti," I add flatteringly. "Nearly twenty years I've waited for this moment. Never tasted pasta like it all these years."

"And you never will either now the multinationals have bought up all the big factories. Ours is only still scraping by 'cause it's so small," nods Don Ángel gesturing with his fork at a spot on his empty plate, which his wife covers with the slice I've just turned down. "Pour Fefe another glass of wine will you Guido seeing as you always have it handy. So we haven't got much for you to go on as you can see. It's a quiet town this is, everyone knows everyone else. People's doors are always unlocked, we leave our cars in the street with the keys in."

"A hen goes missing around here and the whole town's up in arms," intervenes Mati and as nobody laughs at his quip I decide it must be more proverb than wit.

"Exactly," I say. "A crime in a place like this would be far more dramatic. Nobody could ignore it."

"SO WHY DID YOU CHOOSE US? I mean there are so many towns in the province," Don León wants to know now.

"I used to come here as a boy," I reply. "Every summer. That's how Guido and I know each other."

"He's Echezarreta's grandson," Guido chimes in. "Poli's son."

"Echezarreta, your grandfather? Why didn't you say so in the first place? I remember your grandfather well, I remember your mother too. The whole town was terribly upset at the news of her passing. She'd left as a young woman in in ... When was it Nene?"

"Nineteensixtytwo," I beat Nene to it. That was an easy one to remember. It was the year I was born.

"So, Echezarreta's grandson eh? Well well. I've always said your grandfather was the best mayor this town's ever had. Wretched luck his illness. He still had so much to offer. And your dear grandmother?"

"She moved to Rosario remember?" Guido asks him.

"Course I remember, I was asking after her state of health."

"She's fine," I answer. "I dropped in to say hello to her in Rosario on my way here. We hadn't seen each other since Mamá's funeral. She doesn't get about much any more."

"WASN'T THERE THAT case in the days I used to come here about some lad or other, what was his name, who had this problem with someone from town or some neighbouring town, I can't really remember?" I take a pull of wine and blurt out without looking at anyone.

"Know of a case like that Mati?" asks Don Ángel archly.

"About a hundred," his son replies with the same wry chuckle I used to find so winning. "If you can't provide more details ... " he says to me.

"They were both from the town's older families; one, the older one, had *estancias* all over the area and they used to say he had the other one killed because he was—"

"Ezcurra," Guido, laconic from chewing, finishes my sentence for me over the head of his brother, who snaps at him:

"It's not certain he was killed."

"No he just upped and buried himself in Villalba's pigsty and pops out every now and then to light some candles for himself," lunges Guido after swallowing.

"That's for the miracle-loving spades that is. Maybe you go and ask him too," his brother parries.

"Don't start, *che*," their father reprimands them from the head of the table, but Guido's already turned around to explain to his grandfather what the argument's about and the remark sails past him. After serving her grandchildren and daughters-in-law at the other end of the table, Celia finishes her waiting duties and sits down beside her father, who's no doubt repeating to her what Guido's just told him. In spite of coming from almost the other end of the long table, I can't help noticing the intense, almost concerned gaze she casts in my direction.

"So who was he this Ezcurra?" I ask anyway.

"EZCURRITA, YES. Course I remember. From one of Malihuel's highest families, the Alvarados, he was, and the Ezcurras of Rosario. High up a greasy pole they were in those days," says old Don León with a cackle the others smile at out of politeness or approval, "'specially after his father went bankrupt, a good thing old man Alvarado had the measure of his son-in-law and left all his earthly goods to his daughter and grandson. Those two were a real pair. His mother with her frocks from Buenos Aires and her trips to Europe, and Ezcurrita may've been tied to her apron strings but in another way he took after his father, always some big business deal in the pipeline that was about to earn him a hatful and show us once and for all who he was, always about to take up some big post with his friend the governor or his uncle the deputy or his cousin the councillor—he lowered his expectations over the years—always about to leave this town of losers for good. Bye bye losers, he'd say every time he left, and when he came back not a peep. You saw him didn't you Licho that time he gave us the finger from the Chevallier bus."

"No not me," the new arrival whistles through the bristles of his moustache and the gaps in his teeth. "It was you as told me."

"There you go. A finger. Who *hasn't* left Malihuel is what I'd like to know. Eh? But a good dog always comes when called, ain't that the truth. And he always came back Ezcurra did, honking the horn of a new car in broad daylight if things'd gone well or more often than not skulking in the back of the Chevallier bus in the small hours when they hadn't. We'd have him back at this table the next day sitting in the chair you're sitting in now, cool as you like, shrugging off

21

wisecracks and bumming cigarettes, coming out with things like You know, the pull of home ... the old lady—and with a wink—my dear friends. Beto here was one of the gang, he can tell you better than me," concludes Don León as his cellphone starts ringing.

"Los Jaimitos they used to call us"—Beto Iturraspe, a talkative, theatrical lad whose fifty plus years only show when tiredness or distraction slacken his youthful rictus, struggles to speak over the stentorian tones of Don León addressing his daughter—"and we liked the name, so it stuck. There were four of us—an ideal number for a hand of truco, the table at the current establishment and a night on the razz in the one car, either Bermejo's Torino or Batata Sacamata's Chevy Coupé—should be here any minute—orange it was, used to look after it a treat, I don't know if you ever got to see it? Bermejo, Batata, Ezcurrita and me," he muses wistfully, looking resignedly at the other three sides of said table, currently usurped by Guido and Licho and myself. "In the summer our days used to start after siesta, a couple of beers under the pines at the island bar, and when the heat let up, a stroll down the public beach to check out the birds and lay some plans for the night ... Then we'd drop in here and Bermejo, who'd spent all afternoon getting the nightclub ready, would join up with us—"

" ... The infamous Sucundún, corruptor of the Malihuel night," I chime in. "The girls had to leave their virginity at the door from what I heard."

"They used to get it back on their way out rest assured, apart from the odd one that forgot to visit the cloakroom," ventures Iturraspe with a wink.

"What became of Bermejo? Is he still around?"

"Uh-uh"—Guido shakes his head. "He opened a new place in Fuguet where there are enough brothels to deflect the sanctimonious wrath of the female congregation."

"After that we'd move on to the vermouth and play a few hands of truco, it depended, if there was no show on at the lagoon we'd keep going till dinner—the lagoon hotel, of course, where else. At weekends there was always a tango orchestra belting it out or a quartet that could do the odd rock number, or sometimes even a Charleston or jazz band from Rosario. By the small hours the four of us'd invariably be round at Bermejo's sucking on our private bottles and the slags we'd picked up down by the lagoon and when there weren't any going Bermejo'd always come up with a bit on the side to peck at. The first ray of daylight was the sign to leave whatever the night had washed up, in the weeds or the back seat, or if there was any money and the chick was worth it, the mirrored room at the Mochica Motel, and the Torino or the Chevy burning rubber at ninety or a ton ten with the windows down and the cool dawn air clearing our hangovers, waving back at the farmhands and foremen riding their horses to the only brothel in Fuguet or the two or three in Toro Mocho, where there was never any shortage of girls so well-behaved you never needed to argue the toss even over the money. Unless Ezcurrita was around that is. They'd fight to be with him then."

"You remember"—the recent arrival Jaimito Batata Sacamata is bellowing and roaring with laughter—"the time Nori or Dori or Flori—Titín's cousin from Elordi, the one as married Kyke Brofman—was waiting for us in the front seat and Ezcurrita, who'd never seen her before, got in the back, tapped her on the shoulder and went Hi gorgeous, and the bag turned round and grinned at him?"

"Don't say a word. You forgot your make-up"—Iturraspe revives the deceased's quip. "No there was nobody faster than him. And that time we all boned that Otamendi girl? We cut for it and the lucky bastard got to go first as usual and when he comes out he tells me to fetch the razor blades and there's me going What are you talking about you pillock and when I go in the sonofabitch'd left her face down for me on purpose, brother her back was so hairy I had to flip her over to make sure she wasn't a truck-driver!" sighs Iturraspe wiping the tears from his eyes with his index finger and there's me smiling in agreement and Guido nodding and Nene Larrieu leaning on the counter with his tin tray handy and a face that says he's heard it all before.

"THE TOWN PLAYBOY he was, Malihuel's very own Isidoro Cañones. Boy did I know Darío well. We were at high school together till they threw him out that is in second or third grade I think, can you remember Vicente?"

His brother interrupts a fork of spaghetti halfway to his mouth and stares wordlessly at him over the rim of his glasses as if to remind him that none of the elder brothers, set to work by their father at the age of thirteen, have had any access to higher education.

"What about you Celia?" he shouts over to the other end of the table and gives me a wink. But I realise from his tone that the question's barbed.

24

"What?"

"Fefe wants to know about Ezcurra. You got anything to tell him?"

Celia smiles with her mouth only. Her eyes on the other hand seem to express puzzlement or pain. The years had tamed Celia. When I was still a boy she was capable of throwing a fit worthy of a cornered animal, smashing the empty plates she couldn't serve until Ángel arrived, shrieking I want to get out I can't stand it any more I'm dying in this shit hole and nobody cares, and from my place as a guest I'd watch Guido and Mati out of the corner of my eye while they stared autistically at their glasses of Coke, waiting with bovine patience for the storm to pass, which was never very long as Celia had to sweep up and wash her face before the return of her husband, who now insists:

"It's the women in town that remember him best. Half of them because he didn't let them get to the altar as virgins, the other half because he did"—his guffaw finds an echo in the wan smiles of his brother and his son Mati, who now asks me:

"Do you think the house looks any different?"

I find the change of subject annoying so I try not to elaborate.

"Well we didn't have this room for a start when my grandparents lived here," I say referring to the gallery of wood and glass they've built where the old fig tree used to stand. Murderers, I think to myself. "Then there's the pool. The rest's pretty much the same isn't it? Grandma left you all her furniture didn't she?"

"Well she couldn't very well have taken it all to Rosario." Mati defends himself as if I've accused him of something.

Maybe it's something in my tone of voice; we don't seem to get along as well as we used to. Luckily, after spearing and bolting down two balls of spaghetti, his father picks up the thread:

"Now they really hated his guts. Your grandparents I mean. Ezcurra. They used to cross the street to avoid him."

I've just forked in the last mouthful of spaghetti—*Number Three Pasta Nests* I was told when served—so I can't answer straight away, but by the time I finish swallowing I've been overtaken by a vision of the past, the first of many—perhaps too many—I'll experience during my stay in Malihuel. I'm walking along the shaded side of the street holding my grandmother's hand, playing at jumping from one broken flag to another without stepping on the grass, when I suddenly find myself being dragged into the blinding sunlight on the other side. Walking towards us is a smartly dressed young man who, clearly amused at the situation, directs a sardonic smile at my grandmother and, from beneath his raised sunglasses, a conspiratorial wink at me. I look up at my grandmother's face and it's flushed with rage, paralysed between the urge to lash out and the glaring vow never again to direct another word to the man whose white-clad back now recedes nonchalantly into the shadows he's just made his. And my grandfather, that or some other day, slamming his fist on the lunch table and choking on his bean stew spluttering "That sonofabitch! He'll get what's coming to him that sonofabitch will!"

"Fancy a little more Fefe?" Celia's voice startles me from behind.

"No, thanks, I'm full," I tell her. So that was Ezcurra. I'm getting something now, a picture at least.

"Still eat like a bird I see. I remember that so clearly. You never did use to eat much and always put lots of salt on your food. Remember Papá how much salt he put on everything?"

"Do I? We used to have to fill the salt cellar every time he came to dinner," Don Ángel slaps me on the shoulder. "Fefe you sonofagun, we thought we'd never see you again!"

"The stuff life throws at you eh?" I mumble idiotically while Celia clears the table with the help of Guido's wife, and Mati's wife cleans up her children's mess, the youngest of whom asks her for the nth time that night, "Who's that Mamá?" and she gives him an answer I never quite catch.

"What about the other one?" I say.

"Which other one?" Don Ángel comes back.

"The one who had him killed ... or run out of town," I add out of deference to Mati, who's just back from the bathroom. "Who was he?"

"Old Rosas Paz?" he asks me as he sits down. "Owned half the county he did. His heirs have carved it up now. Didn't you see their town on your way here? It's the stop before as you come in from Rosario. Rosas Paz it's called, just like them."

I nod and insist:

"So why did he take it out on Ezcurra?"

Don Ángel takes the floor:

"The feud between them went back a long way, maybe even to before Ezcurrita was born," he explains as the women start serving dessert, a home-made flan with *dulce de leche*, which Celia's good memory has prepared especially for me. "Ezcurrita's grandfather, Don Alejandro Alvarado, used to buy the wheat crop off Don Manuel's father—or was it Don Manuel's grandfather? Can you remember Vicente?

27

It makes no difference, the moment these fights between families start nobody remembers how … The Alvarados owned the mill over by the station. Errrm, let me see, till around nineteen thirty I reckon. Old man Alvarado got fed up of the anarchists always walking out on him and set fire to it. They can go to Alcorta and cry for all I care was the memorable phrase he came out with the next day. You could see the flames from here my father used to say. He always remembered that day because they had to get their flour from Toro Mocho after that. Old man Alvarado cashed in the insurance money and set up a convenience store … on the square on the side where the soda factory is today. Have you taken him to see it yet Mati? The mill I mean … Theeey're the ones, where the steel-grey silos are. The whole lower part of the building—the brickwork—was salvaged from the old mill. If you look carefully you can still see the scorch marks. Apparently there were some wagons of grain too that belonged to Don Manuel parked right there on the tracks and one of the explosions from the blaze set light to them … Old man Alvarado couldn't admit responsibility of course, he wasn't about to go and tell everybody he'd torched the mill himself, and of course then it was open war. That, as far as anyone can tell, is where Don Manuel's beef with old man Alvarado started. And with the grandson … I reckon it started when Ezcurrita took up as a journalist. Before that, I've no idea. It was just like Ezcurrita to take up journalism and set about savaging Don Manuel just for kicks," says Don Ángel.

"Ezcurra, that's right, poor lad. Making a film about his life are you? Oh, because I was told … I remember his newspaper articles well. Don Manuel Rosas Paz used to collect them and keep them in a binder he was more reluctant to show than the Church with the Turin Shroud," some days later the bald skull of Malihuel's pharmacist Don Mauro Mendonca will beam, greenish in the neon light from outside. They called me from the *estancia* once—urgent; I shut up shop there and then and drove the medicine over myself. My reward, once Don Manuel was back on his feet, was to see it. It was a legal double-ring binder, I can't really remember if the covers were black or not, more of a blue colour I think, difficult to say after so many … I don't seem to … of course of course. Right. The newspaper cuttings were stuck on card and kept in plastic envelopes to protect them. A quick glance through wasn't enough, no—line by line I had to read them while he sat there the whole time watching me, frowning over his oxygen mask and wheezing. I clearly remember there being several blank pages at the end of the folder, in plastic envelopes too, awaiting any future articles. You'll understand, he said to me when I closed it and handed it back to him, the boy leaves me no choice. If I don't do something now it'll be too late, he added, and I realised his haste had less to do with the blank pages than with the blue cylinders containing what was left of his life and with the intolerable idea of him going first and leaving the other to dance on his grave. What I want, he said to me on my way out, is to burn that folder and forget there was ever a time when anyone could even *think* that of me. He didn't need to explain," the pharmacist will explain, the

29

green of his skull deepening as the rain starts to fall on the other side of the pharmacy window, "the prerequisite for him to carry out that private and perhaps melancholy auto-da-fé. I think deep down he may eventually have developed a fondness for the binder don't you? I mean if you'd seen the precautions he took when he handled it. Perhaps he was disappointed the articles had stopped appearing, because it had been something like a year by then since poor Ezcurra had decided to toe the line and stop poking his nose into his business. Perhaps Rosas Paz decided to do something when he realised how futile it was to go on waiting. What? Errrm, I don't know, he must just have burnt it, unless he asked to have it buried with him. The articles were from a newspaper that's closed now, what was it called, let me see … "

"*La Chicharra*," I'll tell him, being in possession of them by then. "I managed to lay my hands on quite a few. Ezcurra had a special talent for headlines it seems."

## THERE'S A ROTTEN SMELL IN MALIHUEL

"WHERE DID YOU GET THIS?" I jubilantly ask Guido the evening he stops by with the gift after his pasta deliveries around the towns at our table in Los Tocayos, where, a few days after my arrival, I'm now one of the regulars.

"Toro Mocho," he proudly replies. "Finished my deliveries early and thought I'd pop into the library. They didn't have the complete collection but it should do for now. I'll take you with me if you want to go yourself one day … Yeah, I only photocopied the pages about Malihuel. They were the ones Ezcurra wrote weren't they Beto? Iturraspe nods

and beckons to me with jutting chin to let him take a look. I
hand him one of the identically headed pages at random—

*LA CHICHARRA*

A WAKE-UP CALL FOR THE COMMUNITY

"Is that Ezcurra?" I ask him.

I'm pointing at the signature at the foot of the daily leader—
"*BROKEN CHAINS—A HORSEFLY TO GOAD THE FLANKS OF
THE SLEEPING MULE OF MALIHUEL.*" Iturraspe nods with a
nostalgic smile.

"Listen to this, listen," I insist, including Nene Larrieu,
who puts his cloth for polishing the glasses on the counter
and walks over intrigued. "'This pampas plutocrat, whose
legendary family fortune has been built on the blood of
Indians and Christians and the tears of orphans and widows,
now wants to usurp one of the high seats of office to which
this most fertile of provinces elevates its favourite sons. And
what credit, what merit, what service to his country or his
native soil does this self-proclaimed lakeside Pericles, this
Lycurgus of the plains, this Santa Fe Solon set before us to
show he is worthy of such an honour? The gallantry and
punctiliousness of that Rosas Paz who paid a pound apiece
for Indian ears, which his devoted great-grandson still keeps
in a glass case in his study as a family relic? Who, moreover,
does he suppose will support his hilarious candidature with
their votes? The descendents of the proud gauchos banished
to the frontier for the sole crime of wanting to work the
land that this hypertrophied Orion wanted for his cattle?
The grandchildren of immigrants, easily gulled in their new
tongue, who naively accepted provisional deeds of ownership

31

for land that, once rendered productive by the calluses of their hands and the sweat of their brows, would be wrested from them by the lawyers of our aspiring cereal Cicero? Santa Fe must indeed be saintly in its faith if we are willing to place the lofty fate of our province in his hands. Will the town of Malihuel, which legend and history have enshrined as the Fuenteovejuna of Santa Fe, consent to kissing the clay feet of this golden calf?' Where *did* he get that style from?" I ask when I finish reading.

"Rosas Paz's own speeches," comes Iturraspe's incisive reply, puncturing the rhetorical force of my question, "in the days when he was running for senator in the province. Listen to this one—'obviate' … 'laudable' … 'moral prostration' … 'emolument' … 'sempiternal'!" he exclaims triumphantly. "I'd forgotten that one," he smiles as if he's just bumped into an old friend.

"What about this?" I ask incredulous in my mirth: "'Are we in need of a new Christ to visit Malihuel, scourge in hand, cast out the merchants from the temple and lash new stripes into the hides of these ruthless pampas tigers … '"

"Oh now that one bears the hallmarks of Professor Gagliardi," pronounces Iturraspe. "He used to lend Ezcurra the odd hand with the articles. We all did actually. We'd meet up here say and put words in his pen. That bit about the lakeside Pericles was mine, for example. Used to split our sides laughing I swear. We never thought it would end so badly."

Unable to stop I read on:

"'In these days of quick capitulation and shameful moral surrender, one man stands erect, immune to the corrosive gilding of corruption. And that moral fortitude, neither consumed nor undermined, let it be called "quixotic" by the self-righteous revellers in self-seeking lucre, a herd of bimanous pachyderms, quick of tooth and castrated of conscience ... ' Are you telling me someone could have taken this seriously enough to have its author wasted?" I finally exclaim.

"If there was one thing old Rosas Paz didn't have," Iturraspe replies, less cheerfully this time, "it was a sense of humour."


THAT NIGHT I'D HAVE TIME to read through the rest of the cuttings. The anachronistic anarchist rhetoric of the early articles lasted a few more months and would occasionally resurface, but it was becoming more and more obvious that Ezcurra had found a new style, albeit not of his own making. It was still broadly in the same spirit; it was the diction and the emphases of certain turns of phrase that had changed spectacularly. Rosas Paz had become an "exploiter", an "oligarch", a "sepoy", a "traitor", an "imperialist", and his victims, the "suffering people", the "working class", the "shirtless", the "poor" and the "proletarians". Ezcurrita was learning a new language and, like children or foreigners, in his enthusiasm he sometimes applied words haphazardly to all kinds of situations and objects. Then suddenly, nothing. In his last year working for the paper: *National School No 7 Celebrates Golden Jubilee—Malihuel Girl Named Provincial Honey Queen—Outstanding Performance From Two Messenger Pigeons—A Circus Worth Seeing.* Toeing the line. The dates said it all; the only unfathomable thing was that, after putting up with all those weighty allegations, Rosas Paz should've wanted to do away with him when he was only writing about basketball tournaments and school shows. I put down the wad of articles at my bedside and lie there staring at the shelf of their cuddly toys in the children's room, where I've been lodged, forcing them out to camp in the living room. Through the wall I can hear Mati and his wife locked in an argument that their confinement and the need to keep it down make all the bitterer and more exasperated. I can't hear the words but I know I'm the cause.

"WHEN THINGS STARTED GETTING UGLY," Don Ángel continues between mouthfuls of flan and *dulce de leche*, "I don't know if they'd been tightening up on Ezcurrita at the paper or what but he certainly learnt from his mistakes and as far as I can remember he never picked on Rosas Paz again. Tried to stop before all hell broke loose. But it was too late by then wasn't it. The damage had been done. Know what it reminds me of?"

"A CHIHUAHUA YAPPING at a Great Dane through the railings." Don León hands me the same version shortly after he and Licho join the table, order a Ferroquina and flick through the sheaf of photocopies. "And now the gate's open the little pooch stops yapping and reckons it's not too late. Should've stopped sooner. Yes, course I remember, Don Manuel loved to repeat it. He even had a saying, how did it go? Something about dogs and days … "

"Every dog has its day," I throw in. "It's an English saying."

"Must have picked it up from your great-grandfather. And you know what Don Manuel used to say then? He's had his day to bark, now I want my day to bite. And he was right in a way, can't say he wasn't. Ezcurrita was the cock o' the walk as long as he thought he was safe, but as soon as the boot was on the other foot he clammed up, not another peep. But Don Manuel was left seeing red and wanted blood. Ezcurra got that wrong, dead wrong. He took patience for weakness. I mean Don Manuel could have sent a couple of heavies anytime to a nightclub to knock him about and pass it off as a drunken brawl or smash up the printing press in Toro Mocho but he never did. What Don Manuel wanted was for everyone to know he was right. What he wanted was justice. A public example. It was a matter of honour. His good name had been besmirched and the stains could only be removed with blood. Had these been other times he'd've challenged him to a duel but Don Manuel had a very fine almost exquisite sense of ridicule and he wasn't about to become the town laughing stock. He wore the judges down trying to file a lawsuit, libel and slander I suppose, appearing in person when his lawyers came back empty-handed. He especially targeted Dr Carmona, wouldn't give her a moment's peace," he says and breaks off in annoyance to answer his cellphone, which has been clamouring for his attention from his jacket pocket for several sentences. "Just got here," he says into the phone, "wait for me, don't know, another hour or so," he says fending off what's apparently a demand from a woman who, seeing as he's a widower, can only be his daughter, then starts discussing building work on the beach resort as we all patiently sit there, knowing he wouldn't want us to carry on without him.

"BETWEEN YOU ME and the gatepost I can tell you Don Manuel wasn't the only one that wanted to pay Ezcurra back," Guido will confide to me one night after dinner at his house, one of the identical prefabs on the Banco Hipotecario block, located as far away from his parents' place as the town allows—a mere seven blocks at most. I'll move in there at his invitation recommending the beneficial effects of childless solitude on my work, a suggestion Mati and his wife would second with nodding enthusiasm. Guido's wife Leticia will offer me coffee, I'll accept and Guido will go on with his tale: "There was a society, Don León and Casarico were in it for sure, and the Chief of Police too they say, and … Carving up tourist plots down on the shores of the lagoon, where Don León's got his resort now, on that little fringe of woodland the floods didn't get. Ezcurra was flogging that dead horse Expotencia to them and they bought it hook line and sinker. Remember Expotencia?" Nodding, I'll pull a stapled sheaf of photocopies out of my folder, heftier now than at its last public appearance.

*We all have the good fortune to be present at the birth of one of the most promising stages in the history of our nation, a stage in which the former colony is finally beginning to develop into Argentina Potencia, the world power we all long for. At last the dark days of surrender and corruption are coming to an end. Now begins a radiant time of justice and prosperity, of which Malihuel, the demographic, economic and geographical hub of Argentina, must be a part. Separated from Buenos Aires by three hundred and twenty-three kilometres of smoothest tarmac, and from Rosario by one hundred and twenty kilometres of magnificent highway, Malihuel is a beautiful town nestling on one*

36

*of the banks of the lagoon of the same name—that giant pupil at our country's heart that was witness in bygone days to the excesses of the unbridled savage and today sports the robes of loftiest civilisation, and the solidest, most shining creations of the restless and eternal human mind. There, by its dreaming shores, a valiant chieftain, lord of our wide open pampas, fought the last battle in defence of his native soil, falling to defeat by the bamboos that spat fire wielded by the white man, uniformed and disciplined in laws that he—a free bird—knew nothing of. But his example lives on, as does that of the heroic gauchos that followed him, figureheads of the struggle for independence. Today, after more than a century and a half, that struggle is about to end in victory. That is why Malihuel, the administrative centre of Coronel González County—the richest of the richest farming region on the face of the earth—has a duty to lead this great march into the future. And so Expotencia was born. Expotencia, the greatest open-air expo in the country—farming machinery in action. Expotencia—a unique showcase for the breakthroughs of today and the promises of tomorrow: cutting-edge irrigation systems, seedbed plots and agrochemicals, cattle shows and competitions, demonstration dairies, intensive cropping, latest-model machinery in action, technical lectures and a full agribusiness, stockbreeding and agroproduct technology portfolio. Over fifty stands, two hundred lovely lady-promoters, twenty telephone lines, a press room, musical numbers, a Provincial Soya Queen Contest … All this and more at Expotencia '73! Santa Fe's leading farming and industrial show. Expotencia—yet another attraction to the 45,000 hectares of salt, iodised and curative waters, the golden sands filled with happy laughter and the lapping of waves, the modern ballrooms where social life is free to blossom and flourish, the hard-fought yet harmonious sporting competitions, the internationally renowned shows by artists and musicians … these are the attractions that have made*

37

*Malihuel Argentina's foremost inland beach resort, visited year in year out by an endless stream, over half a million strong in the summer months. This is when Expotencia '73 will open up its doors—an event your grandchildren will one day celebrate as the dawning of a new age. The year 2000 will find us united or downtrodden. And if we are to find union and avoid division, now's the time to start. If you believe in Malihuel and in Argentina, don't miss the boat. Sign up for Expotencia '73!"*

"Where *did* you get that from," Leticia will ask me intrigued.

"Clara Benoit," I'll answer.

"Ah, the famous lagoon files."

"Reckon it had anything to do with it?" I'll return to Guido.

"When you look at it Ezcurra lost just as much money as they did if not more. This is what happened. He'd brought some people over from Santa Fe who were going to make the blessed flood canal we'd been promised since the colonial days—one day they threw a party at the Yacht Club and everything to celebrate the project going through. And there it is, still approved. Without the canal to control the floods there were no plots and Ezcurra promised to speed up work on the canal if they came in on Expotencia. So in the end the guys from Santa Fe turned out to be involved with the Montoneros or something like that and lasted all of two seconds in the provincial government, the whole Expotencia thing collapsed and on top of losing everything and being up to his eyeballs in debt Ezcurra ended up being tarred as the town lefty. He wanted to rub shoulders with the town's big cheeses and wound up … I'm not saying his partners in town wanted

his blood the way Don Manuel did. But when the chips
were down they weren't going to bend over backwards to
save him were they."


"SORRY, I'M AFRAID I'm not convinced the articles had
anything to do with it. Don Manuel wasn't one for wasting
powder on *chimangos*," pipes Licho after Don León hangs
up, running a polite finger over the pile of photocopies on
the table. "But Don Rosas Paz did have two granddaugh-
ters of courting age that's for sure—one, Elvira, ended up
marrying a French agronomist with BO; the other, María
Luisa—Pipina they called her—was left on the shelf. They
were always coming into town whenever there was show at
the lagoon—anything to get away from the *estancia*—and
knowing our dear Darío's reputation … "

"Nice theory," rasps Iturraspe, "if it wasn't for the fact
they were both so ugly just looking at them was enough to
make a bull a bullock, and for that at least we have to give
the deceased his due—he had good taste. The thing is," he
says to me as he turns round, "everyone's got their theory
but actually nobody really knows why Rosas Paz had it in
for Ezcurra."

"Be that as it may," Don León now goes on, who ever since
Licho's interruption has been looking daggers at the table
in indignant silence, "Don Manuel decided to speed things
up. He was dying, or at least he thought he was. Pulmonary
emphyteusis he had and had to go everywhere with a nurse
and a blue cylinder. Used to call it the "heir-scarer". Even
went out hunting he did—he'd plant the nurse and the blue

cylinder in the back of his pick-up and shoot anything with legs, wings or fins that moved, edible or not, anyway he couldn't touch any of it on account of his diet and what the farmhands didn't take was left for the dogs ... partridges, martinetas, ducks, hares, armadillos, caracaras, herons, lizards, possums, plovers, owls ... " Don León interrupts himself to wet his lips in his second Ferroquina.

"*Chimangos*?" I ask giving Licho a wry sidelong glance.

"*Chimangos* too. In the country if it ain't got horns it's a pest, he liked to say. Anyway duelling had gone out of fashion, quiet revenge wasn't his style and there was no joy to be had from the legal system. So that left the police."

"MALIHUEL POLICE HEADQUARTERS," says Don Ángel referring to the building less than a block away that, together with the courts, occupies an entire block, "is in charge of all the police stations in the county including the ones in Toro Mocho."

"One of the privileges we have as the oldest town in the area," adds his brother Vicente with a smile, taking a sip of after-dinner coffee. "This is where they lock up all the lags."

"When they lock them up that is. The police chiefs are appointed in Santa Fe and are generally from thereabouts. They don't stay long, a year or two, and they're sent off to thieve somewhere else so the area can recover. Like crop rotation," chuckles Don Ángel at his own joke. "That's what I'm telling you, Superintendent Neri was different."

"That's what my grandfather always used to say," I impinge. "That he was a different breed of policeman. 'The finest police chief in Malihuel's history.' Was he really that good?"

Don Ángel and Vicente glance at each other to see who'll answer:

"Don't know about the other towns see, that'd be asking too much. But we're quite certain he didn't lay a finger on Malihuel," answers Don Ángel for both of them. "Don't shit where you eat right? He was a sort of local Robin Hood Neri was. Stole from the rich towns and gave to the poor ones," he chuckles again.

"Most police chiefs are just passing through"—Vicente completes his brother's thought. "They don't hobnob with the local population and get out as soon as they can. There are those as prefer a police station in Toro Mocho to the headquarters here. But not Neri. Actually I reckon he'd grown rather fond of us," he ventures and glances at his brother.

"He was more devoted to the town that's for sure. It was his last destination and he'd decided to stick around with his wife when he retired. Had no children did they Vicente? They'd started work on the house and everything, two storeys it was going to be, the first in town. Don't know if you noticed it when you used to come, on the right as you come up the lagoon road. You can see the foundations clear as anything. You should take him to see it Mati if he's so interested in the story. Why not go tomorrow now you're here?"

"One of Malihuel's big tourist attractions," whispers Mati with a wink that attempts to be conspiratorial.

"I DON'T KNOW about the best, no, that's saying a lot, but he certainly was different. Not at all like a copper. He and Professor Gagliardi used to play chess at that window table there. Gagliardi had several regional tournaments under his belt but the Super didn't always come off worse," recalls Don León, sipping his brimming Ferroquina in Los Tocayos. "And here in town he never missed a trick. If the owl in the belfry winked Neri wanted to know which eye. I don't know if he was as honest as they say but at least he was efficient. And had an education—you're the one as knows Nene—was he actually a lawyer or not?"

"The proverbial three subjects short of his degree."

"So why didn't he finish?" asks Iturraspe.

"Gave it up apparently when his old man got blown away. Another copper. Only child, father a hero, mother a widow. That was *his* version at least."

"But?"

"Goodness only knows. Didn't have it up here if you ask me and the excuse fitted like a glove."

"You'd be better off sticking to what you know and going and fetching me some smokes from Chacón's. Tell him to put them on the tab"—Don León puts the sceptic in his place.


"SO HE WAS having this house built on a policeman's salary was he?" I ask Mati next day, one cold, grey Saturday, after his father's finally worn him down.

"He had a cheap source of labour," Guido winks at me.

"The cons," I say to confirm. They smile in agreement.

"Got them to paint the headquarters first mind. The way it is now, that was the last time it saw a lick of paint. Had them classified by occupation and milked the lot for all they were worth. If you ask me that's how it should always be right? Get them doing something useful while they're in," airs Mati.

I nod, much as I beg to differ. I don't feel up to arguing the toss.

"The master builder was from Elordi remember?" Mati addresses his brother. "Used to work for Titín and had a fight with his cousin I think it was. Killed him with a Bic to the jugular. That's accuracy for you. When he got out he'd developed an attachment for the town and wanted to stay but there was no work."

"He had to pay the architect though. Couldn't find anything to arrest him for," cracks Guido.

"And the materials I should think," I butt in. "I mean if it was going to be such a luxury home … "

"It was even going to have a pool, the first in town. We've got several now though, now we've lost the lagoon … Too bad you didn't come in summer 'cause otherwise … " starts Mati and stops, studying the ground plan possibly with a professional eye.

Now that I was seeing it I remembered it clearly—the cement floors cracked apart by weeds and undergrowth, the walls shrouded in hanging gardens of campanulas. As teenagers we'd played one last rubble war here, which was cut short when Guido sent a brick flying into his brother's forehead and we all ended up at the little ward with Doña Isadora giving him first aid. I look at Mati in astonishment, then at Guido. Has it taken me twenty years to realise my great childhood friend wasn't Mati but his younger brother?

"So why did they leave?" I ask. "The Neris, I mean."

"Actually I can't really remember but I think the Ezcurra affair had something to do with it didn't it Guido?" Mati asks his brother, who he seems to get on much better with outside the family circle. "Ezcurra had something to do with it I'm sure."

"HERE IT IS SIR ... " Nene Larrieu will remark, plonking the stained cup down on the table, " ... an ex-presso for an ex-con."

"Don't you ever get tired of that joke Nene?" Haroldo Cuesta, the ex-con in question, will reply to him the day he made his way over to the bar at Licho's invitation, and then to me, "I was in the jailhouse from January sixty-six to June seventy-seven, I'll never forget. Then I was sent to Coronda for another year and eight months. Nothing political. Rustling." He will explain: "Got to eat. So yeah I got to know the headquarters from the inside back in old Hog Neri's day."

"Is that what they used to call him?" I'll ask.

"He liked to throw his weight around," the ex-con will expand. "Not just anybody mind. Never laid a finger on any of us; we weren't worth the trouble. He only dished it out to the hard nuts, the heavyweights, the ones who stood up to him ... Getting smacked around by Hog Neri was a mark of distinction, a blessing from the bishop. 'I moved all the way down here because I was told this town had real men in

44

it,' he'd say. 'So let's see where that good ol' Malihuel grit is shall we?' I think deep down he liked it when you stood up to him. He showed you more respect after that. As I said, the man was naive."

"Naive? Why naive?"

"'Cause he thought we felt the same way. The badge wasn't enough, no, he wanted us to respect him as a man too. Always had something to prove did old Hog."

"AN UPRIGHT MAN, a decent man," will be Dr Alexander's diagnosis when I visit him. "The day he left town he wore the same suit he was wearing when he came. How many people can you say that about? Superintendent Neri was an exemplary human being. Ehhhm, where's this going to be published? Ah. No, because I'd been told … "

"DIDN'T NOTICE THE SUIT. Couldn't take my eyes off the Torino Grand Routier he'd picked up in Fuguet. Brother what a set of wheels!" Iturraspe will remark when I tell him the story.

CITING ASSORTED FATIGUES, they've retired for the night— Vicente, Mati's grandfather and Mati's wife, who, having lashed her husband with several withering looks, has taken the children to sleep at the house next door. Toying with the last threads of our flagging after-dinner chit-chat, that leaves Don Ángel, the dutiful Mati, the rather livelier Guido and

Leticia, Celia, who's toiling in the kitchen and resurfaces every now and then to offer another round of coffee, and myself.

"He had Don Manuel breathing down his neck for a whole year Superintendent Neri did. What he was asking him to do was straightforward enough—drag Ezcurra out of his house kicking and screaming and put a bullet in him there and then for all the world to see. He'd have settled for less earlier. But now the military were in power Don Manuel wanted to have his cake and eat it. All that waiting had whetted his appetite."

"Withdrawal symptoms," I remark. "Happens to the best."

"So I reckon he dealt with them direct," Don Ángel goes on, "when he saw the police chief playing hard to get. He had his contacts Don Manuel did that's for sure. And that's where things got complicated see. We're not talking about just any old spade either mind you. An Ezcurra no less, one of the Ezcurras of Rosario, and an Alvarado on his mother's side. Right here in town. If the Super did what Rosas Paz asked him the whole town would be down on him like a ton of bricks. And if he didn't the military would run *him* out of town, and what was the use of that, 'cause Greco wasn't going to turn his nose up at the chance."

"Who?" I asked.

"Oh didn't I tell you? Greco's ... Neri's boy he was. Subsuperintendent Greco, he stepped into Neri's shoes as chief when he retired. He ended up sticking his oar in too."

"BETWEEN A ROCK AND A HARD PLACE," confirms Don León, sprawling in his bar chair, and lights his 43/70 after offering them round, while everyone gathered around him nods almost imperceptibly. "He was a few months off retirement and thought he'd make it through by passing the buck, but he didn't. He'd decided to stay on in Malihuel as well. And I'll tell you something else. Just between ourselves I'll tell you something as lots of folk don't know—he intended to stand for mayor when your dear grandfather's term was up, 'cause by then he was having health problems that'd force him into early retirement if I remember right. Had the slogan sorted out and all, the Super had, told me in private he did—'Firm hand, clean hands'. Not bad at all eh? But Rosas Paz set the cat amongst the pigeons. They were ruining his prospects as mayor before he'd even got started. And there was something else—there'd been pressure to move the headquarters and the courts to Toro Mocho for years. Think where we'd be now— no government offices, no island beach resort … Because my place for now … You lot'd be the only ones left eh Guido?"

"The whole town hanging by a thread of spaghetti"— Iturraspe steps in in Guido's stead.

"So in a way Neri was thinking of the common good as well," Don León pursues his dissertation. "I'm not justifying him, just explaining the circumstances, because as an outsider and twenty years after the event it's easy to judge, but you had to be here to really understand. The Super himself told me it's just the kind of excuse they're looking for, saying no is like handing the headquarters to Toro Mocho on a platter, and if the headquarters goes the rest goes too. Malihuel can afford to lose one of its citizens but not one of its main sources of gainful employment. Maybe looking at it like that there's a positive side to it right? It was a price that had to be paid. Ezcurra was a sacrifice for the good of all."

ONE NIGHT OVER A FEW WHISKIES Guido and I stop up late talking, mulling over football matches in the church field, summers at the lagoon, games of hide-and-seek at siesta time in the empty factory ... He goes quiet at one point, looks me in the eye for barely the time it takes to blink, then fixes his gaze on his glass so intently it looks as if he's speaking to it: "I never told anybody," he begins, "maybe that's why I can remember it all so clearly. I'd found the best place to hide, somewhere none of you lot would dare come looking for me, and I'd just got settled behind the stairs to the mezzanine when the door opened and in came Grandpa followed by this big guy. Only after they closed the door did I see it was the Superintendent. I huddled down afraid they'd hear my heart beating, you know how Grandpa'd get if he found me in his office. From my hiding place I could see his face in the lamplight—set lips, frowning eyebrows, clasped hands resting on the glass of his desk, and the other's back, the triple roll of his neck against the edge of his suit, a hairy hand clutching a collection of pasta samples that he pretended to study while he waited for Grandpa to start talking. I told you to come at this time Superintendent, he said eventually with a gulp, so we won't be disturbed. I hope you don't mind the dark, we'll be cooler in here. How can I help you? It's a delicate matter, Neri began, choosing his words carefully, and fell silent again. I knew Grandpa's face so well, I could see how hard he was trying to hide his concern. What is it pray tell, he said to him. One of the lads from the factory's got himself into trouble. If it's a matter of a few pesos to bail him out ... The back of the Super's neck said it wasn't. He paused before saying Don Genaro, please. Can you see me coming all the way

48

over here over something like that? To collect a few pennies? Please, Don Genaro. Over one of your workers? Actually I find it less upsetting that you take me for a bent cop than a lightweight, and Grandpa goes What then? Come on, spill the beans Superintendent. Listen Don Genaro, Neri said to him, you know the score. The Province's new police chief is an artillery colonel, a hard man, what more can I say? And I saw Grandpa's moustache quivering with the effort to control himself and a dark circle appeared around each eye. It's about my boys, he eventually stumbled out. What did you come to tell me? That one of my boys is in trouble with the military? They're family men all three of them, they've never been involved in politics or anything of the sort, they haven't the time with all the work they've got on. What's there to explain? They aren't even students, there's only one of them's finished high school, and the Superintendent goes Settle down Don Genaro, it isn't about your boys. Who *is* it about then? My wife? Grandpa burst out laughing in relief and sat there with his mouth open, smiling. Let's get down to brass tacks Superintendent. Tell me what you're here for. Don Genaro I wanted to ask you about the Ezcurra boy, you know him, Señora Delia's son, the Superintendent said to him and Grandpa goes That's why you woke me up from my siesta? To talk about Ezcurra? I don't know what kind of a mess he's got himself into now but I've never had anything to do with him. I used to have dealings with the father true enough but never with the son. Nor did my boys thank goodness. They're up and working when he's on his way to bed. Ezcurra's grandfather used to sell us flour but that must be more than forty years ago. So? That's exactly what I've come to talk to you about, the Superintendent said to him. You, sir, are one of the distinguished citizens of Malihuel, your family's been here since last century, your factory feeds many a family ... Indeed, and we own half the town too, Grandpa interrupted him. You've probably heard, what they don't say is that we earned it all by hard graft. Don't tell me my family history Superintendent, I'm afraid I know it better than you do. Where does Ezcurra come into all this? And the Superintendent says, As you've just pointed out he's from an old-time Malihuel family as well. And before I take a decision I thought it wise to talk to people whose opinion might tilt the scales if it comes to it. However, I will have to ask you to act with the utmost discretion on this matter. What we say mustn't go beyond these four walls," Guido says the Superintendent said, and his eyes widen as if he's still hiding behind the stairs, spying on the broad shoulders of the deliberately spoken policeman and his grandfather's growing confusion through the gap between the wooden steps. "I'd have nothing to tell even if I felt like it Superintendent," continues Guido in his grand-father's words. "Was it Ezcurra asked you to come and talk to me? If there's one thing everyone knows about me it's that I don't like beating about the bush. If he's got something to ask me why doesn't he come in person? Please, said Neri, raising both palms towards Grandpa, if there's anyone who mustn't find out it it's him. Not even Don Manuel can find out, and Grandpa goes Oh Jesus you should've said so in the first place. Listen, you know what I think about the quarrel between those two? I don't give a tinker's is what I think. They can kill each other for all I care. Ezcurra senior was

50

a serious hard-working man who had some bad luck that's all, but his son's a loose cannon. Spent all the money his grandfather left him, conned half the town, and then to cap it all he went for Don Manuel quite unprovoked. Now he's in trouble. Well if he's in trouble he had it coming. And all I've got to say about Don Manuel is he'll be calling the shots in Malihuel the day the cows get the vote. If the people in this town spent half the time working as they do sticking their noses into other people's business we'd be up there with Toro Mocho or Fuguet instead of being where we are, off the map, if it weren't for my factory and your headquarters, he said without pausing and fell silent. So I have a free hand do I? the Superintendent asked. Grandpa stared hard at him for a good while before answering if you ask me … Listen Superintendent, I won't get in your way. If you get in mine, if it's about my boys or my employees then we'll stop and talk. Otherwise what Ezcurra, Don Manuel and you want to do with your lives is your own business. When they left," Guido tells me, "I came out of my hiding place and went back to find you lot, you were all still looking for me. I reckon it must have been the last time we played hide-and-seek in the factory. We were getting too old for it."

While he'd been talking I'd been studying one of the old laminated plastic spaghetti catalogues that served as place mats. The specimens were classified with entomological rigour, yellow lettering on a blue background: *Number Seven Hatchets, Number Twelve Friar's Sleeves, Number Fourteen Gunshot, Number Fifteen Partridge Eyes, Number Twenty-Five Ave Maria, Number Thirty-One Pamperitos, Number Forty Argentinas alla Napoli.* Above the list was a logo with a globe and a strand of spaghetti

51

running around the equator. Over the North Pole ran a banner that reads "*Round The World*" and another under the South Pole that says "*Tuttolomondo Spaghetti*".

"There's something I don't understand," I eventually say, far more disconcerted than I'd anticipated. "Why did Neri go and ask your grandfather of all people?"

Guido looks at me for a second, perplexed, before answering.

"He didn't just ask Grandpa," he says. "I thought you knew. Neri did the rounds of the whole town before he made up his mind. House by house. To see if people agreed with him wasting Ezcurra."

# Interlude One

THE TOWN ITSELF *is a square, ten blocks by ten. Fewer than half show any trace of building, a sure sign that the town never managed to fill out the ground plan drawn up by its indifferent or over-optimistic surveyor; unlike other surrounding towns built on the same plan that ended up outgrowing it and imposing their own outlines on the pampas, Malihuel has never lived up to its map. The centre, as you might expect, is occupied by two blocks of humid, tree-filled square around which the main buildings are distributed: the two hotels, the local Council offices, the church, the Tuttolomondo pasta factory on the opposite corner and, as you go down Comandante Pedernera Street, the police headquarters, the primary school and the old cinema (nowadays a cultural centre). If the square is the centre of spiritual and public life, Veinticinco de Mayo Avenue is the main artery of Malihuel's commercial life—spread along its length are Ferro & Brancaloni's butcher's, the concrete arcade of the new coach terminal, the supermarket, Sacamata's Stores, Fischer's Hardware, Mendonca's Pharmacy, on opposite corners the Kawasaki Bar and the closed-for-refurbishment Makumba (the erstwhile Sucundún), the Los Tocayos hotel-bar and Chacón's kiosk adjoining, the imposing armoured corner of the National Bank, and the two service stations (Shell and YPF). The rest is in the adjacent streets:*

53

two or three more general stores, butchers' and kiosks, the corner of the Yacht Club with its basketball and tennis courts, Dr Alexander's surgery, the barber's, the ladies' and men's gyms, prudently separated, the post office, the courts on the same block as the police headquarters, the Indiana Jones Video Club and the satellite dishes of the cable station, the telephone exchange and Ye Olde Tuttolomondo Ice Cream Parlour next to the Banco Provincia on the corner, a low, brick building with a wooden door and bars on the windows from the days of mounted bandits. Two blocks from the square, towards the lagoon, stands the relic of an even more remote past—Malihuel's watchtower, the cornerstone of at least one of the five vertices of the boat-shaped fort founded by the Viceroys on Ranquel Indian land. You only have to look at it to get a precise idea of what this corner of the world must have been like in those days—standing atop the platform the eyes of the lookout, if tall, would be at most five metres above ground-level; only a landscape drawn with a spirit level and absolutely devoid of even the slightest suggestion of a tree could be effectively guarded from a height lower than a two-storey house—which, as its inhabitants will often tell you, are nowhere to be found in Malihuel. It used to be possible to go up the church steeple and enjoy a vast three-sixty-degree panorama of the lagoon, the neighbouring towns and the surrounding countryside, but no one keeps count any more of how many years it has been since its only visitors are the parish priest, who can negotiate the crumbling stairs in the dark, and successive incarnations of a pair of large white owls. But it isn't for the lack of sweeping vistas that the inhabitants of Malihuel languish; it is impossible to find a street corner from which you can escape the sight of open country in all four possible directions. (There are no streets in all of Malihuel that aren't parallel or perpendicular—the Hispanic infatuation with the checkerboard saw the pampas as the perfect submissive body for the privileged exercise of its perversion.)

With the exception of the eucalyptuses of the Colonia and the age-old specimens that give the square some shade, the trees lining the streets of Malihuel are spindle-trunked and stunted, apparently intimidated from growing any taller by the surrounding plain. But dotted anarchically here and there—one in the cemetery, several in assorted houses and gardens of the well-to-do, and a whole procession along the unbuilt dirt street that skirts the town out by the lagoon—rise the sturdy boles of Saharan palms, whose exotic crowns, silhouetted almost black against the feeble charm of a sunset sky, turn Malihuel into an oriental desert town. These and the relative age of its buildings lend Malihuel if not a measure of beauty then at least of poise.

On the north-east side of downtown Malihuel are the new commercial high school, whose ugly concrete edges are unmellowed by the surrounding young olive trees, the identical white boxes of the Banco Hipotecario houses, and, after an isthmus occupied only by Malihuel's second primary school ("the little school"), the Colonia, a rectangle five blocks by ten cut in two lengthwise by the train tracks and the station, within which you find a scattering of small dwellings, shacks, ruins (including those of two passenger hotels) and patches of waste ground.

The Colonia sprang up at the turn of the century and grew at the feverish pace of the railways, and with them, as the trains first stopped carrying passengers, then freight, it slowly flagged and faded. Two new developments have appeared on its dirt streets in recent times—the green-roofed, brick houses of the FONAVI housing estate and, separated from the station by a lush grove of eucalyptus, a round-roofed, corrugated-iron shed, which is home to the Spiritist Society and hub of the cult of Palmiro Raulí, the prophet of Malihuel, who draws pilgrims from all over Santa Fe and neighbouring provinces.

To the north stand the brick-and-earth mounds of the Federal Shooting Range—now closed down—and the silos of the Bullock

Cereal Company, which rise blinding and incongruous from the scorched brick walls of the old Alvarado mill.

Three sets of tracks converge on Malihuel Station, which would make it one of the best connected in the country if the passenger trains still passed through. Perhaps because there is something palpably grand-sounding about them, the locals still use the old names for the branch lines: the Santa Fe Western Railway, which brought the first train from Rosario in 1886; the Great Southern Railway, which, as it advanced towards Río Cuarto in 1890, laced together the towns of Alcorta, Rosas Paz, Malihuel, Elordi and Toro Mocho; and the Argentine Central Railway, which connected Malihuel with Pergamino and Buenos Aires in 1894. The station itself is built in the omnipresent English style, with wrought-iron colonnades and swags of metal fleurs-de-lys along the cornices, a clock with no hands, huge and white like a full moon, and rooms higher than they are long. Of the original installations only the old postbox is still there (albeit painted yellow), leaning like the Tower of Pisa on its rusting base, where every year's end the children of Malihuel post their letters to Father Christmas and the Three Wise Men.

There are four paved roads that lead you out of Malihuel. After the concrete arch announcing your departure, Veinticinco de Mayo Street forks in two—eastbound it leads to Rosas Paz and Alcorta to join up with the Buenos Aires-Rosario expressway; southbound it breaks into a tight chicane that connects the triplet towns of Leopardi, Dupuy and Bullock before meeting the section of Route Eight that leads to Pergamino and Buenos Aires. Northbound is the road to Fuguet, which at the time of the great floods kept what was left of Malihuel in contact with the outside world, and westbound along Veinticinco de Mayo Street leads to the cemetery and the lagoon road, which, after skirting the new beach resorts (Benoit's and the Yacht Club's) and passing through Elordi, meets Route Eight on the section heading to Toro Mocho and Río Cuarto.

*An officially closed short cut skirting the lagoon allows truck-drivers to dodge the toll road between Bullock and Toro Mocho; facing each other on either side of the short cut are the Mochica Motel and the tyre-repair shop, which everyone in town knows simply as the "road whores' place". Strewn along the length of this byway—which has more potholes than tarmac—are the relics of Malihuel's golden age: the beginning of the causeway that once led to the island beach resort, the ruins of the hotel rising out of the water like a fortress, the posts of the street lights for the plots that never were, the entangled skeletons of rusting farm machinery and decaying stands that still await the opening of Expotencia '73. As in all small pampas towns there is so much space available that the new never has to replace the old; it is added on. So from the nineteenth-century watchtower to the yellow hulk of the old power plant, which fell into disuse when the high-voltage power lines arrived just over a decade ago, everything that has ever existed in Malihuel endures, as it does in the minds of the townsfolk, who make the stubborn exercise of memory part of their everyday sport. Malihuel is a permanent museum of itself, and its history—which barely features in the official records—persists, writ large on the surface of the earth in its obstinate calligraphy of twisted iron and concrete.*

# Chapter Two

I N WINTER, the tearoom of the Malihuel Yacht Club is a cold, depressing place, with barely a few white Formica tables streaked with grey, surrounded by black tube chairs upholstered in red plastic, huddled in the centre of the room. The high, livid walls display an ancient calendar, courtesy of Ferro & Brancaloni Butcher's of Veinticinco de Mayo and López, the snow of which has been yellowed by the years; a sepia photograph tinted with essential colours (green for the treetops, blue for the water, yellow for the buildings, red for the roofs), showing the island's beach resort in its glory days, a black-on-dayglo poster announcing the participation of Las Karakaras ("All the Way from Córdoba!"), La Sonora Malihuense and Diógenes "El Lagunero" Aulicino at last carnival's dances. Don Eugenio Casarico, the Yacht Club president back then, today merely the owner of the franchise for the tearoom, tells me of the carnivals of twenty years ago. "Those carnivals at the lagoon," he reminisces, "tourists'd come from all over the province and from neighbouring provinces, like the beaches of Mar del Plata the lagoon's were, you should've seen it at night," he tells me, and once again

I don't remind him I did. "Your grandfather was always a friend of the Club, as well as a life member and, going through some old papers a few days ago I found his membership card of all things in a drawer, which we'd never got around to giving him; the previous mayor on the other hand had declared war on us, he and his Council said the Club was a bastion of unfair anachronistic privilege that deepened the social injustices at the heart of our community, I mean it's not as if it's the Jockey Club or anything, you can see for yourself how modest our facilities are, even the milkman was a member, and that lad Ezcurra in his leaders calling for the people to 'tear down the wire!' and 'get their feet wet on the wild side', the shower of arriviste brats, as if the Club hadn't been founded by their fathers and they hadn't been members since birth, sheer demagoguery like everything in those days, the 'Montonero Council' they called it, all that 'for the people what is the people's' palaver but, as far as I know, they were never seen rubbing shoulders with the spades down at the public beach resort, which was bare as a bone scorched by the sun, and only the stunted willows for shade, the Council had to replant them come the start of every season because none ever made it to the end of the season. That's what we had the wire fencing put up for, the lagoon's ours and we wanted a bit of peace and quiet to enjoy it. Don't think that's why I bore him a grudge, I've always ridden any wrongs with my head held high, which is why when Superintendent Neri came to see me I put all grudges and personal interests aside and begged him, pleaded with him to reconsider his decision—already final mind—which he'd only made public to scratch a consensual itch. I even offered to talk to Rosas

60

Paz myself, whom I sympathised with from a certain point of view, to smooth things over, at least enough to dissuade him from a course of action he might come to regret, but the Superintendent objected—if Don Manuel gets wind of it it could make things worse, his military friends may take measures that wouldn't benefit either side. Far be it from me, Superintendent sir," says Don Eugenio he said in that conversation with no witnesses, the highlights of which he now offers up to my good faith, "far be it from me to dictate to you how to go about your duties, but wouldn't it be enough to give the boy a fright, something to make him see the error of his ways? Especially seeing as he's calmed down since the new authorities took over, well, anyway, perhaps just a warning … A fright Casarico? What did you have in mind?" Don Eugenio tells me Superintendent Neri replied a little snidely. "Shall I send Officer Rama over in a sheet to sneak up on him and go boo? We're not curing his hiccups Casarico, we're trying to find a solution to a problem, a permanent solution. What I want to know exactly is whether I have your backing or not"—and Don Eugenio goes quiet after repeating the words from twenty years ago and runs a trembling hand over his leathery pate, his vaguely bulging eyes reliving either the humiliation or the fear, I can't tell which. Feeling awkward I get up from the table to study a wall covered in framed photographs, most of them so old it's difficult to tell from their general sepia uniformity which ones were once black-and-white and which colour. One in particular draws my attention—it shows one of the tables in the bar, around which four men are playing a hand of truco, apparent from the distribution of the cards and the white beans and the victorious smile worn by my grandfather in the foreground as he shows the seven of coins he's about to win the hand with for himself and his partner. Their opponents, also half standing, hold up their cards to the camera, shielding them from the other players. They aren't hard to recognise: a Don León with undyed hair, my present company and my grandfather's partner, the only one who isn't showing his cards—his broad, seated figure stares out at me with eyes of unfathomable pitch.

"I don't know this fellow," I remark, pointing. Don Eugenio comes over to the wall and screws up his eyes, first at the image in question, then, even more perplexed, at my face.

"I don't understand," he says.

"This one," I repeat. "My grandfather's partner. Who is it?"

"Neri," he replies. "Superintendent Neri. Who've we been talking about all this time? Wasn't it him? Weren't we talking about Neri?" he asks and asks again, without a trace of irony, just to make sure his incipient dotage hasn't got the better of him again.


"CASARICO? Told you that? Very odd *che*, Don Eugenio's memory must be going, sounds like he's going gaga on us. But anyway anyone in town can give him a hand if he needs it jogging, 'cause even people who hadn't been born know he was one of the first to give Ezcurra the thumbs down. There was no need to say anything, Casarico'd had it in for him ever since Ezcurrita was in the Council and waged war on the Yacht Club"—Iturraspe, with eyebrows arched, would feign an astonishment he doesn't really feel a couple of nights later at the table of Los Tocayos.

"HE'D ALREADY MADE UP HIS MIND about Ezcurra, no one'll persuade me otherwise, when've you ever heard of a police chief knocking on people's doors and asking them for permission, least of all in those days." Don León rearranges his buttocks on the bar chair in Los Tocayos, rests his elbows on the table, and leans confidentially forward. "Mark my words Fefe my friend, what Neri wanted was to kill two birds with one stone, find out if Ezcurra was working alone or if there were others with him and see if he could reel in someone else to boot. It's the only way to explain it don't you agree? The survey wasn't about him, it was about us. Ezcurra's fate was signed and sealed, nothing you could've done or said would've changed it, the only thing you'd've achieved by defending him was to be tarred with the same brush. I realised straight away, Neri might've been a sly old fox but he wasn't pulling the wool over *my* eyes. He came to see me at the bar on the island, a weekday it was, Tuesday I think, 'cause the beer had run out and the order didn't come till Wednesday morning, I had a licence to run the power plant and the bar back in those days, did you ever? … " I answer that I did, recalling a high counter I had to stand on tiptoe to rest my elbows on, a huge wooden fridge, the metal tables on the sand under the shade of the pines. "We chatted about this and that, don't ask me what, I knew what he was up to and I was ready for him, but Neri wasn't saying a word. Course he was doing it on purpose to make me feel uncomfortable, playing cat and mouse like, but forewarned is forearmed and when he started rubbing his butt end round and round the ashtray and saying Listen León my friend there's something I want to

63

talk to you about I was on my guard and I said to myself mentally let's see if you can trip me up. This Ezcurra lad, right, you know him better than I do, what can you tell me he says to me and I go Only what the whole town knows Superintendent, no more no less, and he goes And what might that be, whereupon I gave him an outline, I mean I had to give him something or he'd've smelt a rat: his role in the Council, his journalism, his business dealings, his run-ins with the fair sex. That's odd, the Superintendent replies, I always thought you two were friends and I go I don't know who can've handed you that story, Superintendent," Don León tells me and then adds, "I still wonder today. At first I suspected Casarico, who was Chairman of the Yacht Club at the time and had started legal proceedings against me supposedly for failing to meet the conditions of the franchise, which he wanted to get his hands on himself … A long-drawn-out lawsuit that benefited neither party it was, still involved in it we were when the great flood of eighty-three swallowed up everything—the power plant, the bar, the whole island— and we didn't have anything to fight over any more." Don León chortles philosophically and goes on, "Perhaps it was a lesson to us all, let bygones by bygones, why keep poking around in lost causes, but Casarico was actually one of the first to be consulted and no one'll persuade me otherwise, he was the one as fingered me to the Superintendent. I can forgive, Fefe, my friend, but not forget. And I've got a memory like an elephant I have," says Don León.

"THE WHOLE TOWN'S RESPONSIBLE," Mauro Mendonca asserts while the winter rain runs down his pharmacy window. "Neri made quite sure of that all right, by making us all accessories I mean. Which doesn't exempt us from blame by any means. At the very least we erred by omission; if we did nothing to condemn the poor boy, we didn't do enough to save him either. Imagine if we'd all answered Neri's surveys with a resounding no, it would've been a very different kettle of fish. His methods were of course based on the police strategy of questioning witnesses separately and using the supposed allegations or betrayals of one against another. Neri subtly led every new subject he consulted to believe that the previous ones had given their approval—or acquiescence at least—and I can vouch for it … From one person to another he gradually spun his net and we're responsible at least for that—for acting as supports. And as is often the case with such traps, the harder you try to wriggle free, the more caught up you get … At one point I had this outlandish idea of turning the tables on him, fighting fire with fire as it were, and conducting a counter-inquiry that reflected our true position as a community—because if Neri's visits connected us all, they only served to divide us … So, once his visit was over, I approached two or three of my neighbours, dependable folk—I won't name names—and, with extreme caution, I made some enquiries of my own … One of them flatly denied any knowledge of the affair even though everyone knew not just that the Super had visited them, but the date and time of day too; the other two were evasive, vague, wanted me to tell them where I stood, put my cards on the table first, but I wouldn't give them the pleasure; from that day on our mutual trust gave way to mutual suspicion for many years to come ... Years later one of them would confess to me that he thought I'd been sent by Neri that night to check on the truth of what he'd told him and that that was why he'd been so guarded ... What Neri was doing was so extraordinary, so unprecedented, that it wasn't surprising most people felt that there was something fishy going on, that behind every one of his questions there might be another question, the real one, one that wasn't about poor old Ezcurra, but about ourselves."

"LOOK AT IT THIS WAY. How many died in Argentina then? Thirty thousand you say? I think that's stretching it, there can't have been more than ... say, ten thousand—just to make my argument more mathematically elegant. Because unless I'm mistaken the population at the time was twenty-five million, you remember don't you? 'Twenty-five million Argentines off to win the World Cup.' So, if you work out the ratio, you're talking about one victim every two thousand five hundred inhabitants, correct me if I'm wrong. And here in Malihuel we had just one and there were three thousand of us at the time. In other words we short-changed them, especially when you think that Malihuel's the administrative centre of the county and ought to have set an example. I know what you're thinking," Don Honorio Moneta rashly claims in the plush living room of his Rosario apartment, which his comfortable pension as manager of the Malihuel branch of the Banco Nación allows him to enjoy in peace and quiet, and whose doors—the front door, the lift door and the door to the private landing graced by Monet's *Poppy Field,* spotlit by a little brass wall lamp—have been opened to me by the ministrations of my grandmother, who I've come to visit on a weekend break. "You find my line of argument cynical, and I'll admit to you my young friend that so it may seem at first sight. But you're young and can't remember what our country was going through. I don't mean to justify what happened, simply to point out that what happened in Malihuel happened throughout Argentina. That's what I'm saying, if we're going to judge Malihuel, we have to judge the country as a whole. Malihuel isn't an island and if things are the same everywhere else, why not here too?" he says and then smiles pensively and strokes the velvet of his armchair, faded by the sun from emerald to moss green. "Gracious me. It's been more than ten years since I left and I still say here instead of there. People have short memories. You had to live through those years, occupy an exposed post like mine before you jump to conclusions. Every day lived was a day stolen from the hold-up or kidnapping the guerrillas had planned for me, and the nightmares wouldn't let me sleep at night. A moving target, that's what I felt like at the time. A moving target. Ezcurra may not have taken up the gun—I'm not so mean-minded as to deny the fallen enemy the benefit of the doubt—but it was his preaching and the preaching of others of his ilk that trained the sights on those of us who held the fate of the community in our hands. So I'm not ashamed to have given my consent."

DR ALEXANDER IS THE OWNER of Malihuel's private surgery on Belgrano Street, right next to the Yacht Club, which he acquired over thirty years ago, along with the licence and patient portfolio of old Dr Rocamora, of whose lack of medical wisdom and hygiene the town still has a mouldering recollection. As if wishing to differentiate himself from his predecessor as much as possible, Dr Albino Alexander is as spotless and distinguished as his name suggests, and accompanies his deliberate speech with modest gestures of his long, white hands, which bespeak asepsia and talced-up latex gloves; beneath the discreet varnish of his fingernails, pampered weekly by Malihuel's redhead manicurist, it's impossible to spot the slightest trace of dirt. Dr Alexander's practice plays across clinical medicine, traumatology, obstetrics and, somewhat by ear, the other branches of medicine. Along with the surgery and keeping up a well-established local tradition, Dr Alexander took up the post of police doctor; under normal circumstances he would have been responsible for examining Ezcurra's body and issuing the relevant death certificate. If he didn't do so, he deigns to explain to me in memory of my grandfather, taking up precious minutes from treating the pneumonias, influenzas and winter colds that clamoured for his attention, "it was because Ezcurra never was in the hands of the police, dead or alive," he claims and asks if I take sugar or sweetener in my tea. "You've probably," he supposes, "heard some of the tall stories going round town on the subject, suppositions and conjectures that insult the good name not just of the dead, who can't defend themselves, but of people who work selflessly and unstintingly for the common good. People only remember doctors and policemen," pronounces Dr Alexander the Police Doctor, "when they're in trouble. And the suppliant, once sated, waxes critical. Gratitude is more volatile than ether, and the cured patient forgets to pay the bill." He pauses to take a sip of his tea and I take advantage of the lull to ask the obvious. "He was killed by guerrillas," replies Dr Alexander with enviable aplomb. "Murdered," he goes on, "by his own companions, probably after one of those shoddy parodies they were in the habit of calling 'revolutionary trials'. I'm reliably informed," he adds, "though I can't reveal my source— professional ethics you understand—that the boy sincerely regretted his participation in that criminal organisation and decided to 'open out', as people used to say in those days. You'll have heard of a hypothetical meeting with the chief of police. Well, for once our small-town tongue-wagging is true. What they don't say—what they can't say because no one has access to first-hand evidence, as I do—is that those meetings were to reach an arrangement over the conditions of Ezcurra's surrender to the authorities. His regret being so deep-rooted he wasn't content merely to change tack in his life; he'd also set himself the mission of redeeming his past. To put it another way, he was willing to talk, tell them everything he knew, even name names, something that many would call treason, but which I call integrity or courage because it was a decision taken not out of fear but private conviction. But Ezcurra and the chief of police both made a mistake, a mistake the Ancient Greeks used to call 'hubris', a term that can be translated as an 'excess of confidence'. They thought Malihuel would be a safe place to wait while negotiations developed; they presumed that here, surrounded by the scrutinising gaze of friends and neighbours, in a small town where a new face never goes unnoticed, he'd be safe.

There are still people who claim the guerrillas were on the back foot by then; but you only have to look at the case of our unlucky neighbour to refute them. On the retreat? An organisation so powerful it even had ears in the smallest towns? Ears no news escaped? On the retreat, when they were capable of bursting in armed to the teeth and perfectly synchronised in broad daylight, and to everyone's horror, abducting one of the town's most prominent inhabitants, who was in police custody at the time? How many people in this town, where everyone knows everyone else, must have acted as secret informers, splitters and collaborators for the operation to be carried out successfully in the very midst of police headquarters? That's where your investigations should be leading, as you seem so determined to dig up our past. For once we could hear both sides in this country where the winners make history and the losers write it. But of course, were we to attempt to do so we'd soon run into all sorts of obstacles. The vested interests are against digging up anything from the past that might leave them exposed, they talk of reconciliation and closing the wounds"—to which he as a doctor answers: "Before healing a wound you have to open it, clean it thoroughly and cut away what needs to be cut away, otherwise what you get isn't a scar but an abscess, a fatal gangrene. Yesterday's terrorist wolves are wearing today's democratic sheep's clothing, and what they used to rob toting guns they now filch with the white glove of the conjuror," illustrate Dr Alexander's whiter-than-white hands, holding aloft the object he's been toying with since the start of our interview, a gilded letter-opener in the shape of an outsized scalpel.

70

THE KNIFE BLADE strikes the chopping board with the force of a guillotine, cleanly separating a T-bone from the rest of the ribcage. Florencio Brancaloni casts a critical eye over the cut and sharpens his knife with several swift strokes down the steel. Only then does he answer my question.

"Ezcurra was a shit, always was, always will be, I've never been one for keeping my mouth shut. Now because of what happened they're all showering him with flowers, next thing you know they'll want to make the poor soul a saint, but nobody lifted a finger to save him back then and rightly so. I'm telling you, and I don't know what the dickens you've got to do with any of this, I'd already heard there was a *Porteño* city-slicker in town asking about the poor soul and I go Oh yeah? bring him on, I won't mince my words, I'll tell him what everybody thinks but doesn't dare say—that the military, the police or whoever it was did us a favour."

He wipes his hands on his white ochre-smeared apron and stares at me defiantly, hands on hips, through the curtain of sausages, black puddings, chitterlings and cuts of rump and flank.

"Evil tongues say evil things about Superintendent Neri I know, talk about kicking a man when he's down. But my father may he rest in peace knew him well and I can assure you Malihuel's never seen another police chief like him. But of course he—the man who kept law and order and brought all the crooks and troublemakers to book—gets stick for enforcing the law instead of taking backhanders; but cops these days all they care about is lining their own pockets so people just slip them a few pesos and they turn a blind eye. He didn't consult my father 'cause he knew exactly what

71

he'd say. I can still see him clear as day my old man, coming back from work, shouting from the kitchen sink where he was washing his hands, Looks like they're finally going to get Ezcurra off our back, I don't know who'd told him, makes no difference, everybody knew by then."

Brancaloni looks at me with his globular eyes, two perfect discs of dull blue on turgid white, threatening to pop out of their sockets like the eyes of the two lambs hanging head-down on either side of him.

"That sonofabitch Ezcurra"—he launches into him again, kicking the twenty-year-old corpse as if it were still lying there on the ground—"that scumbag shat on half the town and nobody'd touch a hair on his head, laughed in our faces he did and not a peep, but my old man never took any shit and his son's a chip off the old block, I swear if Ezcurra walked through that door now I'd smash his face in, like that I would, without a word to him, whack!" he exclaims and illustrates his point with a thud of fist on palm. He's getting heated, and the real smell of quadruped blood and the imaginary smell of human blood have sent him into a frenzy like a shark in a documentary, and I'm beginning to wonder if it would be too risky to wait for him at closing time and follow him into the dark alleys of the Colonia where he lives and where I'll stand a better chance of snapping his scrag with a discreet brick. "We could do with another Superintendent like Neri I tell you to clean out all the scum around town and I'd be first in line to hand him the list. Fuck could this town do with a clean-out. If there was one thing Neri got wrong it was that he didn't go far enough. Greco the one who followed him did a bit better but didn't give a toss about the town—all he wanted was to sell us out and hand the headquarters over to Toro Mocho where the big money was. And the ones today you can forget it. Go to the butcher's on the next block, look at the cuts and if you can find any public-health labels I'll give you a side of beef. Don't even know what colour they are, one big illegal country carve-up it is. Think the cops care? Charge them the same as they charge me sir, side of beef a month, and me with all my books in order? I tell you sir," he tells me with another swing of the pendulum between formality and informality, a common affliction of bullies with an inferiority complex, "there's a lot of hypocrisy in this town. And anyone who tells the truth makes a lot of enemies, but that's me for you, can't change, chip off the old block I am, can't keep my mouth shut, what can you do," he concludes and before crossing the curtain of multicoloured strips with my little packet of T-bone steaks I cast a final glance at the unwholesome pink and grey marbling of the cow tongues on the steel tray, studded with tiny pointed cones and scraps of salivary gland adhering to their roots, whose mute dithyramb has in eloquent chorus accompanied their master's voice.

"SUPERINTENDENT NERI LIKED chess. And in chess he had a fondness for exotic gambits," Professor Gagliardi will tell me at one point of my last afternoon in Malihuel. "He'd rightly assumed that the procedure for picking someone up in a small town, where not even a hen can disappear without creating a stir, couldn't be the same as his mentors had developed for the big city, or indeed for larger towns like Villa Constitución or Toro Mocho. Remember? Let's say you were living in an apartment block. You'd always found the upstairs tenants a little odd. One night you heard screaming and shooting and the crunching of splitting wood and next morning when you ventured out from under your bed the concierge downstairs informed you your suspicions were well founded. Within a month the new neighbour had moved in, and because of the military moustache and his whatthehellyoulookingat expression you asked no more questions. And that's if it happened in *your* building, because if it'd been in the one on the corner you'd never even've heard about it. No, after pondering the matter at length, Superintendent Neri's twisted but obstinate brain came to the conclusion that that wasn't viable here. In any other town in the county it'd've been a piece of cake, as the local police would point the finger at the Malihuel headquarters; but here in Malihuel there was no one to pass the buck to. What I can vouch for is that Neri tried his level best to get the Rosario Regiment to come and pick him up—he'd do the tailing for them and guarantee the area'd be police-free and they'd do the dirty work and take him far away, somewhere it couldn't be pinned on him. But it was no use. They wanted him to do it, in person, with his own people. It wasn't personal, that's what it was like everywhere. A kind of blood pact, with other people's blood of course. When the clean-up was complete and the claims started rolling in after the return of democracy, they wanted to make sure the fussy ones couldn't hold their hands up, point the finger at others and say Wasn't me."

MALIHUEL'S BARBER is an old-timer with neatly trimmed hair and a flaccid, harmlessly depraved expression, who answers to the vaguely incredible name of Eufemio. Seated in one of the two antique pedal chairs, I let him adjust the apron around my neck and say yes thanks to the manicurist's fancy a coffee, with her outrageously turquoise apron and furious red hair, and number three to the old-timer's question. "Of course I do, how couldn't I? He always had his hair cut here," he answers mine. "You're? ... Oh yes, I've heard something about you now you mention it. Is it for some magazine? I don't know what I can tell you, we didn't know each other any better than townies usually do, it's impossible to be strangers in a small town as they say right? He came in for a trim a few days before, that much I can tell you. Nothing particular about his conversation—if he knew something or had been warned, he didn't let it show. Except for one thing. He kept on about how this time he was back to stay. Unusual for him, he was always on the verge of leaving. It's time to settle down Eufemio, he told me—that's my name, Eufemio—while I was cutting his hair. Maybe I'll get married, have a family, be someone here, he told me. It was like he'd found his place in the world, you know like in the film, and he wasn't going anywhere"—Eufemio précises the deceased's words as the clippers buzz across my cranium lifting clumps of tousled greying hair as they go. "I didn't pay much attention at the time but in the days that followed, 'specially after what happened, his words took on another meaning and I realised what he'd been trying to tell me. He knew what was coming, he knew perfectly well. It isn't true what people say about nobody warning him. How couldn't he know with so many people—not all as some say, but a lot—in the know? Whatever people say, I'm certain he knew and decided to stay anyway and face the music. Perhaps in the knowledge that it was hopeless, but possessing a quiet fatalism that wasn't devoid of heroism. He was hell-bent on staying in Malihuel, dead or alive, and that's what happened. They couldn't send him away so they had to kill him. He was no victim," claims Eufemio, putting the finishing touches to my fringe. "In a way he had the last word."

He swivels the chair round and shows me the short-back-and-sides in a hand mirror. The little mirror also catches the flame-haired manicurist's enthusiastic look of approval in the vast wall mirror.

"EZCURRA'S ALIVE AND WELL and living in Casilda," Licho's voice drops to a conspiratorial whisper. "I have it on good authority." He turns his snout towards a mockingly attentive Iturraspe and says as if trumping him with the ace of swords, "Tonito. Know him? Saw him in Casilda he did. He's married, looks like he finally settled down, and he's got two children—boy of seven, girl of five. Works in a real-estate agency on that boulevard, Colón Boulevard, and Tonito was passing and spotted him through the window, but Ezcurrita had customers and stopped him in his tracks with a gesture. Tonito gave him a wave … and you know what he did? He winked back," argues Licho, exaggeratedly shutting one eye to illustrate. "No, they'll never catch Ezcurrita that easily I've always said so, always did his surname proud he did. You'd have an easier job catching an eel with soapy hands. All that malarkey about Don Manuel and the police was just a story he made up to dodge the creditors and start afresh somewhere else, wipe the slate clean. Fooled the lot of them he did, I know what I'm talking about, can you picture Ezcurrita sticking his head in the lion's mouth on his own, being bamboozled, him of all people? He waited for the right moment and scarpered. Alive and well he is, I'll bet you the shirt off my back. The Devil looks after his own," he says and drains his glass of Fernet.

"What about the body?" Iturraspe asks.

"What body?" Licho says dumbly.

"The one the dogs dug up, out at old Villalba's place. Who was that?"

"No idea. Ask El Peludo, he'll be able to tell you."

"The gravedigger," Guido clarifies before I can ask.

"While you're at it you can ask him," Licho concludes, leaning over with a cigarette in his outstretched lips for Nene Larrieu to light, "why the north wall of the ossuary collapsed. There were stiffs to spare in those days. Got hold of a whatdoyoucallit an NN they did and gave him a name and surname. Ezcurra and Neri must have come to some arrangement, that whole circus of the inquiry was just a smokescreen."

"I'M DISAPPOINTED," I tell Guido and Leticia over dinner, "with people in Malihuel. When I was on the way here I was worried people wouldn't want to talk, that they'd be wary of an outsider like me poking my nose in. Particularly when I started asking about Ezcurra. I rather hoped I'd get threats or warnings like 'Leave town before sundown', or that I'd come up against a wall of silence, or get dirty looks at the very least. Nothing. They're all so helpful, so friendly, so willing to welcome me, to talk openly. I was expecting a conspiracy of silence not a conspiracy of chattiness. I must have watched too many movies right? Foreign movies. You don't think it's odd? Or do I have a gift for making people open up to me? Now I come to think of it it's not the first time."

"It's winter, people get bored," Leticia opines through a mouthful of No 12 Friar's Sleeves Tuttolomondo tagliatelle. Guido swallows before adjusting his posture, a signal he has something juicy to add. Behind him a colourful television presenter hosts a brawl between tight-fisted housewives on *The Price Is Right.*

"Don't flatter yourself," Guido tells me. "Bad-mouthing your neighbour's an addiction in this town and all they see in you's an ear. A tender little newborn virgin ear. The tongues start wagging when they see it coming, wriggling around in their mouths like mad. Can't control themselves. So don't go thinking they're doing it to help you or even to ease their consciences. They're doing it because it's stronger than they are."

ON THE CORNER of the telephone exchange—a building clad halfway up in imitation brickwork forming a clumsy tetris against the cement—the orange diving bell of the Entel phone box has been replaced by one of the new rectangular blue ones, but it's too cold to talk out here, so I go inside and ask for a booth. Paula, my wife, asks me how

78

I am, if I'm having a good time, when I plan on coming back, whether I miss her. Fine, yes, dunno, lots, I reply, and to my two-year-old son, who clamours for the phone with whoops of joy, I say soon, very soon. I hang up with a strange unease in my chest, somewhere between annoyance, hostility, perplexity and guilt, yet none of the above. With every passing day my current life, our shared daily routines, my work, the house we live in, our neighbourhood, the whole of Buenos Aires blurs and dims, and as if in some transfusion of reality, Malihuel grows in specific weight and density, hardening slowly, inexorably, like cement. Maybe there always was a life here for me, a parallel life running from one summer to the next while I was away, like a reflection of my other life—a faint, ghostly reflection, like the ones in shop or bus windows. A life that I might have lived had my mother not left Malihuel so young, and which, after nearly twenty years' absence, must have faded to almost total transparency, like a vampire without blood; it must have given up all hope, when one day like any other it saw me get off the coach at the new terminal and leapt on me with all the greediness of so long a famine. I know there's only one person I can share this peculiar uneasiness with and, in pessimistic resignation, dial the number of my friend Gloria. Miraculously she's at home and delighted as always to hear my voice, asks me how I'm doing, if I'd found out everything I wanted to, who I'd been talking to and if I'd remembered to send her regards. Fine, no, several and yes, I twice told the truth and twice lied to even things out. She put the girls on and, guessing it was me, they fought over the receiver with that peculiar whooping

79

of theirs, and I promised to bring them presents when I got back, counting on the inevitable hamper of Tuttolomondo Pasta that accompanied me in the luggage rack, every summer on my way back to Buenos Aires. The assistant whose open palm receives the shower of coins my call has cost can't be much over twenty, although her glasses, her tight but dishevelled bun and her shapeless brown pullover add a few more years. Looking more closely I see five earrings studding her left earlobe, and a small blue butterfly tattooed between her thumb and index finger on the other hand. She half-heartedly answers my questions about the old location of the telephone exchange without deigning to make eye contact. Nor has she ever heard of my grandparents, nor predictably enough of the Ezcurras—mother or son. She's from San Rafael in Mendoza and lives in the Colonia, where her father has been stationmaster since the privatisation of the railways. She doesn't know and doesn't want to know about Malihuel's past, or much about its present either. The whole family dream of being moved on, anywhere, but she's set a date—"Next year," she finally looks up at me to say, "I'm twenty-one, and I'm going back to Mendoza if I have to hitch there. If we'd at least been given a house here in town," she says apologetically. "When it rains a lot like now in winter I sometimes have to get off my bike and carry it with mud up to my ankles 'cause it's impossible to pedal." I hang around for as long as I can, waiting in vain for her to match my curiosity and ask something about me, so I ask her another question about her. Soledad, she answers.

"WE NEVER THOUGHT HE'D DO IT, 'specially when he started his enquiries," Don Casiano Molina, the owner of the Shell franchise, tells me as his employee replenishes the gas I've used over the last few days in Leticia's Fiat Uno. As word of my almost all-consuming interest in the Ezcurra case has spread through the streets of Malihuel like wildfire, I find people increasingly launch into well-rehearsed speeches after I've barely opened my mouth. Sometimes they bring up the subject before I even ask. "If Neri'd wanted to, we reasoned, he'd've kept the biggest secret and later confronted us with a fait accompli. All that idle chatter threw us off the scent. We all thought his bark was worse than his bite, least I did. I still think Superintendent Neri's hand was forced by circumstance even now and I still have my doubts about him doing it. If you ask me I reckon Subsuperintendent Greco acted off his own bat and that, faced with the fait accompli, Neri was forced to take the reins so that word wouldn't get out a subordinate had gone over his head like that. Neri was a different kind of policeman," rattles the prattling head of Don Casiano, and for the nth time I'm subjected to the irrefutable evidence of the foundations of Neri's future house, the freshly painted headquarters, the selective honesty with which the Superintendent courted Malihuel's tradespeople.

"EVERY CLOUD HAS A SILVER LINING," someone or other said to me in one of the countless conversations. "If the Ezcurra business hadn't happened we'd never have got Neri off our backs, we'd still have him as mayor, the people would have voted him in, believe you me, aren't you fed up of hearing about his honesty, his uprightness, his authority, his love for Malihuel? Poor Ezcurra, I know it's no consolation, but he actually took a weight off our shoulders."

"I DON'T BOTHER ANYBODY and nobody bothers me," is all Don Porfirio Dupuy, the spectral landlord of Los Tocayos, has to offer when I ask him one afternoon we're alone in the bar.

"NO ONE ASKED MY PERMISSION," says Eduardo Rufus, the owner of La Bonita, the largest slice of the carve-up of the mythical *estancia* with its own horizon, named La Catalina in honour of my great-grandmother, Señora Kathleen Doyle de Bullock, on his way through Malihuel. He's agreed to meet me out of deference to Don Brendan Bullock's memory, for whom his father worked as an administrator. He's very pleasant to me and insists I'll be welcome at La Bonita whenever I feel like it. But on the subject of Ezcurra I can't get anything more out of him than that first phrase. He's very talkative about everything else though. "Things weren't that good around here; a lot of land got salt-logged in the floods and to clean it up … We picked up a bit again with the soya but Rosas Paz's heirs … I always said to them, whoever puts their money in cows loses, but they wouldn't listen to me and La Bonita just went on growing with the land they kept selling to me. Would you credit it, they wanted to do up the *estancia* for tourists, it's all the rage these days you know, they put new rooms in the *estancia* house and a swimming pool, spent a bomb they did and what for, who's going to come out here, tourism for spades is all we've got, for Benoit's beach resort. Course they'll drive brand-new imported four-by-fours in what little land they have left. Me I'd rather stick to my old Rastrojero and have more land to drive around in."

"POLITICS DIDN'T ENTER INTO IT," clarifies Clara Benoit, Don León's daughter, in the half-finished ballroom-cum-bar of the new resort, down by the shores of the lagoon. "It was an excuse. Darío was killed because he was full of life, beautiful and didn't give a damn. And it was the women who killed him, contrary to popular belief. Not, as rumour has it, the famous seduced and abandoned ones—no woman's heart, in a body touched by his, could ever again beat against him. They couldn't even feel jealousy, except maybe towards his mother. No, it was the others that were jealous of him, the ones he'd never touched. They were the ones who finished him off—a conspiracy of jilted hopefuls egging on a flock of imaginary cuckolds" —she breaks off for a minute, exhales smoke from her cigarette and through the broad windows her gaze loses itself in the heaving, leaden expanse of the lagoon, skirted on the horizon by a crooked brushstroke of distant trees. "Darío was the last good thing to happen to this town. That's why they killed him. In a dead town the living only get in the way."

"I CAN TELL YOU A THING OR TWO ABOUT ONTIVERO," says Ortega, the owner of one of Malihuel's two hotels, the one opposite the church on the other side of the square, the

Malihuel Grand Hotel. "Ezcurra was having a relationship with his wife, you know … The police chief didn't have to put himself out over Ontivero, he went to the station himself he did. The cuckold's revenge, let's call a spade a spade. Not that the Super'd take any notice of such a nobody, he should be grateful he saw him, but anyway, the bandwagon might've belonged to Rosas Paz as they say but quite a few grabbed the opportunity and jumped on didn't they. I'd like to see what that rat says now, if he still has the face to say he had nothing to do with it that is. Don't get me on about folk here … Have you talked to him?"

"Not yet," I tell him, and to loosen his tongue a little more I grill him again about his hotel's capacity to accommodate contingents of pensioners from Buenos Aires sent over by the imaginary firm I've just invented. They say all sorts about me in town now anyway.

"WELL, A FRIEND, I wouldn't call him a friend … " Tararira, the video-club owner, qualifies my hasty assertion during a pause in the three series of bench presses I'm spotting him at his request. At the suggestion of Guido, who's an assiduous regular, I've taken to spending my downtime in the Malihuel's men's gym. "I knew him right enough, we all know each other in these parts. But that's as far as it went. And as for telling him, telling him … What was I going to tell him? I didn't know a thing. Let all those good friends of his warn him. Why didn't they go and tell him? Anyway, anyway, if Ezcurra'd been in my shoes I tell you, and me … I mean, if I'd been the target … D'you think he'd've stuck his neck out to warn me eh, think he wouldn't look after his own arse first? Eh? And what about you? Eh? You were here too if I remember right. Why didn't *you* warn him? 'Cause otherwise it looks like all of us here have to provide you with explanations but what about you eh? Yeah yeah. You were too young. And someone else was too old and someone else was too fat and someone else overslept and couldn't make it. We've all got excuses. Anyway, listen, I got nothing against you, my folks were good friends of your grandparents and you probably came round to our house and all, but what are you doing here now? The subject was closed, we'd turned the page and all moved on with our lives, and now you keep banging on about it. Another twenty years and somebody always on and on about the same old thing bada-bing bada-boom? What've you got to do with any of this? What the hell does Ezcurra's story matter to you eh?"

His bad blood makes me feel tempted to drop the hundred kilos of rusted weights on his chest, but because there's a grain of truth in what he says, I restrict myself to surreptitiously pressing down on the bar every time I help him lower it, and even say come on, one more, last one, make the ten, while the veins on his face look increasingly like chitterlings and a number by Gilda fades out over the speakers and one by Las Karakaras starts up.

"I CAN TELL YOU A THING OR TWO ABOUT ORTEGA," says Ontivero, the owner of one of Malihuel's two hotels, the one opposite the school on the other side of the square, the Las Delicias Hotel. "Ortega's wife was still up to it in those days, a right slag she was, and Ezcurrita you'll probably have heard if you've been asking around didn't need asking twice when it came to totty. When the dog's dead, the madness is done, the naive Ortega probably thought, as if by wiping the other one off the map he'd wipe away the stain on his reputation. I'm not saying that's why, what police chief would look twice at him let's face it, but you can bet your life that when Don Manuel whistled he was one of the ones as came running. I'd like to see his face when he's asked. Have you spoken to him yet?"

"Yes," I reply.

"And what did he say?"

"Same as you."

Ontivero looks surprised.

"Well. Blow me. Well it was about time he came to terms with it. Ah well, each to his … So, tell me a bit more about these pensioners, let's see … "

AT NIGHT, after I switch off the light, the voices won't let me sleep. As if all their echoes were ringing together inside my skull, the voices I've heard during the day make themselves heard again, arguing ill-manneredly, interrupting each other, contradicting each other, each trying to drown the others out, trying to gain my approval, my attention, or just my ear. They've detached themselves from the bodies that anchored them and now run free through the overrun garden of my mind, forcing that crucial silence that precedes sleep further and further away. Through the wall I can hear the rhythmic jingling of Leticia and Guido's bed, but, for all its vitality, the noise doesn't move me or dispel the feeling that I'm lying in a tomb, condemned to listen to incessant murmurings from neighbouring vaults.

So I switch the light on again, get up and get dressed as stealthily as possible so as not to disturb my generous friends' post-coital bliss, and checking to see I haven't forgotten my cigarettes and lighter, I go out through the front door and pat the heads of the three dogs—Tuqui, Botita and Titán—who get up and wag their tails when they see me. One of the undeniable advantages of lodging on the outskirts of town is that you only have to cross the street to be out in open country. Beyond the fence post where I rest my lighter and cigarettes there is nothing but the shadows of groves of trees, more sensed than seen, and a horizon barely drawn by the beginning of the field of stars. The sounds, on the other hand, are unusually crisp and crystalline, as only the inimitable acoustics of a winter night in the country can make them: the lurchings of the dogs sniffing around excitedly in the patches of weeds, the whispering of the wind stirring the leaves of distant trees, the scattered and occasional crickets, the fleeting hoot of an invisible owl, perhaps one of the eternal pair from the church bell tower. Sharpening my ears I can make out the distant roar of a truck on the highway, the brief low of a cow startled from sleep, the panting of the dogs, my own breathing; and if, on merging with the background, they give way to the returning voices, I reinforce them with the crackle of the glowing tip of my hard-drawn cigarette or the twang of the wires tautened like guitar strings by the cold.

When they've occupied my head entirely and displaced the very last of the invading voices, it will be time to return my shivering body to the comforting warmth of the sheets.

"I WARNED HIM, course I warned him, it'd've been criminal not to, even with the risk involved. What I find hard to believe is nobody else did. This was his home town, a lot of the people who turned their backs on him had been friends of his father's, they'd been to his christening, watched him play in the square, watched him grow up. And it was down to me—an outsider, a newcomer in town back then—to tell him," says Berraja, shaking his head, the owner of the local love hotel, whose rooms—the beds with their lacquered bedheads and plastic-lined mattresses, the worn, red carpets, the odd compass rose made out of offcuts of mirrors, the posters of naked silhouettes against orange-crush sunsets—he wanted me to see before showing me into his office. It's a cold, rainy afternoon, and the surface of the lagoon is raised in little wave points, like gooseflesh, and, every time the wind shakes them, fat drops run down the windows of Berraja's office and trace sinuous lines through the fine spray of drizzle. "But what else could I do, Ezcurra was a regular as you've probably heard," he says with a wink from behind a lens of his glasses. "He was one of the first to adopt me when I came here. Put yourself in my shoes, an establishment like mine in a town like this in those days—those holier-than-thou women with nothing better to do, greed dressed up as local council and police morality, sermons in church for those as went, the very ones who'd head over here when they got out or ask me next day who was with who last night *che*. Ezcurra wasn't bothered about any of that, just the opposite, and what I wonder today is of all those young girls who opened, well, let's say their hearts to him not one, not even for those couple of hours of happiness they spent together, had the common decency to tell him? Or perhaps that's precisely why—they may've been afraid Ezcurra'd let the cat out of the bag afterwards and go shooting his mouth off about who'd warned him? Or it may've been out of spite or revenge or morbid jealousy?"

"But you warned him," I intervene.

"I told him, course I did, I told him to look after himself, that there were people in town who wished him ill, that he'd be better off going away for a while, far away, but he, you probably know what he was like from what you've been hearing, he got worse, dug his heels in, he said Tell … I can't remember who he said, Tell whatsisname that if anyone's going to have to leave town it'll be him, and tell them from me to find someone else to tend to his horns, I've done my bit." Berraja smiles as he recalls, and mumbles, "Real piece of work that Ezcurrita."

"But you set him straight? You let him know the problem was with the police?"

Berraja's initial hesitation gives me the answer his words try to correct.

"A nod's as good as a wink," he finally manages to articulate. "I didn't spell it out to him, the name, if that's what you're getting at. But I was certain he'd understood at the time. Subsequent events proved I may've been mistaken, but then it was too late to correct my mistake. I did a fair bit, while his lifelong friends, his partners, his neighbours, even

his relatives left him to his fate without so much as batting
an eyelid. If Ezcurra'd been less pig-headed, less proud, less
omnipotent, he'd've realised straight away. But there's none
so deaf as those that will not hear you know. Besides, they
were both customers," he adds unnecessarily.

"Both?" I ask.

"Ezcurra and the Superintendent. They're both dead so I
can permit myself the breach of confidence, though I can't
do the same about their partners of the fair sex you'll understand," he says in a winking tone, which fortunately his eye
refrains from backing up. "What's more, that week halfway
through the week, they ran into each other here one night
at the entrance—Ezcurra on his way out, the Super on his
way in. I was a witness. You can just imagine, by that stage
there was nobody who didn't know what was afoot, not even
Ezcurra, or so I thought, though I'd mistaken what was sheer
foolishness for courage. The glances of the men who'd be
victim and executioner crossed for a second, you could hear
the toads croaking in the lagoon in the silence that ensued.
Then Ezcurra acknowledged the Super with a nod and a
half-sardonic smile and left with his bird on his arm. The
Super left his—always the same one, methodical the Super
was—and came over to the window. Does he know anything?
he asked me with his eyebrows. Not from me I gave him to
understand, shrugging my shoulders, and he believed me.
I swear, for a moment there I was afraid he'd rumbled me,
went weak at the knees I did, I can remember as if it was
yesterday, soon as he'd gone after his *chinita* I had to sit down
and have a couple of whiskies before I could carry on."

"AND CLOTA, poor thing, so fond of God's creatures she was, 'cause she couldn't have children I say, well she did have one that died young she told Chesi and me once and they couldn't have any more after that one or didn't want any, I'm not sure, you know Fefe when there's a misfortune like that you try to avoid the subject; and just imagine us asking her husband—a very helpful man the Superintendent was, but with secrets not just professional ones, wait I'll tell you in a minute, he couldn't keep that one from us, silent as the grave he was, and I reckon that that must've been why she was so fond of animals, full of cages the house was and a pair of little plovers loose in the garden and sometimes even a martineta which didn't last her long see on account of the possums and you can't keep them in the hen coop 'cause the hens'll kill them her husband used to bring them back for her when he went hunting famous for his aim he was if he wanted to he'd kill them and if he didn't he wouldn't and take them back home as a present for his wife. But her favourite was the little dog she was given when they first moved to town, by ... oh of course your grandparents what a scream Fefe I was about to say the Echezerretas as if you didn't know them I'll forget my head next but your Auntie Porota's getting on," my grandmother's friend, whom I've always called Auntie, will say to me, and her sister Chesi will look up from her knitting and smile. "Adored that little dog she did, from being a puppy she'd make it talk like a person you know Mummy Mummy give me those ickle bonies from the barbie Clota'd pretend the little thing said what was it called Chesi and she'd take it out for walkies oh you know with little bows on and all dolled up because truth be told it was a lovely gesture of your grandparents' but the little tyke didn't have much of a pedigree to be honest and well that's what I wanted to tell you her husband also had one of his own not much of a pedigree either I can tell you why would I beat about the bush Fefe dear we can call things by their names a bit of *chinita* fluff she was and to make matters worse she was so young coming out of school in her white pinafore, she must've been around fifteen then but she was still in sixth grade, didn't have much up here, worked for me at one time she did and I had to send her back. So she'd come out of school and make straight for the headquarters, but that wasn't enough for him, he had a room booked in that hotel on the highway, I don't know if you saw it on your way into town … Can you imagine Fefe! A hotel room, and all for a *chinita*! And poor Clota, how couldn't she have known, she was bound to. She played stupid poor thing. But then she wouldn't've been the first, or the last, there are times that look, all sorts goes on in these towns we'd prefer not to know about."

"EZCURRA USED TO DO HER, know what I mean?" Sacamata junior asks Guido unnecessarily and winks at him. "That *chinita* of Neri's, La Nena they used to call her. Got enough for the first one?" he asks his partner, Licho, who mutters, "They're yours," eyeing the only card on the table, my dodgy six of cups. "That's the reason the only reason Neri whacked him. Mum's the word," he says and plays a knave of clubs. "That whole circus of the general inquiry was to hide his real motives," he goes on and I make the most of the opportunity to give Guido the signal. To get our opponents to bite he opts to bait the hook in silence and make the first with a three of coins to distract them. "Rosas Paz's request suited him down to the ground and if he played hard to get it was only to throw people off the scent. To the girl he … Call!" he abruptly orders his partner, who shakes his head.

"They're loaded Batata," he mutters sceptically. "They're trying to draw us in."

"Nah bag o' nails, look what they played. Call I'm telling you," he insists, and as a man resigned to his fate, Licho calls an *envido* that Sacamata and Guido promptly double and triple. "Thirty-three," I say first, having led, and after the superfluous "They're good," Licho plays his three of swords to match my lead and rescue what's left of the hand. Six beans slide my way over the table.

"They don't lie but they are tricky," Licho reflects philosophically, and Sacamata junior adds, "Don't worry, we'll get our own back in the second. What can they do to us with the seven of cups and where was I oh yes if you don't believe me," he says to Guido, "explain that business about La Nena got off lightly she did with a man's haircut, shorn for a whore she was and that's as far as Neri went, after all anyone who'd stoop any lower for a *chinita* looks like a right berk," he concludes, while I turn up the corner of the six of swords and give Guido the signal for the seven.

TO SEE IF I CAN LET OFF some of the accumulated anger that's starting to blind me, I decide to go out running one afternoon with Guido along the edge of the lagoon. Charging into the wind, which is like a hand on my chest pushing me backwards, skipping over strips of tyre, rusty tin cans and dead caracaras littering the verge, I rattle out what's been eating away at me before I run out of breath.

"I'm beginning to think," I tell him, "they're not far wrong—the people who say Neri—wanted to spare Ezcurra—He might've really—meant it—he might've really believed—that by telling everyone—they'd stop him—and in a way—he became the instrument—the executioner, but not the judge—of what the people wanted—that it was Malihuel, not him—that decided Ezcurra should die—and that afterwards" (I've got a pain in the pit of my stomach now) "they washed their hands—saddled him—with the blame" (I can't draw a full breath) "they made him a scapegoat—and they bad-mouth—him—to cover up their tracks—and he—by killing Ezcurra—was only—complying with—the will—of the people?" I finish with a wheeze and pull up, panting, unable to go any further. Jogging on the spot, Guido offers to wait for me. We haven't yet completed the first of the eight kilometres he normally covers. I tell him to go on alone, that I'd rather take advantage now that it isn't too far to walk back, and once his energetic figure disappears round a wooded bend in the path I light up and smoke my cigarette leaning against a post, watching the waterbirds take off and land on the steel-grey waters of the lagoon.

"BEHIND EVERY ONE of the Superintendent's questions," states Don Augusto Noel, now as then owner of the Trigo

Limpio bakery, 'Malihuel's Number One', "there was a veiled threat. Know what he suggested when it became clear I was reluctant to give him the support he was after? That if we didn't sort things out ourselves the *milicos* would move in from Rosario and quite a few more would end up carrying the can. The righteous end up paying for the sinners was how he put it, who knows how he told them apart. Know what else he said? I can remember him standing there clear as daylight. Better if this matter remains in police hands Don Augusto. You know what the difference between the *milicos* and the police is? Us policemen fish with a hook, the *milicos* use a net. It's up to all of you," Don Augusto recalls, tongs in hand, before asking me, "Shall I put some vigilantes on too?"

AND ONE NIGHT, a Saturday as it happens, my mind, blunted by the exponential proliferation of voices, reaches saturation point and I take to the streets in search of some relaxation too disgraceful to confess to my hosts, who, since my arrival, have generously granted me the use of either of their two Fiat Unos, though out of deference to Guido's extra headlights and souped-up engine I always take Leticia's. I park half a block from the infamous Kawasaki Bar and the moment I'm inside I confirm that the good townspeople have been understating their execration. The Kawasaki is a godforsaken dive within whose walls bedecked with cave paintings of fluorescent rockers and laminated posters of motorcyclists and motorists painted in primary and complementary acrylics circulate twenty or so longhairs in leather jackets and big-collared shirts unbuttoned to the sternum, followed around by a barely less numerous band of little cumbia-dancing spades flaunting rotund thighs beneath their skimpy miniskirts or an abundant volume of buttock moulded by the biting white cloth of their trousers. The jukebox oscillates between heavy-metal numbers—outdated before they became dated—and the usual cumbia rhythms. The drinks lined up behind the precarious bar are unalleviatedly foul, and the service slow and gruff—the place is, from one end to the other, exactly what I needed and I soon find what I came looking for. Precariously balanced over the black hole of the toilet I separate two lines of charlie, cut with that other, unnamed soap powder that never passes the test in the TV ads, and further emboldened by a shot of gin I go up to the only face I recognise in the crowd. If she can't tell from my sudden verbal outpouring and my sparkling corneas, she must have a very good nose because, after a few minutes, she accepts my proposal unquestioningly and walks at my side the few blocks that separate us from the darkest dirt streets. For half a joint of the more than decent local weed and what's left of the soapy coke she lets me fuck her against the shadowy corner of a deserted hallway; I could have driven her out to the Mochica but I'm aroused by the echo of my vague teenage memories, and the cold on her nipples that no bra separates from her T-shirt. It isn't love, but for once it spares me the tiresome process of spanking one out in a house not your own. Two days later, when I go into the telephone exchange, Soledad predictably pretends not to recognise me, or more accurately, pretends only to recognise the man who makes regular if ever less frequent visits, asking for a booth to call Buenos Aires.

"No FILES," Leticia warns me, wolfing down one croissant after another, having been kept at the court until four without lunch. "Nothing before eighty-three. They were all lost in the floods, ours and the police's. When the flood waters went down we discovered that the ones below the waterline had turned to pulp and those above it were covered in enormous pouffe-like balls of furry green mould. The shelves were made of wood and sucked up the water like a siphon. The ones in the Civil Registry and the Inland Revenue fared better—they're a bit higher up and have metal shelves. They lost documents dating back to the days of Comandante Pedernera and the foundation. Anyway at best you'd've been able to confirm there wasn't anything there about the Ezcurras. None of that was recorded in the guards' logbook and no files were opened, not a thing. I couldn't say if they kept parallel or secret files. But nothing for you or me or even the judge to've looked at."

"*Che* tell me," I tell her, "you work there, I mean you're right next door aren't you? Can't you get me a visit to headquarters, an interview with the current chief, or some other? … "

"Sure, course I can, I'll talk to the judge, I shouldn't think there'll be a problem," Leticia enthusiastically agrees, and we fall to discussing the subject. When he gets home and we tell him, Guido buries the plan with a shovelful:

"I wouldn't tango with the cops if I were you."

"IF YOU WANT TO KNOW what was going on inside headquarters," Iturraspe tells me one night when not even all the gas fires in Los Tocayos can keep the glacial cold at

97

bay, "the man you should talk to's Sayago. He was a cop back then and word is that he was well in on it. Know where to find him Guido?"

"In the FONAVI social-housing estate right?" my friend replies.

"Lives in his sister's house you know the one behind Ña Agripina's. But don't go and see him there, he'll smell a rat and you won't get a word out of him. Get him to come here and offer to pay for his drinks. It can't fail."

ÑA AGRIPINA, the local healer, is no dishevelled, toothless, wrinkled Indian crone as folklore dictates, nor does she drag sandals across the tamped-down dirt floor of an adobe shack. On the kitchen walls of her little house in the FONAVI district, within its green roof and bare bricks, there are no painted-plaster statuettes of St George, or red candles, or pygmy-owl feathers: two little old china figures talking on the phone, connected by a black flex, a rectangular tray with a tropical sunset in furious oranges and blacks, a wall clock in the shape of a gigantic golden wristwatch that in mythical times may have graced the wrist of a Titan. She herself is on the diminutive side, her dyed, spongy hair in an abundant perm over her heavily made-up eyes and mouth, her cream rayon blouse separated from her double chin by several ropes of fake pearls, her feet embedded in faded, bunion-battered flat-soled shoes.

"I remember you well," she says to me the moment I walk through the door, I sit down and thank her for the tea and petits fours she's honoured me with. "Your grandmother called me once to cure your bellyache. No, not by pulling the skin on your back; the seamstress's tape measure. It works every time. Don't you remember? Darío often used to come and see me yes," she remarks, sipping her sweet tea from a blue cup. "Potions for the girls he used to ask me for most of all, concoctions for his binges, balms for the occasional dose of clap. He was as young as you now. You have to watch out for the drugs Fefe," she says to me without pausing, in the same amiable monotone of tea and petits fours. "The spirit of the drugs is climbing up your back like a creeper. You can carry on with the marijuana for now, better not drop her all of a sudden 'cause she gets very jealous, but watch out for the others, especially the mineral ones. Minerals are terribly ruthless, they're capable of anything just to live a while. What was it you had in your head? A bullet?"

"A piece of helmet."

"He came to see me that week, but the moment he walked in I realised the die was cast," she returned to our initial topic of conversation in the same natural tone, making me wonder if I hadn't hallucinated her warnings about drugs, which would have had the paradoxical effect of confirming how apt they were. "The work was advanced, the web"—she interlaced her fingers with their varnished nails to illustrate—"extremely dense, too many people behind it. His shield had already been pierced, he came to me too late. The only thing he could do I told him was to get away before the net closed. The circle I told him had a break in it—the road to Fuguet. Above all he had to stay away from the lagoon, from water. Everything mineral aspires to the condition of the vegetable. And the vegetable to the condition of animals, and animals want to be people. That little girl the other night she's a vampire. She's already sucked the lifeblood out of the Lugozzi boy like sucking on a marrowbone. If you feel the urge to see her again pay it no mind, it isn't coming from you. It's she who's calling you. Put the photo of your wife and son next to your skin over your heart and hold it there. He couldn't say no when a woman called to him. He couldn't even say no, not even to Mother Death. What could I do? He turned to me the way you have but he came too late. Don't repeat his mistakes Fefe. Don't let the new moon find you in town the way it found him. When the new moon caught up with him there was nothing left to do. You were in touch with Gloria a while ago weren't you. I can see her every time you smile. Send her my regards when you see her again. And don't pull such a scared face. Nothing of what you confide to me, nothing of what you don't confide to me but I can see anyway—you know what I'm talking about—goes any further than this," she said and traced the outline of the round table with her finger.

"AND ONE DAY at noon on my way to the lagoon I cross the square at siesta time, sun beating down, and I see some kids playing and for some reason or other I stop and watch them. It was like hide-and-seek but in reverse—they were all counting and one was hiding. The one hiding 'was Ezcurra' and had to get to the Comandante's statue before the others caught him. See what it was like Fefe?" Iturraspe asks me one of those afternoons in the bar. "Even the kids knew."

"'Cause that's what began to happen, in the middle of the week," Carlitos "Turquito" Majul, heir to the old general stores of Babil "Turco" Majul, the one over by the watchtower, tells me in the gym. The exercise is a shoulder press and this time it's me who's being spotted. My body still aches from last time. "Ezcurrita might have been lots of things but slow on the uptake he wasn't and it began to dawn on him something was afoot. Now even his friends crossed the street to avoid him and when he came into Dad's place say for cigarettes everyone in the queue'd stop talking. I remember him sitting at the table in Los Tocayos—one of the last images I have of him—his feet stretched out the way he always used to, drinking a beer on his own and smoking with his head down trying to work things out. He looked up in hope when he saw me and I signalled to him I'd be right back, but I didn't show up again. Behind his back there were these two lads playing Foosball sort of robotically 'cause they couldn't take their eyes off him. He must've been the only one in town who didn't know by that stage—and his mother of course, who unfortunately was out of town. People were running from him like the plague and nobody had the common decency to at least tell him why. Till somebody plucked up the courage, or maybe it was more than one, I hope so, I don't know what you've heard. They say there was a letter too, my old man used to say."

"Wouldn't he be able to remember who sent it if we asked him?"

"The only thing he remembers these days is Syria," he replies, helping me to stow the weights I'm groaning under.

"KNOW WHAT THE FUNNIEST THING IS?" Carmen Sayago, the reformed ex-police officer will ask the day my promise to buy him some drinks clinches his decision to visit our table in Los Tocayos. "The Ezcurra lad came to us of his own accord. Someone must've tipped him off and he went right up to the Superintendent there and then. Ended up shouting at each other they did; there was—must still be—a window in the door to the chief's office, it's always open in summer and you can hear everything through it. The second Ezcurra stepped inside he squared up to the Superintendent he Did I hear you've been asking about me around town? If there's something you want to check on about me why don't you come and ask me to my face? I've got nothing to hide and if the law has a score to settle with me I want to know about it he rattles off and the Superintendent when he can get a word in edgeways says to him a bit sad like The law's got nothing to do with it lad, things have changed around here too. Or don't you know what's going on everywhere? And Ezcurra goes You can't compare, those are communists and guerrillas. I'm one of the most influential figures in the town, not some spade who you can push around. You mess with me and you'll end up with the whole town against you I give you my word and the Super goes Let's see if I can talk some sense into you lad, there's a time to defend your honour and another to save your sorry ass and I reckon you're mixing them up but it wasn't any use and I don't know if you ever met Ezcurra but there was nobody could hold a candle to him for pig-headedness, even on his way out he turns round and I was born here he says to him, my mother was born here and my grandfather too. We built this town from nothing and now you, who breeze in through one door and out through another, you're playing the big boss? Keep on messing with me and you'll be the one who ends up leaving! Screamed at him he did in front of everybody and though the Super tried to laugh it off afterwards saying What a fucking joke and shaking his head this one's as much chance of saving himself as a headless chicken, but if you ask me he never forgave him for that one. But in a way he was right, don't you reckon Chief? I don't mean it was right what they did to the Ezcurra lad but he was sort of asking for it. Going and squaring up to the chief of police like that right in headquarters just when the other one held his life in the balance and was making up his mind."

"And wasn't that going to get him into trouble?" I'll intervene when the ex-corporal pauses to practise an avid piece of cunnilingus on his upturned glass of *caña*.

"They wasted him didn't they? Ain't that enough?"

"Neri I mean. He practically alerted him to the fact."

"See Licho? Ain't that what I've always been telling you?" Then back at me, "The Super wanted to save him if you ask me. If he'd skedaddled to Buenos Aires or Rosario or even Alcorta he'd've been out of our jurisdiction and we couldn't've laid a finger on him. If the military or provincial headquarters found out Neri was going to be in a right fucking pickle, but there you are. He was up a what's it called a cul-de-sac but he was even willing to run that risk long as it gave the lad a chance. But it's no use with some people right Don? There's no way to make them understand," Carmen Sayago will say with a broad grin, which given his lack of teeth looks heroic at least. "'Nother round Maestro?"

103

"Nene," I'll bark. "Keep an eye out for my friend's throat over here, don't let it get dry will you."

THE GATHERING AT LOS TOCAYOS BAR has stretched into the small hours, as we await the ex-policeman, who always ends up standing us up. Guido left a while ago to answer the call of his occupied bed; Don León Benoit and the bar's landlord muttered their vague farewells and retreated too, one to the catacombs of the premises, the other to the biting cold of the street. That leaves Iturraspe, who's got nothing better to do, Licho, living in hope of scoring another drink; Nene rock-steady as ever at the counter, and myself. Then one of the doors onto the main street opens—enter a fat man with long curls and a moon face as white as an unbaked pie crust, his eyes and mouth looking for all the world like the slits in the dough. We're introduced, Bartolo someone-or-other, currently employed at the Tuttolomondo factory, pasta-nests department, and once he's drawn up a chair they put him in the picture. "Sayago," he laughs hoarsely with a triple shudder of his double chin, "good thing he didn't show up, he's on my blacklist he is, one of these fine days I'm going to cut him into little pieces. Fancied my ladyfriend he did and chucked me in the can to get me out of the way, the royal sonofabitch, came looking for me at the Sucundún on my birthday, 'cause we was drunk according to them but it was 'cause once I was eighteen they didn't have to report to the juvenile judge. Couldn't wait another day he couldn't so I copped a beating with sticks and boots, lovely present, and to cap it all he locked me up with the vice cons he did who didn't fuck me by this much," he says bending his index finger inside his thumb to illustrate. "That's an easy one"—he answers Nene's question—"eighteenth of December nineteen seventy-eight. I'll never forget it as long as I live, nor'll he, since he stopped being a cop I lay him out flat once a year, out of principle. I'm told he takes a detour all the way round the block just to avoid going past the factory door. Anyway I got off lightly all in all, I mean look what happened to Ezcurra. You related or something?" he asks me and I say, "No." "Friend of Guido's," Iturraspe explains, and Gordo Bartolo says, "Oh right"—pat on the shoulder—"if you're a friend of the little boss's say no more. Oh so you're the one who's going to make the movie"—he looks at Licho, then at me to seek confirmation—"if you need someone to play the lead look no further. The Ezcurra business you mean? Well not much, just what anybody knows, they locked me up in Greco's day and that all happened before. What was him before Greco called? He had to be taken down a peg or two for sure but they went over the top. A good hiding would have done I say, no need to go that far. They showed no mercy did Rosas Paz and Echezarreta, took full advantage of the fact they had a free hand."

"Who?" I take a moment to ask, long enough to register Nene, Iturraspe and Licho's panic-stricken exchange of glances.

"The Rosas Pazes were the biggest ranchers in the area, not any more, and the Echezarretas—"

"I know who Echezarreta is," I interrupt sharply. "What I want to know is what ... why you said he ... that Rosas Paz and he ... " I've suddenly developed a stutter as my arse rises off the seat of its own accord.

105

El Gordo realises something's wrong, the eyes of his acquaintances confirm it but can't explain what. With a shrug of his shoulders, as if to say too late to turn back the clock, he waits for me to sit back down before he answers:

"Couldn't abide Ezcurra Echezarreta. That's common knowledge isn't it?" he asks his table companions. "I don't know if it was the other one's idea or his, but when Neri came up with that plebiscite on Ezcurra our beloved mayor was one of the most enthusiastic defenders of the yes vote. And if you don't believe me ask Sacamata what he went to buy from him a few days later. Champagne. The mayor sent out for a box of champagne. What were they celebrating? Wasn't Christmas or New Year or anybody's birthday. Find who drank those six bottles of champagne and you'll find who killed Ezcurra, or who wanted him dead at least."

"AND WHAT ELSE was he going to tell me?" I answer in exasperation. "He knows I'm his grandson. What else was he going to say? Yes, I sold him the champagne, a box of Chandon Extra Brut seventy-seven?" We've just left Don Alfredo Sacamata's general stores-cum-minimarket, we walk down the sidewalk under the cowering, indecisive sun, nodding to the greetings of acquaintances, most directed at Guido but a few by now evidently at me as well.

"Fefe"—Guido tries to calm me down—"why believe Gordo Bartolo over him? I've told you, Gordo's a nasty piece of work, I've already had a word with my old man a couple of times to give him his cards, sets himself up as a union delegate he does and fills the others' heads, but my

106

old man says he prefers him because he's a fraud and at the end of the day he can be bought unlike someone who takes it seriously … " He pauses realising the gist of his obsessions has led him away from my own.

"It's all right, Sacamata probably said he doesn't remember to protect me, or to cover my grandfather, or himself. Supposing there was no box of champagne. That it's just another piece of Malihuel folklore. My grandfather didn't toast with champagne, he toasted with a bottle of Chianti he'd been keeping for the occasion since his last trip to Europe. What's not in doubt is that he was one of those who sent Ezcurra to the wall right? The whole town knew and tried to hide it from me. Isn't that right? You too."

Guido walks beside me but doesn't reply.

"YOU'RE SURE, you're dead sure, he doesn't know I'm Echezarreta's grandson?" I grill Guido and let go of his arm when I notice him wince in pain.

"Yes Fefe, I've told you," he answers wearily. "And I've told you what I think. Why don't you leave things the way they are?"

"Because things are for shit the way they are. Come on, let's just ring now we're here."

"Here" happens to be the neighbouring town of Elordi, where Professor Alfio Scuppa, erstwhile head of Fiscal School No 16, which included the high school too in those days, has retired to enjoy—so to speak—his autumn years in the company of his children, who at least as many years ago again left Malihuel in search of broader, or at least more lucrative, horizons. The house, with its flat corrugated-iron roof, its white stippled plasterwork and its railings of iron lozenges, is not unworthy of the prosperous architectural and phonic ugliness of Elordi, which, rather than a typical rural town, looks like a chunk of suburbs transplanted en masse to one of those points of the pampas whose only distinguishing features are latitude and longitude. I ring the bell once, twice, three times, with no result, not even the muffled echo of the ring from inside; having more local expertise than myself, Guido claps, listens, warns me he's half deaf the old man is, claps again until the door opens noiselessly and through the crack a tiny flap-eared old man with a blotchy face like a Jackson Pollock done in melanin on parchment pokes his head out. How angry I am, I think to myself.

"Hullo Don Alfio, remember me?" Guido shouts at the figure that staggers smiling towards us.

"Matías? Is that you?" he asks, his voice tremulous with emotion. Was *this* the man, I ask myself, who was the terror of schoolchildren, who personally combed the streets hunched over the wheel of his Citroën 3CV in search of truants? "I drop in at least once a year but it's no use, he always gets me mixed up with my brother, the model student, who's never been to see him," Guido tells me without bothering to whisper in my ear.

"No Don Alfio. It's Guido his brother, remember me?"

"Of course I've forgotten"—he gives himself away—"I never forget a single one of my old students, every year when Matías comes I ask about you. You used to put me through the mill in your day," he says, then fastens his eyes magnified by the lenses on me. "And you are ... Peralta?"

The inside of the house I find pleasanter, and it isn't hard to see why—on a yellowing plastic imitation-lace tablecloth at an optimum distance from a gas fire that hisses emphatically and keeps the kettle on for maté, shine the beloved and eminently caressable forms of a state-of-the-art computer. Throughout Don Alfio's account I'll cast the longing glances of a castaway in its direction.

"They came to look for me," he explains, his eyes opening wide like a child's. "Dr Alexander, Mendonca the pharmacist, Casarico, Don León, the Banco Nación manager what was his name … Moneta, yes, thank you, you see what old age does to you, there was a time when I could reel off all the classes from fifty-three on, student by student … and Don Julián Echezarreta of course, the mayor, leading them. We're going to talk to the chief of police, they told me, about this Ezcurra boy. We can't sit around with our arms folded with what's going on. Well what can I say?"—he answers a question from Guido—"I was a little alarmed, they'd already killed a nephew of mine in Rosario, but well Ezcurra had been a student of mine as you all had and besides I thought if such important people from town are going there must be some reason for it so I went along. I can't quite remember, Thursday or Friday it must've been, what I am sure about is that classes hadn't started yet because otherwise I couldn't have made it at that time. Somebody'd asked for an appointment beforehand, I don't know who. Neri was waiting in his office with his feet on the desk, that much I can remember, I mean how rude, and his gun too, feigning indifference; if he was trying to put the fear of God in us he succeeded with me. He didn't even invite us to sit down, there were two or three chairs on our side and they stood there a waste of space till the end of the meeting. Up till then we'd been full of resolve, marching along like a platoon under that ferocious sun, who *does* this Neri fellow think he is, he'd have to listen to us now, us Malihuenses aren't the sort to get pushed around, some of us may even've cast a glance at the statue of Comandante Pedernera in the middle of the square to give us strength before going into the gloomy headquarters, well I don't know if you've been told about the Comandante … " he says and I tell him I have. "So far so good," he goes on, "but once we went into Neri's office our momentum evaporated, nobody dared to start, a lot of clearing of throats and shuffling of shoes and nudging till the Superintendent decided he'd had enough fun and spoke. Gentlemen … How can I help you? To what do I owe the honour of this visit? he said and the mayor summoned his courage and says Listen Superintendent, we've come on behalf of the community to bring to your attention the need to do something about this situation we're all so concerned about, or words to that effect, and Neri, his eyes twinkling with amusement, And what situation would we be talking about, Don Julián, who getting bolder said The one you've been consulting us about constantly over the last week, we sincerely hope in good faith, which is why we're here, and the Superintendent as if it were just dawning on him said Ahh … so that's it, you've come about Ezcurra, you should've said, and he frowned—What about Ezcurra? What have you come to tell me? You want me to leave things the way they are? No can do. A decision has to be made and time is of the essence, he snapped at us. The atmosphere was quite suffocating with all of us crammed in there," Don Alfio recalls, "and the ceiling fan barely moving the air and there was me having to stand on tiptoe to see over people's heads, the mayor of all people standing there gulping, Superintendent, I think we can stop beating about the bush, all of us here are figures of some standing in the community and as such we've more than once been obliged to take difficult decisions"—Don Alfio repeats what he remembers of my grandfather's words—"but the idea is not to burden people with problems who've got quite enough of their own, rather to solve them for them. Can you imagine if I bothered you every time I had to dismiss a member of staff? Or if Don Alfio were to ask us one by one for permission to expel a student?" And then Don Alfio says, "At that everyone turned round to look at me but as I couldn't think of anything to say, Casarico or Dr Alexander intervened I can't remember which, Superintendent, they said, what our mayor's trying to tell you is that we don't approve of all this discussion. Shouldn't we be more discreet? There was no need to consult us in the first place, we fully trust your judgement, but now things have got this far let's hope they don't go any further. What are you up to, do you want the whole town to find out?" Don Alfio recalls and adds, "and I still didn't catch on. The mayor took up the baton and went on, Superintendent we've specifically come to ask you to put a stop to the whole affair and Neri says Fine, I get the picture. But who's going to take responsibility where the military authorities are concerned. You? Because I can't see Don Manuel Rosas Paz taking it lying down. Unless of course you risk talking to him yourselves. That's not a bad

111

idea eh? What do you think? You have a word with him and I promise I'll talk to the authorities. Deal? It didn't sound like a bad idea to me what the Superintendent was saying," says Don Alfio, "but in the faces I could see I discovered not relief but panic. I don't think we're seeing eye to eye Superintendent, the mayor stammered and only then," says Don Alfio, "did the penny drop. Had I realised, I'd never have been party to it, but I was already there and it was too late to turn back," he stammers, the growing trembling of his jaw and hands perhaps illustrating his disquiet at the time. "I believe, I want to believe that at that moment they all wanted the earth to swallow them up but it was too late to turn back and Mendonca the pharmacist said Listen Superintendent, this may be a small town but we're aware of what's going on in this country. Malihuel isn't an island, danger lurks here too. Are we going to put our heads in the sand and be grateful that only the neighbouring towns have been affected for the time being? And what do we do when they come for us? It'll be too late. We can't take things lying down. We can't afford to miss the train of history yet again. You know better than anyone Superintendent how much pressure there is to move all the public offices—including your own—to Toro Mocho or Fuguet. A lot of people say this town is dead, and if they take away our status as the administrative centre of the county it'll be dead and buried. Think about it Superintendent. It isn't much they're asking of us when you come down to it, just adding our grain of sand. And the Superintendent had to fight to keep a straight face and then, all innocence, he says to us Oh good heavens. You've come to ask me to kill him then. You should've said. Fine. How do we do it? He sprang it on us and this time it was Dr Alexander with his customary sangfroid who pulled the chestnuts out of the fire. We'll leave that up to you Superintendent. I think I speak for everyone when I say that from now on the less we know about the matter the better. The Superintendent must've decided he'd had enough fun for one day and after thanking us sarcastically for our civic-mindedness he said goodbye and shook hands with us one by one," says Don Alfio and looks in shock at his fragile right hand as if it still bore the traces of the offending imprint. "On our way out," he adds, "we quickly dispersed by some tacit agreement, in case anyone should spot us. I don't remember saying goodbye to anyone."

"And that's all." Don Alfio takes a loud and futile slurp on his empty maté and sits there staring vacantly at it. To escape from myself for a little while, from the boundless disquiet in my chest and the anguish garrotting my throat, I ask him if I can borrow his computer for a while. Delighted to have found a kindred spirit he opens the gates of paradise for me and over the hour I spend checking my mail and answering messages I manage to shake off the asphyxiating feeling that the universe ends at the edges of this quadrangular patch of Santa Fe pampas. Guido sticks around and keeps up a conversation with Don Alfio that this time next year he'll attribute to his brother, and, before we leave, Don Alfio asks me for a favour—can I sort out some problems he's been having opening a short cut to a Web address, which turns out to be a Hungarian website devoted to child pornography. On the way back Guido drives the delivery truck in silence through the brown fields untransfigured by the sunset. "They went to look for my grandfather too, but he wouldn't go," he says at one point. "Not in working hours he told them," Guido adds and I nod as if I understood.

MENDONCA HAD ALREADY MENTIONED something to me about the delegation that rainy afternoon I'd been to see him at his pharmacy: "But there came a point when we drew the line. A delegation of us went to see Superintendent Neri. To ask him to abandon his designs. The cream of the community were there: Don León Benoit, Eugenio Casarico, Don Honorio Moneta, whom I don't know if … oh you do, Sacamata, Senior of course, and your grandfather naturally. Let me see, have I forgotten anyone, erm … I shan't give the names of those who declined to take part so that their memory won't even live on in local gossip … We assembled outside the door of the headquarters as a man, and knocked, demanding an immediate appointment with the chief of police. He agreed to see us when he found out who it was. We want to know what you're up to Superintendent, we began without further ado, and very soon the room was ringing with the yells of half a dozen people heatedly arguing, the Superintendent banging his fist on the desk saying Who are you to tell me how to do my job and us answering If we don't who will and demanding he give his word that things would go no further. He gave it us after a bitter verbal exchange and I now realise our greatest mistake was to trust him, to treat him as one of us, to consider him … a gentleman. He abused our good faith you understand. Gave us guarantees.

It's easy in retrospect to say the military and the police back then lacked any sense of honour, but in those days most of us still thought … I reproach myself bitterly anyhow. Our gullibility cost the boy his life. It's hard to forgive yourself … The chief of police has listened to reason, we informed the town when we left. That may have been a mistake too. We made everyone drop their guard as it were. But we were acting in good faith. Our most serious crime was naivety."

"OH," says Don Alfredo Sacamata senior that night, when our paths cross at the bar table after we've got back from Don Alfio's, "I didn't go. They came looking for me that they did. I don't want any trouble with the police I told them. If you want to go you go. You have to walk on eggshells where things like that are concerned," he pours into the scathing ears of Iturraspe, the indifferent ears of Porfirio Dupuy, the uncomfortable ears of Don León, the irked ears of Guido, the ulcerated ears of yours truly. "It was none of my business after all. I didn't have anything against the Ezcurra boy but—"

"We're not going to start with that again are we Alfredito," Don León interrupts him. "Everyone did what they thought best and your own conscience is the best judge of any mistakes you might've made. The only thing I will add," he says looking right at me, "is that I was there and I saw how your grandfather did everything possible to get Superintendent Neri to change his course. You have my word," he adds unnecessarily, and not knowing what to reply I sit there staring at him for a while; but he doesn't say any more. I thank him for the white lie with a nod of the head and leave my head tilted slightly until they've left.

WHAT I REMEMBER MOST about my grandfather was his ability with his hands, the grace and ease with which he connected with the material world; it was people that were always the problem for him. At the end of the backyard by the chicken coop, with which it shared the same long corrugated-iron roof, stood the shed where he worked. The cement floor always covered in a fine layer of sawdust and dirt, the carpenter's workbench with the edges bitten by countless missed sawstrokes, the lone green lampshade dangling on a long flex strung from the ceiling, the walls and corners invisible behind the profusion of objects hanging or leaning on them, the peculiar quality of the sunlight coming through a dusty window … Entire siestas I could spend studying the various traces of my grandfather's handiwork, like an archaeologist excavating some ruins to deduce from them the characteristics of a world that would never be mine. It was as if I already knew that that ability, that familiarity with the purely material side of things, was forbidden to my purely mental intelligence, not for now but for ever. I, who slip in and out of impregnable software as smoothly as a hand into a silk glove, have always been incapable of hammering a nail without bending it, sawing a plank other than in a zigzag, or unravelling a tangle of string without feeling that it's a living thing whose only reason for existence in the cosmic scheme of things is to exasperate me with an obstinacy I can't help but take personally. So I'd sit and watch him as he worked—I wanted to locate that knowledge, discover what there was in the movement of his hands that made the block of rough wood an eddy of dark water flowing beneath his eyes and fingers, or whether it was his eyes or his hands that possessed the gift of ordering space into precise geometries using just nails and bits of wood and chicken wire. Nothing inert was strange to him—he was equally at home welding and riveting wrought-iron gates and lamp posts as carving a piece of marble for a tabletop or night table, or bending a wooden plank as if it were soft to make a mailbox. And that was why the encyclopaedia of that knowledge, the visible sign not only of everything he'd made, but also of everything he was capable of making, was his shadow board—a vast sheet of wood made vaster by memory, as long as a school blackboard and twice as high, on which all the instruments of his trade were hung within reach of his sure hand, some with shapes so recondite that I could spend hours developing theories about their potential functions, and beside whose complexity, the frequently ordinary use my grandfather's hands put them to at my request was usually rather disappointing. Each one had a precise place assigned to it on the board, a cast patiently moulded by my grandfather that it and only it could occupy. Where someone of a more practical bent would make do with a nail, he'd place a wooden block whose convexity would snugly receive the inner curvature of a saw handle or the concavities of a hammerhead, or he'd cut and bend some sheet metal to provide a made-to-measure resting place for a wrench or a pair of pliers. I sometimes think that nothing in this world represents him as well as that shadow board—it says more about him than all the papers he signed as a provincial lawyer and politician; and I know we never had a better time than when he used to let me watch him work and without any explanation whatsoever, without uttering a single word, he'd show me what the different tools were for and the particular way of bringing out the best in each material. But I've never got to grips with the mute obstinacy of the material world, which must be why I ended up devoting my life to computers, every bit as irrational, capricious and crafty as their makers. And what's true of me, capable of howling insults at the flush button on a toilet because it refuses to stop hissing and dripping, was true of my grandfather, Don Julián Echezarreta, with people. The lowliest member of staff on the ladder was just as likely to drive him to distraction as the provincial governor; his reactions were always disproportionate and turned out to be the death of him. Apoplexy, diagnosed Dr Alexander, not without elegance, and at the funeral, which wasn't here but in Rosario, I can remember my grandmother's stern expression as she told my mother, "Cry all you like but stop repeating 'Papuchi Papuchi' out loud," and how snugly the wax doll fitted into the wood and satin bed made to measure for it. His face wore an almost happy expression; perhaps—a secret kept even from himself—he'd always wanted to rejoin the peaceful existence of inert matter, which had never let him down. He almost always cared about me, but I think he knew I secretly found him a disappointment. He was barely capable of being a grandfather and, for the three long months of summer at least, I asked him to be a father to me as well.

"YOU LEAVING FEFE?" Leticia asks me when she sees me getting my bag together.

"Yes. I'm taking the four am to Rosario, they leave every hour for Buenos Aires from there so I'm told. It's the first one that passes isn't it?"

"The La Verde bus? Yes. There's another at five-thirty I think."

"Two. But I've already bought my ticket for this one," I reply, wrestling with the zipper.

"It's really got to you about your granddad hasn't it. Guido told me."

"Yes. No," I lie, I'm not sure with which word. "I miss home too. I rang from the terminal and when Guille answered I actually got a lump in my throat. And there's such a hoo-hah here over this whole business, it's all getting a bit much to be honest. I may come back later on, I don't know. I need to stop and think for a bit. And I've found out everything I wanted to. I don't want to talk to anyone else, I get the feeling I know what they're going to say."

"Are you stopping for dinner?"

"If that's all right with you. We'll have a send-off."

She waits by the door a little longer out of politeness, and I'm about to tell her not to put herself out and to get on with her things when the tooting of a car horn makes us jump. Through the window we're dazzled by the battery of full headlights from Guido's Fiat Uno, who's already walking in through the front door.

"Sayago's shown up. The ex-cop," he announces exultantly. "He's waiting for us at the bar," he says coming inside

119

and he sees my bag on the bed. "Where are you going?" he asks me.

"I'm leaving. I decided a while ago," I reply, stating the time.

"There's still time then," he says to me dragging my by the arm towards the door he left open when he came in. "We've got more than enough time till four in the morning."

# Interlude Two

D AILY LIFE IN MALIHUEL *hasn't changed radically since my last visit, so it isn't hard to reconstruct what an average day would have been like, twenty years back. To be more illustrative let's choose a weekday; to avoid being too abstract let's say a Friday; and let's put that Friday somewhere towards the end of February—Friday twenty-fifth February 1977. We can place our ideal observer high up at the top of the church spire, from where he would be able to observe everything—all four points of the compass—that goes on in the streets and, in less detail, at the lagoon's beach resort; and for what's hidden under the tops of the trees or in the interiors of the houses, imagination or memory should be enough, as this is an observer who has the essential rhythms of town life written on their body.*

*The day begins at night, as is the norm in towns in Argentina's interior, even in summer. A light comes on—at the Trigo Limpio Bakery. A light goes out—at the police headquarters one dozy officer has replaced another sleeping officer and doesn't want the light to keep him awake. Half a block away the drying fans of the pasta factory commence their non-stop drone, wafting their egg-and-flour breath onto the street. At 4.45 am—if it's on time—the Los Cardales bus from the towns to the south swings onto Veinticinco de Mayo Avenue. These days it stops at*

121

the New Terminal, but twenty years ago it would have driven on for two more blocks, as far as the corner of Los Tocayos, where a shadowy figure gets off, its human form disappearing into the surrounding shadows never to be seen again. Forty minutes later the Chevallier from Bullock follows the same route and, when it sees no sign of a passenger standing on the corner, heads straight on down the Fuguet road, bound for Rosario. Impressions: a watery light spreading from the east, the air still, and cool for the last time in the day, the acoustic depth of the space measured in all directions by the crowing of cocks and echoed by the street lights, as sector after sector of the local grid clicks off. In the uncertain light the tarmacked streets are filled with the silent traffic of bicycles, mainly from the Colonia, converging on the open gates of the Tuttolomondo factory. Down the same street, from the lagoon, lurches the milkman's trap, laden with dented, presumably full aluminium churns. In the gardens of each house it stops at, a covered jug has been waiting since the night before. The sky is criss-crossed by the shooting silhouettes of birds and everywhere the grass bends under the weight of the dew.

About seven, as the sun plucks the first rays off Comandante Pedernera's bronze kepi, the La Capital truck from Rosario via Fuguet and the La Nación truck from Buenos Aires pull in at opposite ends of town. The first drops off the pile of newspapers outside the Casaricos', the other at the hallway of the Dupuys, who will distribute it to whoever has ordered it. Fifteen minutes later the Central Alcorta bus arrives from its namesake, bound for Elordi and Toro Mocho; at most one dozy passenger gets off and steers their elongated shadow towards the houses, if they're from town, or as far as a bench in the square to wait for the shops or offices to open if they aren't.

By half-past seven no dew is left, except at the bases of the thickest patches of weeds, and in the sun-warmed treetops the cicadas start up their tentative drone. Until then the town has just been stretching *and yawning, but now it wakes up properly. Lots of people on foot, a few cars, the odd motorcycle fill the streets; a couple of weeks later and there'll be more activity because the start of classes will add the gleaming white of school pinafores to the bright light of day. The two banks and two service stations open, a few businesses and all the public offices. A handful of cars from neighbouring towns pull up outside the Courts, the police headquarters or the all-purpose building that houses the Inland Revenue, the Civil Registry and the Justice of the Peace's Office. The traffic is fluid because the number of people or vehicles is never large enough for queues or traffic jams to form. Delivery trucks arrive from neighbouring towns and Malihuel sends them its own in return, with the logo of the globe and the question "What kind of delicious pasta shall we eat today?" painted on the grooved metal sides of the trucks. An hour later all the shops are open, the cemetery, the telephone exchange—still called Entel in those days—and the Post Office. This is also the time when the hotel kitchens and dining rooms come to life, with tourists and townsfolk wanting an early breakfast to make the most of the day, which promises to be a bright one: the Malihuel Grand Hotel and the Las Delicias on the square, the Los Tocayos hotel-restaurant and above all the Lagoon Hotel, towards which the trucks and vans that have finished their deliveries in the Colonia and the town advance, along the causeway across the glittering water. The stationmaster opens up his office and waits for the freight train to pass through, and at the now abandoned power plant the nightwatchman sets off for home and sleep, after a few matés with the two daytime operators.*

*By around nine o'clock, when the metallic sawing of the cicadas thickens the air, the heat really has begun to kick in. The* Clarín *van arrives and drops off its bale of newspapers—the bulkiest—outside the kiosk-cum-photocopier's on the corner opposite the Courts. Half-an-hour later, the mail van leaves one canvas sack on the opposite corner and picks up another. By that time the bicycle traffic is all children, who also bring the playground in the square to life. Today being the last Friday of Carnival, many of them are equipped with squeezy bottles and water bombs. In kitchens the length and breadth of town, mothers are washing up the breakfast things and beginning to fill polystyrene coolers with pop, sandwiches, tomatoes and hard-boiled eggs for a day out at the lagoon. On the basketball and tennis courts of the Yacht Club the chairman switches the swags of coloured light bulbs on and off to make sure everything's in working order for the dance that night. A patrol car carrying arrests from other towns pulls up around the back of the police headquarters and toots its horn outside the jailhouse gates. Behind it, while it waits, an orange Chevy coupé chugs and lurches beetle-like down the tarmacked street, turns right at the corner and, after two more gruelling blocks, stops outside a house with a slate-inlaid façade overlooking the square. A figure gets out on the passenger side, shades his eyes from the glare of the sun with one hand and opens the door, without a key. Before going inside he turns round and waves to the occupants of the car, one of whom is in the process of clambering from the back into the recently vacated front seat. The car pulls off with the door still open and one foot sticking out, and over the noise of the engine comes a confusion of intermingled laughter and swearing. The two doors—the car's and the house's—slam shut at the same instant.*

*It's noon, and first the Banco Provincia then the Banco Nación close their doors to the public until the following Monday. An hour later the public offices will do the same; only the post office and the telephone exchange will reopen after siesta. This is the time when the relay stations in Rosario start broadcasting, and in the kitchens of those who have lunch at home television screens flicker into life to accompany the meal*

124

*with their grey silhouettes and almost articulate static crackle. It's still two years before colour TV and ten before the arrival of cable will lend some meaning—other than ostentation—to owning one. At other houses husbands and fathers park outside the door and get out to change, while the family loads up the car and youngsters riot in the back seat. After tactical stops at the butcher's and the baker's, they will join the swollen caravan of cars and even trucks from every town in this and neighbouring counties which converges on the causeway and advances single-file towards the lagoon's two beach resorts. At 1.15 pm, when the Los Ranqueles coach bound for Rosario goes past, it will be fifteen minutes since the DRMCO grader paving the Belgrano Street section between Revoredo and Martínez has stopped work; its two operators take a break from the double reflection of sun and hot tar under the insubstantial shade of the olive trees that line the as yet non-existent commercial high school. Little by little the early din of Malihuel's day dies away, except on the island in the lagoon, where the smoke of dozens of barbecues and the cries of children playing in the water or at Carnival amidst tables and cars rises heavenwards. In the dining room of the Lagoon Hotel most of the waiters wait patiently by the counter; only at night will things liven up.*

*By three in the afternoon it's as if a flash plague had done away with all the inhabitants. The last bus from Central Alcorta bound for Toro Mocho has just passed through without stopping, and the streets are devoid of people and vehicles. They're filled entirely by the sun, the heat and the thunderous singing of the cicadas, the only movement that of a rhinoceros bug lurching over the red-hot sand. The shade, which has been retreating over the course of the day, now crouches at the foot of the trees and in the interiors of the houses, holed up behind closed shutters. All life and movement has retreated to them—in one, a standing fan swings from one side to the other, its breath strafing bodies sprawled on sheets, separated to prevent sweating at the points of contact; in another*

125

one, glued together from head to toe, grunting and groaning in chorus to the creaking of the bed; on a cool-tiled patio children play their silent siesta games among the potted plants; in a darkened kitchen the doñas who can't sleep for the heat switch on the television in resignation and wait for the half-past soap.

An hour later the heat has hardly abated but, as if in answer to some secret call, the streets begin to stretch and yawn. The doors of the post office, the factory and the bar open, a megaphoned Fiat 600 begins to drive around the square, stridently announcing the night's shows down at the lagoon, towards which a last batch of bathers head off to soak up what's left of the sun; the TV drama over, the church bell begins to ring, calling the señoras to five-o'clock Mass and, refilled over and over at the tank in the square, the sprinkler starts roaming the dirt streets, damping down the dust with its open flower of water dodged by boys on bikes and dogs (the first sprinkling evaporating so fast that one inhabitant sitting on a wicker chair on the sidewalk outside her house watches the earth suck up all the moisture and dry before her eyes as if in fast-forward) and the whole town is flooded with the scent of wet earth, which mingles with the honeysuckle, spikenard and jasmine as the shadows lengthen. On the dot of seven the cinema opens its doors for the one-and-only showing on sunny days (a matinee and a late show are added when it rains), welcoming the trickle of cinema-goers who have been killing time in the ice-cream parlour next door, only one of whom—a young man in bermudas and multicoloured polo shirt, carrying a two-flavour tub—walks against the tide and disappears around the corner of the Banco Provincia. The last intercity coach of the day—the 7.20 Chevallier to Rosario—goes past, and in the Council yard an employee uncouples the sprinkler tank from the tractor and couples up the tipper, Friday being trash day. A reddening sun closes in on the horizon and the singing of the cicadas has now given way to crickets

126

*and frogs; first one row of mercury lights, then another perpendicular to it, comes on in the two main streets, the axes of a grid immediately, if more faintly, completed by the light bulbs strung along the other streets and a few moving cars with their sidelights on. Outside their radius, on the closed highway, almost at the edge of the lagoon, a few young couples under cover of the shadows venture towards the Mochica, as does the occasional solitary kerb-crawler down by the tyre workshop to check out the highway whores. Out on the island the power plant shudders and jolts into life, and as it hums the filaments of hundreds of light bulbs glow, going in seconds from red to yellow to white until they disappear in the very light they generate. A bronze-torsoed bather in scarlet trunks steps into one of the cubicles dripping wet, emerges from it in bermudas and brightly coloured polo shirt, sits down at one of the low pine tables and orders a beer. A few families have already struck camp, fathers loading deckchairs into trunks, mothers washing dishes in brown water in concrete sinks, grandmothers towel in hand waiting for the kids to launch the last of their water bombs or take a last dip in the lagoon, while along the causeway the caravan forms of those who want to shower again and change for the nine-o'clock show. By then there'll be clouds of moths and scarabs and other beetles around the spotlights that will turn the open-air stage into a living, crawling carpet beneath the feet of the artists who that night are Los Churrinches (a folk group from Salta), an unknown imitator from Buenos Aires—who, crippled or consumptive (opinions vary), will take the stage on crutches and perform on a chair—and last, before an audience, whose impatience borders on frenzy, no less than Sandro will take to the stage in a triumphant return to the town that gave him a standing ovation when he was a rising star and today has dressed up to fête him in the cradle of his fame and glory. Special buses arrive from Santa Fe and neighbouring provinces, and hoards*

127

of young girls with placards and posters ready to be unfurled at their idol's imminent arrival anxiously scan the clouds gathering in the livid sky and pray for the rain to hold off until the concert's over. It's likely—only likely—that at this stage of the proceedings a young man in an impeccable cream suit with neatly slicked hair, appears in the hotel doorway, scans the gathered multitude with puzzled eyes and disappears again in the direction of the bar.

From this point on it's impossible to say with any certainty what happens. The night may well be unique and so fall outside the scope of a description that, like this one, endeavours to keep to the merely habitual. The artists take the stage a little late, when the audience's rhythmic clapping makes their presence unavoidable, Sandro keeps them waiting even longer and rumours about accidents on Route Eight or health problems gust around the sensitive surface of the crowd; Sandro does or does not arrive and the approaching storm does or does not drown out the girls squealing at the delirium of his show, and at eleven at night the waxing moon may no longer be seen behind the black thunderheads driven by the sudden wind across the sky. The Carnival dances go ahead regardless, the poshest in the function rooms of the hotel with the Boedo Dixie Orchestra, who can switch from a milonga to a foxtrot in the blink of an eye, and the dance for the youngest under the Yacht Club shed vibrating to the rhythms of the Los Machimbres quartet from Córdoba. The night owls end the day—technically now a new one—at Bermejo's nightclub or queuing at the drive-in entrance to the Mochica or scattering to the neighbouring towns, and more than one ends up sleeping it off in a lay-by, where they eventually open their dazed and gluey eyes to the first light of day.

This is as far as we can go then with the description of a typical summer's day in Malihuel twenty years ago, peppered with the appearances of the figure of Darío Ezcurra, which the keen observer

128

*will have been able to spot amidst the anonymous swarming of his fellow townsmen. It is as well not to overlook those instants because, though they may seem habitual, they are nevertheless precious. Tomorrow the observer who wants to trace Darío Ezcurra's trail from noon to dawn, in the complex weave of Malihuel's inhabitants', will search in vain.*

# Chapter Three

" I WAS IN THE FORCE *che* but it ain't the same thing as being a cop though. It's common knowledge my old man was the one as got me into the force, I couldn't kick up a fuss about it could I. You're from Buenos Aires, maybe you don't know what it's like here. A son follows in his father's footsteps, part out of obedience, part out of need. If he don't like it he's got to leave. If the father's got a business the son inherits it, if he's got a farm the land, if he's got a council job he tries to get his son a job there. Correct me if I'm wrong Don Guido."

"You aren't," he replies laconically.

"That was my case. They give up a lot for me and sent me to the Virasoro Academy, a policeman's salary's barely enough to get by on as I'm sure you know and there were eight of us, my five sisters and me the only boy, I couldn't very well refuse. A policeman all his life my old man was and proud of it. You wore the badge with honour in them days, not like nowadays when people see a cop and think 'criminal', and they ain't far wrong, let's face it the only difference between a thief and a cop these days is the uniform. I expected something different when I signed up, thought

they'd all be like my old man. Never forget his face I won't
the first day he saw me dressed in blue, chest bursting with
the pride of … But anyway, that's not what you called me
here for is it. To tell you about my life. Ask me whatever you
like, I might be able to give you something useful."

We're sitting at our usual table in Los Tocayos. Nene
Larrieu's already poured the first round of drinks: vermouth for
Iturraspe and Licho, gin on the rocks for Guido, Argentinian
Scotch for me and Legui *caña* for Carmen Sayago, the elusive ex-policeman who's finally deigned to grace us with his
presence and is willing and able to talk. He doesn't look too
intimidating; just the opposite in fact—a squat Indian-looking
type with submissive manners and shifty eyes, uncombably
tangled hair, dressed in a brown pullover with stripy sleeves
and trousers washed to some colour beyond the spectrum,
who, with a timid, caried smile, asks: "They're on you ain't
they Don? 'Cause me like, if I can't land the odd odd job I
can't afford to eat. If I'd of carried on in the police I'd of made
sergeant by now at least, not a fortune but enough to make
ends meet. Still I don't regret my decision. When Greco got
promoted to chief I knew my days in the force was numbered.
One of the old guard Superintendent Neri was—good fellas
like my old man, who could never adapt. Had Greco under
his wing, grooming him to take his place. That's what usually
happens, 'specially when the retiring Superintendent's thinking
of staying in the area—puts his man in the headquarters and
stays a part of things … But of course while Greco was going
yes sir no sir three bags full sir he was looking for somewhere
to stick the knife in, lots of games of chess with that whatsisface
but if you play chess with a cheat … "

He finishes his glass instead of the sentence, smacks his lips and puts it down with an insinuating thwack. Nene Larrieu arches his eyebrows and I give him the go-ahead. Sayago gazes with glee at the honey-coloured liquor filling his glass and running thickly over the edge into the saucer beneath.

"Ah, that's better, my soul's returned to my body. Shivering all day long I been, just couldn't get warm."

"There's a lot of flu about," opines Licho, sipping his vermouth.

"And I've got the best remedy here," replies Sayago, putting his lips to the brimming glass to take a sip. "Where was I?"

"Greco. Neri," supplies Iturraspe.

"Right. Everything Superintendent Neri did Greco un-did. Gang of thugs, that's what he turned the county police into. Didn't give a toss about law and order Greco didn't, or guerrillas for that matter, the only thing he was interested in was lining his pockets. Mortgaged his old folks' house to pay for his promotion and his assignment can you believe? Everything in his headquarters was arranged with money. Kept a pad of accounts on his desk he did—so much from bookies, so much from tarts, so much from dealers, so much from truck-hijackers, which in this area—"

"They call us the Bermuda Triangle around these parts," Guido interrupts. "We once had a whole truckful of merchandise vanish into thin air. Driver and all."

"Oh, no wonder we had spaghetti at headquarters two months running. Only joking Don Guido, no need to look at me like that. As I was telling you Don, Greco ended up buying one of them pocket calculators that'd just come out—big square one with little red numbers I remember it was—at it all day he was with his little gadget. Only thing that mattered to him about the police stations in the area was that they came up with the readies between the first and the fifth, he'd pocket his share and send the rest to the big pricks in Rosario, and not so much as a thank you to the men on the beat who sweat and stick their necks out to get it for him. Got land all over the area Greco has, and several nightclubs, and a security firm in Toro Mocho, but if an ex-policeman who's risked his life for him goes and asks him for a job you think he gets any help? Treated like a dog he is. A man who doesn't know what loyalty is can't be a policeman I say but that's how it is—so I left. Wasn't going to sully the uniform my old man give me you can be sure of that. Ah well, can't complain. Short but all the sweeter for it innit," he innovates, tilting his glass for some time so that the last drop oozes thickly down from the bottom, and then excuses himself to go to the bathroom dragging his feet, his upper body in advance of his hips in the convex bulge of the chronic alcoholic.

"What did they kick *him* out for *che*?" I ask the others out of no particular interest.

"Used to pocket the pay-offs," Licho declares. "And someone went and tipped off Greco. Can you imagine. They gave him his marching orders and a real going-over. Split his head open apparently, serious it was. He says he started hitting the bottle after that, and it must be true 'cause he ain't stopped since has he."

"Didn't want to know him any more," Iturraspe adds meditatively, "his old man didn't after he was dismissed. Kicked him out of the house and from then on every time their paths crossed—several times a day in a town like this—he'd look the other way. Moved to Casilda when he retired, with his wife and single daughters; Carmen and the two married daughters stayed here. It's thanks to them he's still alive. *Che* it's bloody cold in here isn't it. If you can't turn the burner or the gas fire up Nene, why don't you set fire to a couple of chairs? We're freezing our arses off in here."


"THINGS REALLY STARTED warming up around then I can tell you, the heat was vicious and didn't let up even at night and what between that and the waiting everybody was worn out and bad-tempered, waking up before dawn in the hope of some cool air or the news that it was all over. Lots of people didn't care how by that stage, you know like when a loved one's suffering and there's no hope left and the only thing you ask is for the suffering to stop once and for all. And now with the weekend approaching there was also the eagerly awaited Friday show, none other than Sandro in person was going to perform there you know where yes at the island hotel and then the scaremongers some saying that he's not coming and others that he is but the storm'll keep him away. And most people thought don't know why but they were all convinced the Ezcurra business would be put off till the next weekend, as if it'd be suspended because of rain, it got mixed up in their minds with the show," El Turquito Majul had told me the afternoon we did some circuits together in the gym—I haven't felt like returning since.

135

"AND ONE FINE morning I remember it was dead hot and the day starts with more hustle Subsuperintendent Greco's in and out of the Super's office and calls are coming in from Rosario and word starts going the rounds from office to office—it's today. But only then in all the toing and froing does the Super answer someone as stops him with a blink and this is it, confirmed from one end of headquarters to the other, particularly when he calls in Sergeant Chacón and says to him Sergeant he says to him put a couple of officers on Ezcurra's tail if he takes a dump I want to know about it and by noon that day which was well never mind a ... wait gimme a second Wednesday no Thursday—"

"Friday," intervenes Nene Larrieu from his post behind the bar.

"Friday, that's it. Don't miss a trick you don't do you eh Nene? Had to be a Friday or Saturday 'cause of the show at the lagoon. Bet you don't know who was on that night? If you don't believe me ask them. Know who was on? Tell him Nene."

"He already knows," the memorious waiter clarifies.

"Sandro, that's who. The Gypsy Man in person. Just picture what this town was like in them days, I don't mean like Buenos Aires but just picture it. So anyroad as I was telling you by noon Friday the news had spread and the whole town knew didn't they. The dog's day'd come."


"HE WAITED LIKE THAT TOO," Nene Larrieu said to me a few days ago, when, bored of my daytime zapping in Guido and Leticia's kitchen and not feeling like going over to the factory to borrow their creaking computer for a while, I wandered over to Los Tocayos in the hope some-one would turn up, 'that dog's day' as they call it, for his mates Los Jaimitos to come. They'd already stood him up at the lagoon and he came in early to see why. Maybe something's happened to one of them? he said to me at one point and I couldn't stand it any longer and I said, I said to myself, I've got to tell him and God's will be done, when I see a patrol car going past behind him without him noticing, crawling along like this past all three doors and through the last one Chacón the one who now owns the kiosk next door and was sitting in the back puts a finger to his lips. Ezcurra didn't notice a thing. Sat there waiting for quite a while but word must've got around that he was here 'cause not a soul came in the bar and it must've been around eight I reckon he said I'm off home for a shower before the show, let the lads know if they're looking for me and he left through that door over there. And that was the last time I saw him."


"SHEER COINCIDENCE," exhaled Jaimito, Sacamata junior soon after arriving, feigning a bodily relaxation belied by the cold gleam in his eyes and the rictus of his mouth. "Bermejo was away on business in Rosario that day, I had my old man down with otitis I think it was and had to look after the store, and my friend Beto here … What was it you had on?"

"Had to take Mamá to the specialist in Toro Mocho. She was in a really bad way by then," and he added unnecessarily in a barely audible voice: "Died a year later."

137

"You see?" boomed Sacamata in confirmation. "We liked a good time it's true, but we weren't kids either. Bermejo was pushing forty, you and me were going on for thirty, and Ezcurrita was around … "

"Thirty-four," I beat the infallible Nene Larrieu to it.

"Didn't I tell you Beto? If he carries on like this our friend Fefe here'll end up knowing Ezcurrita better than any of us. That's what I'm saying, we weren't kids, we all had responsibilities. Not Ezcurra of course, he was our very own Isidoro Cañones, he could afford not to. But the rest of us had work obligations or family obligations, like Beto with his late Mamá. I mean the razz is the razz and graft's graft right? That's something Ezcurrita could never grasp."

"I couldn't say anything to you in front of Batata 'cause he still goes crazy nowadays if anyone dares to insinuate," Iturraspe whispered when we were alone, "but what you're thinking's the truth. We did everything we could not to run into Ezcurrita all day. It wasn't 'cause we were scared—least not in my case—it was 'cause we were embarrassed. If I hadn't told him anything by then how would I find the face to tell him now? He'd never forgive me for not warning him earlier. What if nothing happened and I'd burnt my boats with him over nothing? I clung on to that hope, it was my last card … There were so many reasons to be hopeful. I don't think Neri thought about it beforehand, too Machiavellian for a cop's brain, but paradoxically enough the result of his enquiries was to convince everybody that he wouldn't do anything in the end see? His bark's worse than his bite people were saying, so we inadvertently gave him the go-ahead … "

"You were his friends," I opined.

138

Iturraspe automatically opened his mouth to speak but no sound came out. All his vanished eloquence rose to his eyes. I changed the subject as a mark of gratitude for his silence.

"IF ANYONE sent him a letter as they say ... "—the pharmacist Don Mauro Mendonca had seemed to hesitate—"it wasn't me. I phoned him. He answered and I quickly outlined the situation for him and suggested that the best thing he could do was to leave town for a while, and the province too to be on the safe side. Then I hung up."

"You didn't tell him who you were?" I couldn't help asking, knowing full well the answer would be:

"Are you mad? Knowing what a blabbermouth Ezcurra was the first thing he'd do would be to tell the whole town I'd told him. I did what morally I had to and warned him that's all. The others didn't even do that."

"LOOK HERE KIDDO," says the last Jaimito, Bermejo, a fifty-something mahogany-dyed Pappo clone in black leather jacket and dark glasses to match the daytime half-light of his locked, empty nightclub. Through the black-painted windows comes the busy sound of traffic and pedestrians with which the not-quite-town of Fuguet does its best to drown the memory of the days when the Agrofé farm machinery and equipment factory was open and they vied with Malihuel for its administrative supremacy of the county. "I agreed to see you 'cause Beto Iturraspe, who's a friend of mine, asked me to, but to be honest the less you remind me of the better. If there's one thing I don't regret in my life it's leaving for good, don't know how I stood the place for nearly fifteen years. This may not be New York but at least they let you work, and live as well, which is a luxury in itself. I'm a believer," he says, tugging at a thick silver chain and disentangling a little medallion of the Virgin Mary from the others—a swastika, a yin-yang and a Megadeath skull nestling in the fuzz of his chest—then kissing it, "but I couldn't set foot inside the church there without being a dartboard for Father Raneri's sermons," he says and I stifle a remark about his pitted cheeks being proof of the current Malihuel priest's excellent aim. "So as you might've guessed I don't find the idea of this little chat very exciting, nothing personal I can assure you but still … What do you wanna know?"

I tell him. He shakes a crumpled pack of black Particulares under my nose until a reluctant cigarette pokes out. I decline. He lights up.

"Ezcurra was a burnt offering," he exhales, "and anyone as tried to save him was going to drown with him," he continues, his composure apparently immune from the almost physical way his metaphors cancelled each other out. "'Specially me. Superintendent Neri wanted to run me out of town so he'd get the holier-than-thou female vote. Twice the pigs raided my place with people inside, trumped up one charge for drugs they did and another for underage drinking, it sucked up the month's profits to pay off a shyster and get myself off the hook. Not to mention the money for the first to the fifth."

"I thought Neri didn't take bungs in Malihuel."

Bermejo laughs hoarsely, coughing smoke. I'm a tad disappointed none of his stained teeth are gold.

140

"That story still doing the rounds is it? What a shower." He adjusts the bridge of his glasses with a jab of his index finger. "He'd go easy on butchers and grocers and tighten the screw on me and the Mochica and the bookies. It's easy for some. Singled me out he did. It got so bad I started winding myself up about how they'd do me in in a blind alley, that's why I've taken the precaution of carrying a piece ever since," he says flashing the butt of a revolver under his jacket. "In the end Ezcurra was the one as copped it, but it could just as easily've been me. He had me in his sights I tell you. With Greco it was all a lot easier. If you coughed up on time he left you alone; if you didn't you'd had yer chips. Everything clear as daylight. Even used to stop by the premises and have a few drinks with the good fellas. Straight up and down he was. Back there they say he ditched them in the flood. Good for him's what I say. I'd've burnt down anything sticking out of the water. What?"

I repeat the question, a bit louder the second time.

"I was over here trying to close a deal on some premises. Wanted to get out of there at all costs. And if I'd've been at Ezcurra's side when they grabbed him you know what"—he dramatised with index finger and thumb at right angles— "Two birds with one stone. Look, with the pigs you don't have to use tongues but you do have to learn to live together. In my line of business you can't afford to have them breathing down yer neck. Bad for business. The fuzz are people just like you and me when you come down to it, and over the years they lay down certain ground rules that both sides learn to respect. And incidentally my good friend Ezcurra conned me over that Expotencia deal as well, never saw a red cent of that dough again I can assure you. Short reckonings make long friends as they say. Well they didn't in this case."

"AH, THE BLESSED LETTER," Don León Benoit had smiled understandingly, who'd turned up a while after Sacamata had left. "Yes, I heard about that too. There was no letter, least as far as I know. The lengths some people'll go to to salve their consciences. If you asked back in those days people would swear on God, the Virgin Mary and all the saints of the year that the letter didn't exist but that anyhow somebody else'd written it. Ask people nowadays, the way you are, and they were queuing up outside the Ezcurras' front door, all clutching their envelopes to slip underneath."

"SO AS SHOWTIME APPROACHES like the Super sends out a car and we get in me, him, Sergeant Chacón and some cop from Leopardi driving his name'll come to me in a minute. The lagoon says the Super and there's me well chuffed 'cause I wouldn't miss Sandro for the world. The causeway was like this, bumper to bumper it was and we radioed ahead to the unit stationed on the island *che* set up a roadblock this way and the Super goes stick the siren on and off we set down the oncoming lane. The grain of sand as we called him look at that eh I just remembered they had him located at the hotel bar, put a man on all the exits and if he moves stick close to him the Super said, we'll be right there."

"Ezcurra'd gone to review the show," Iturraspe supplies rather gloomily.

"Why grain of sand?" I ask.

"Dunno, it was the Super's name for him God knows why, and we all started using it 'cause he seemed quite fond of it. The grain of sand, good God. The things you remember eh? And we sat there waiting for I don't know what, the Superintendent said we wait and nobody was going to ask why, then we spotted Mayor Echezarreta approaching through the window, he was yer grandfather am I right in thinking? Gor my throat's drying up with all this talking. Not used to it."

Nene Larrieu responds to my nod. Without looking at anyone in particular as he pours he remarks:

"Looks like the drinks are on tap tonight."

Sayago grins happily at him then turns his eyes back to his glass. Once again he bows his head with devout lips to the trembling golden rim.

"I WROTE HIM A LETTER," Clara Benoit had confessed. "I don't know if it's the one they're talking about. Probably never opened it, he was used to getting letters from his … I even tried to change my handwriting so he wouldn't recognise me, tried to write like a man. I've never understood why men's handwriting comes out one way and women's another."

"So you didn't sign it," I'd said to her, trying not to let my disappointment show.

"No," she'd replied. "If he'd known it was from me he wouldn't have believed what it said. He'd've thought it was another one of my desperate ruses."

143

"NEARLY CALLED OFF it was the Los Churrinches' set, they used to be called Los Atahualpas and they must've changed their name to get off the blacklists, but someone recognised them and went and told your grandfather," Iturraspe takes advantage of the lull in the conversation to insert, "remember Los Atahualpas Licho?"

Licho begins to whistle a catchy tune and Nene Larrieu supplies the missing lyrics.

> *"Through the jungle of Bolivia*
> *he advances with his rifle*
> *A new knight ups the ante*
> *no lord the Comandante*
> *He's the revolution's armour*
> *And his name is? … "*

"*Che* … what was it called?" asks Licho.

"*Zamba rebelde*," Iturraspe replies. "So when your grandfather found out the Superintendent was at the lagoon he went right up and asked him What shall we do and the Superintendent goes Not now Don Julián and your grandfather went on blaming the artist's agent saying he'd acted in good faith till the Superintendent got tired of telling him all right and yelled you can play the bloody communist march for all I care, I've got more important fish to fry today." Sayago has weathered the interruption by taking off one sneaker and, with a pained expression, fiddling with a toe sticking out of his holey sock:

"Anything the matter?" Licho enquires politely.

"This ingoing toenail's killing me."

"Better kill it first then," quips Iturraspe. "Once a cop always a cop eh?"

Sayago works out from his tone that it's a joke and laughs without getting it. He takes the opportunity to regain the limelight.

"And there we were still waiting when we see one of the doubles approaching from behind and Subsuperintendent Greco gets out on the passenger side—"

"One of the what?" I ask.

"Doubles. Unlicensed vehicles. This one was a Dodge Polara Greco'd confiscated for his own personal use, a set of wheels that'd of won more than one race with a guy with balls at the wheel, so anyroad like Greco comes over to the window and says Excuse me Superintendent I was held up but I haven't been briefed on the operation, maybe the Superintendent didn't tell him on purpose, It's all right Arielito don't worry about it or something like that actually I didn't pay much attention 'cause I was looking through the back window to see if Sandro was coming, pink limousine with real diamonds on the tyre covers I'd been told though some said he was coming straight by helicopter which was going to land on the hotel roof, sounded odd to me though 'cause to do that they'd of needed permission and we hadn't been informed; everybody on tenterhooks 'cause the support acts had finished and I reckon I've never seen so many people at the lagoon, and I was thinking let's leave it for another day or else they might lynch us Superintendent sir I was thinking when I hear the Subsuper insist The men are at their posts sir and the mark has re-turned to the hotel bar do you want me to give the order

all grovelly and sucking up like and Neri goes to him It's
all right Arielito, Arielito, that's what he used to call him,
It's all right Arielito we're going to get this over and done
with and we headed to the hotel the Super and Arielito go
inside with Sergeant Chacón and me and this other guy
stand lookout on the door outside just in case but nothing
happened can't of been inside two minutes they can't when
the three of them come out with Ezcurrita sandwiched
between them looking more lost than a dog in a bowling
alley I mean if so many people'd warned him he must at
least of seen it coming right? If he really was as cute as
people say he was. The moment he sets foot outside he
starts spotting familiar faces What's wrong don't let them
take me he tells them Whatsisface tell Mamá, Soandso tell
Thingumajig to come over to the headquarters with Dr
Someoneorother and them all going Yeah yeah take it easy
while they were looking for somewhere to scarper, but of
course it was hard going for them with the pressure of all
those people, worse with the ones furthest away fighting
to see, 'specially the ones who were from out of town and
didn't know, they wanted to get a closer look at what was
going on and then as usual some big mouth starts shouting Sandro! It's Sandro! and then there's no stopping it
when the running starts and the jostling that tell you the
avalanche is coming right? Operations with crowds are
the most difficult see they get out of hand at the drop of
a hat we get special training at the academy but anyroad
like at the ground right I'd like to see you cope with thirty
thousand monkeys screaming their heads off, enough to
make a brave man piss himself I was saying my prayers I

tell you I'm not ashamed to say it right then we were more scared than Ezcurra you can bet yer life if you like and I reckon that must of been when it got pretty much impossible for us to find a way through 'cause we'd left the car by the causeway with the guy from Leopardi his name'll come to me in a minute and the people were pushing us the other way somebody's attention lapsed somebody tripped and before we know where we are Ezcurra gives us the slip and shoots off towards the stage and the stalls where all the people he knows are the town's VIPs here's a riddle for you chief tell me what they did you'll tell me they shielded him with their bodies they hid him they yelled at him to at least escape? Did they fuck! What they did was scarper, couldn't run fast enough they couldn't, and to make matters worse they was tripping and falling over all the chairs there like a possum in a henhouse Ezcurra was with all the commotion he caused," the ex-policeman recalls with a throaty laugh. "When you tell it like that it makes you laugh, I swear it does sir, but it was pretty nasty too to be honest." He pauses for a moment to recover his gravitas and drains what's left of his *caña* while he's at it.

"You see anyone laughing?" says Guido gruffly. "Apart from you I mean."

Sayago gives a servile smile, laughs off his remark, senses a warmth and goodwill in the atmosphere that are merely the product of liquor in his bloodstream, looks hopefully first at me, then at Nene Larrieu, who goes and gets a fresh bottle off the shelf.

147

"I HAD THE CAR NEARBY," Clara Benoit had recalled, biting her cuticles, looking out of the window and down at the table in the freezing half-finished building of the new beach resort, "and when I saw what was happening I started to shout Over here Darío, this way, don't let them take you, but there were so many people screaming and shoving that he couldn't hear me, I don't even think he noticed me except one moment when a swirl of people brought us a little closer and I shouted to him again to come with me, that if he let them take him they were going to kill him. This time he did hear but they must've been the very last words, because instead of following me he made a break for it and tried to climb onstage." Clara's voice was at breaking point and I shifted uncomfortably in my chair and offered her a cigarette in the hope of heading off her crying jag in time. It worked. "That was down in the stalls, almost everyone there was from town or at least members of the Yacht Club, he knew them all personally, a lot of them all his life. Why didn't anyone else try to help him?" she asked me after two or three drags. I looked at her without answering.

"AND THEN I dunno what must of got into him to make him climb on the stage, from where we were fighting our way through the crowd we could see him trying to jump up onstage and then he makes it and stands there like he's dazzled by the spotlights, missing a shoe he was and one sleeve off his jacket, but the people in the crowd, particularly the ones too far away to see properly, started shouting San-dro! San-dro! 'specially the birds, you know how they get over the Gypsy Man some of them were already waving their knickers round their heads shouting Get yer kit off Roberto! Fuck me! stuff they usually save for the end of the show and then I reckon it was Greco and Sergeant Chacón and the guy from Leopardi his name'll come to me they get up onstage too and they go and pull Ezcurra to the floor and start laying into him. That did it. People thought we was beating up Sandro and wanted to arrest him or something and launched themselves to the rescue, and once the avalanche come there was no stopping it nearly brought the stage down they did, we was lucky to get out alive mind, you ain't got no idea what it was like."

"We were all there," Iturraspe remarks, including me out of politeness. "There were several casualties. Good thing the sand was there to cushion the falls otherwise there'd have been a lot more."

"My uncle broke a leg," Guido says to me. "Remember?"

"Who? Talito?" Of the three brothers he was the one I had least to do with.

"No," exclaims Guido, a little more perplexed. "Vicente, Vicentito's dad, who was with us. Don't you remember?"

Now it's my turn to look surprised. But I still manage to get out:

"You know what, all this you're telling me, you can't expect me to remember every—"

"But Fefe, you were there. You were with us that night. You saw everything."

He hasn't finished his sentence, but I already know it's true. That and not the dubious narrative gifts of the ex-corporal was the reason why the scene was so vividly painted in my imagination. It wasn't imagination. It was memory. I'd been there, just like the rest of them. I too had witnessed what happened. Not just that night, the night they removed Ezcurra from the lagoon. I'd been there all summer. How could it have been otherwise—I used to come every summer as a boy and spend three long months of the summer holidays, at my grandparents' house by the lagoon. How could I have forgotten? When I finally come out of my daze, I notice the silence that's fallen around the table. Stunned, with everyone waiting for me to say something, I'm barely able to ask:

"What about Sandro's show? I can't even remember that. What happened to the show?"

"Sandro couldn't make it," says Licho softly, squashing a butt end against the ashtray.

### IDOL FAILS TO SHOW,
### BUT GOOD TIME HAD BY ALL

*Once again a good time was had by all yesterday at the booming beach resort of Malihuel, with yet another of its famed musical offerings, whose fame has jumped the borders of the province time after time. Once again the responsibility of opening the soirée fell on the square shoulders of well-known Coronel González LT 29 Radio announcer, Sr Elbio Limongi, who introduced the show in brief but heartfelt words, thanking the plentiful throng for turning out. With a quite outstanding performance at the last edition of the Cosquín Festival, the outstanding musical ensemble Los Churrinches brought us all the colour and joy of the traditional music of our northern lands, playing classic compositions from their repertoire like* El quirquincho *and* Diablito carnavalero, *which the audience accompanied with enthusiastic clapping. Given the profusion of insects blanketing*

150

*virtually the entire stage—a problem we have raised in our column on other occasions—it's unfortunate they didn't perform a stomping malambo as well. Next up was comic Ziggy Estrella, who delighted old and young alike with his famed imitations, the most applauded of which were those entitled* Fasting with Mirtha Legrand, The Pink Panther Strikes Again *and* Raffaella's Party. *And so we came to the most keenly anticipated moment of the night, the return of the incomparable "Gypsy Man" to the stage that saw his debut as an artist. And, as our headline suggests, our idol may have failed to show up, but it didn't dampen the general jubilation. Only a series of stampedes and jostling, which the efficient security operation of our forces of law and order successfully contained before it escalated, was the all-too-understandable outcome of the audience's disappointment on finding out they would have to postpone—hopefully not for long—the long-awaited reunion with their elusive idol. It would, in any event, be extremely gratifying if the show's authorities and impresarios were to inform the population through this or any other medium they deem fit about the fate of our absentee. Where was he when everyone was looking for him? Where is he now? What does the future hold? Will we ever see him again? These and other questions disturb the peace of our daily comings and goings. For we are all aware that, where information is lacking, rumour runs rampant. We hope that Malihuel Festivals' next offering will afford us no such similar surprises.*

"Who on earth wrote that?" I'll ask a few days later.

"Iturraspe," Don León will reply. "The newspaper editor had come all the way from Toro Mocho for the show and offered him the job as editor of the section there and then. Iturraspe accepted, on a temporary basis, to cover for his friend he explained, and the editor, going along with him, said Right, sure, by all means. That was how he ended up with Ezcurra's 'Malihuel Page', it was his till the newspaper folded donkey's years ago now."

"And there was no reaction to this article?"

"No, people were expecting it. I reckon they could've waited a little longer right, at least till the Ezcurra boy was ... I mean the patrol cars hadn't finished crossing the causeway yet at least as a matter of form don't you reckon?"

"No, I mean because of what it says at the end. It isn't talking about Sandro at the end."

Don León will stare me in surprise, then grab the stained photocopy I hold out to him and, donning his spectacles, will read it laboriously, following the lines with his finger and mouthing the words as he goes. When he's finished, he'll hold it out, take off his glasses and say:

"You're right *che*. Well I'll be ... What a crafty old fox Beto turned out to be. No nothing happened. Nobody picked up on it."


THE PLACE where the events took place is long gone. The island, the causeway, the concrete pavilions are part of the bottom of the lake, from whose surface all that sticks out is the power-plant building, a few upright pillars, which at a distance could be dead tree trunks or lamp posts, and of course the three-storey hulk of the hotel, one of whose lateral walls has given way, leaving the halls, passageways, corridors and rooms open to view, like a doll's house. Emerging from the rocky base of its own rubble, its angular forms and the sunken cubes of the windows suggest more a prison or fortress built on a bluff than the hotel where I had dinner so many times with my grandparent—the tango orchestra or jazz band playing on the bandstand in the dining room, the marble staircases and the velvet curtains. It's difficult now to believe any of it actually existed; not even my memories feel like my own—maybe they belong to my friend, Gloria, who told me them four years ago, the day we met quite by chance and discovered our common past in Malihuel.

"SOON AS WE GOT HIM in the car he went quiet and we'd barely laid a finger on him eh. He was sat there between Chacón and me mind, not on the floor or in the trunk, sat on the back seat the way it should be, and the Super in front not saying a word, the whole causeway dead quiet, and only when we was on the road into town did yer man decide to say anything: What am I being charged with? he comes out with and the Super Being a dickhead he says to him and didn't say another word. We entered headquarters directly through the jailhouse gate and that's when I thought you're a goner lad 'cause that's what's done if they don't want a new prisoner to be entered in the warders' log. I'm not saying the Super had already made up his mind to waste him just that he was covering his back in case he had to. Told us to throw him in the pigsty and just as me and Chacón was about to give him some the Superintendent tells us to stop. Anyone lays a finger on him while I'm not here's in for it he said and headed off to headquarters. Superintendent, wait, Ezcurra said to him. Aren't I entitled to a phone call? I want to speak to my lawyer and without turning round Neri goes

You've been watching too many movies lad and walked out. I was at headquarters all night 'cause the sergeant'd given me detention for some daft thing or other can't even remember what it was now, you know what cops are like, and poking my head round the door I could see the Carnival parade heading down Veinticinco de Mayo and the music and the lights of the party and I got to thinking about the poor guy locked up there and all his friends out on the razz like nothing'd happened, if there'd been just one who'd of come to see him or ask about him not that they'd of been let in mind 'cause officially there were no records of Ezcurra—he wasn't there—but anyroad nobody tried. Nothing surprises me nowadays, life's shown me too that when you're down on yer luck people treat you like a dog, just look at me I mean. While I was in the force everyone wanted to be my friend, bought me drinks, laughed at my jokes, and I'm not saying the birds were all over me but they did look twice, but it's all water under the bridge now. Ended when Superintendent Neri left town, if I'd been a bit cleverer I'd of gone with him. Now he *did* appreciate me, liked me to brew a maté for him and have a chat, not just like a boss to his subordinate, it sometimes felt more like a father to his son. He didn't have any children you know. If the Super'd stayed on a while longer at headquarters I could of been a very different person than what I am today. Someone everybody respected," he says, scanning the audience to test their reaction. Only from me does he get a look of hypocritical understanding. He empties his xth glass, only Nene can keep track by now, and with his next one I replenish my whisky glass and Licho his vermouth. "Greco's the one to blame"—Sayago harps on the same string—"Greco fucked my life up. I swear sometimes I feel like going and finding him and sticking a forty-five right here in his gob and telling him Come on then, say what you used to say about me to my face eh? I swear I wouldn't give a toss what happens after that long as I see that shit Greco shit himself I'll take what's coming to me. Once—"

"Ezcurra," I interrupt him.

"Yeah, sorry about that sir"—he smiles his servile smile—"it's just when I get worked up the Good Lord himself can't stop me. Well in the small hours when the Super gets back the first thing he asks me was whether anybody'd come to ask about Ezcurra, and me I go No news Superintendent sir thinking he'd be relieved, but instead I thought I could see something like disappointment on his face. Went straight to his office he did and locked himself away in there all morning. They say he was calling Rosario, the *milicos*, to come and take him away, I dunno. Don't go thinking I knew everything going on just 'cause I was there, it wasn't like that—I was just a corporal, I'm only telling you what I saw. The only thing I know is the *milicos* didn't show up. Left us holding the baby they did. I was dropping so I found an empty cell right next door and slept like a suckling pig and round about noon it must've been I was woken up by the prisoner screaming for them to call his lawyer, call his mother. You understand? He wanted his mummy. I reckon it must of been the heat, the pigsty was a little two-by-two room in those days with no windows and a corrugated-iron roof which at the hottest time of day heated up like you wouldn't believe and when it was your turn to dish out some pig—"

"Dish out what?" I interrupt.

"Beat the inmates to death," Guido translates.

"Not always," Sayago clarifies. "Sometimes we never even touched them, you'd just leave them there for a few hours and they'd squeal all by themselves they would, the ones who knew what the score was that is. But Ezcurrita didn't, what would he know. So the Super had to come and spell it out for him didn't he so he'd understand, shut up then all right. Still it couldn't go on like that. All the common criminals listening in see, some who might be out shooting their mouths off on the street in a few days and to make matters worse the day after was visiting day. So the Super decided to move him. Problem was where to. He locked himself in his office with Greco who'd been there since the early morning too and when they came out you could see they had it all sorted and went to fetch him with a couple of low-ranking officers and took him away in Greco's double this time not a patrol car, must've put him on the floor I reckon 'cause it was after siesta by then and the streets were beginning to fill up with people again, and it wouldn't do to go parading him round the streets like a carnival queen. The town'd seen quite enough the night before."

"Where did they take him?" I ask to confirm what I already know.


THE OFFICIAL NAME of the dirt street skirting the limits of the railway station is La Niña, but everyone calls it Eucalyptus Way. Guido and I will stroll between its tall, peeling trunks, submerged in the glittering green light and the murmur of the wind, impregnated with their scent as it blows through

156

the treetops. A little further on the abandoned freight wagons stand on a stretch of disused siding. Wading into the weeds, getting my pants soaked to the knees with dew, I'll scan the corrugated-iron sides of the nearest one, lead grey where it isn't eaten away by rust. There are holes through which an adult body could easily fit and, poking my head through one of them, when my eyes get used to the half-light raked by sunbeams, I'll make out the signs of recent occupation—old newspapers, sheets of cardboard, soot-blackened tin cans. I'll get hold of one of the rusting metal edges and effort-lessly pull off a piece, which will crumble like puff pastry between my fingers.

"Could this have been the one?" I'll ask.

"Who knows. The metal's had twenty years to rust. Could've been any of them. Does it matter?"

"I guess not. And I don't think our friend will want to tell us. How many ribs did you say?"

"Three."

"Think we're a few short?"

I'll manage to get a smile from him. The situation will make me feel a little selfish. At the end of the day, when this story's all over, I can go home and say fuck them, but Guido has to go on living here. And you never know with cops.

"There won't be any problems will there?" I'll ask. "With the cops I mean."

"I've taken care of it," he'll reply. "They stopped by the factory yesterday."

"You didn't say anything," I'll protest. "I swear I—"

"Wasn't worth bothering you about. I've told you, it's all taken care of."

"How much?"

"A hundred."

"I'll give you half," I'll offer, reaching for my wallet. And then he'll look me in the eye and grin from ear to ear, like when we were kids and had got into a spot of bother.

"Please," he'll raise his hand to reject the offer. "The next one's on you."

"THEY PUT AN OFFICER on guard for the night, Ramírez or Rodríguez, can't remember. Poor Ramírez, the slapping he took. But you got to understand, Saturday at Carnival time the whole town's out on the razz and down at the binge at the sports centre nearby the air blew him the music of the dance and the whiff of skirt up for a fuck and him all on his tod in the derelict station, with nothing but the toads for company and the snivelling of the bloke in the wagon, which only stopped when Rodríguez went and banged on the side with an iron bar. So he did a bunk, gave the padlock on the sliding door the once-over and went off to the sports centre to find his girlfriend and a couple of bottles of red. That's right, took them back to the train station—he might of been thoughtless but not irresponsible—and he opened up another of the wagons for his own private party. He was woken up in the small hours by Sergeant Chacón kicking him in the head. He got out you dumbass! He got out! He was shouting at him and threw him out of the wagon half bollock-naked as he was and arse-kicked him along the tracks." Ex-corporal Sayago chuckles again and, when he manages to stop, he looks at us with tear-filled eyes and then at me:

"'Nother round Maestro?" he asks with a naughty wink. He's beginning to get matey, it's time to call it a day. But what can I do?

IT MUST BE ABOUT twelve blocks from the abandoned wagons to the entrance of town, but they're dark blocks, where a dead light bulb can sit in a street light for months— almost vacant blocks, with dirt streets so seldom trodden that they're sometimes overgrown with grass from sidewalk to sidewalk—so there's nothing strange about no one seeing Ezcurra on the first leg of his getaway. What is strange is that he didn't head for the paved road, where his chances of stopping a passing car and getting away from danger would have been better; the most plausible explanation being that the odds of a patrol car, or someone who'd call one, going past were equally high. What is certain is that between the time they locked him up in a freight wagon and five o'clock, when they got the call at headquarters, any trace of his movements was lost. The people at the sports-centre festivities, which lasted until six in the morning, will assure you he didn't come that way, and you'd better believe it, because for all the boozing and the debauchery and the costumes, the figure of Darío Ezcurra, with bulging eyes and missing a shoe and a sleeve, his clothes stained ochre from the beating and from squeezing through the rusting metal of the wagon, can't have been a sight easily overlooked. And without a precise time of escape, it's impossible to say how long he was wandering about for, who (if anyone) he turned to for help, how many doors (which stayed shut) he knocked on before he resurfaced at the little first-aid ward, where you could always find a light and a duty nurse on at the weekend.

"I CAN TELL YOU THAT," Guido had told me at the table in Los Tocayos a few days earlier, and Leticia, who was with us, along with the perennial Licho and Iturraspe, nodded gravely. Leticia's one of the few women from Malihuel who dares to sit at the eminently male domain of the tables in Los Tocayos—says she prefers men's company to the harpies who only gather to tear strips off other women (her for example, for being here now) and the men certainly appreciate hers, which they flatter with compliments and lighted lighters and even the odd glass of something, with prior permission from her ever-present husband, who proceeded to relate the events of the small hours that final Sunday. "I worked as a volunteer driving the ambulance for two years, not in those days of course but later on, and one of the two nurses, Doña Isadora de Mendonca, the pharmacist's mother, who's dead now, told me the story. It was getting light, she said, she'd nodded off reading the magazines opposite the door, which used to be left open in summer, with just the strip curtain, when she saw him appear through the coloured fringe she nearly had a fit from the shock, because like all the others she'd already given him up for dead and the man staring at her from the door looked more like a ghost than a living human being. Help me Doña Isadora, I'm hurt, he managed to get out and she reacted, his voice still coming from this world. She half carried him to the first consulting room, laid

160

him down on the stretcher, undid his shirt and washed his face and body with some gauze soaked in distilled water to see how bad the cuts were. He had two deep ones on his scalp that he'd got on the edges of the corrugated iron when he stuck his head out to scream for help, and another in his groin which was still bleeding badly; the rest was grazing. Call Soandso or Soandso she says he kept repeating, Tell them to come and fetch me, tell them to tell my Mamá. But she was worried about the wound on his leg and decided to call Dr Lugozzi, who was in charge of the little ward till the cancer took him."

"He realised he was going to die when he saw his tests," Leticia intervened, and Guido gave her a stern look before going on:

"The doctor came straight away, in the first pair of trousers he could find and his white coat flung on any old how, with his hair all standing on end from bed and his eyes red he grabbed her by the arm and dragged her into his office. Are you crazy? How come you let him in? Don't you know he's wanted by the whole provincial police force? This man's a fugitive from justice and we have to report him rightaway! And she says Doctor, look at what they've done to him already and he says you want us to end up like that too? Go and ring straight away and from the next-door room she heard the doctor saying to him take it easy Darío, Isadora's calling your family, come here and I'll fix you up, and three minutes after hanging up the nurse heard the squeal of brakes and the slamming of car doors. It's only six blocks from the headquarters."

"Didn't Ezcurra do anything?" I asked.

Guido, Leticia, Iturraspe and even Nene Larrieu looked at each other for a few seconds before one of them dared to reply. Only Licho, who thinks Ezcurra has a wife and children in Casilda, stayed out of it. It was Leticia who finally plucked up the courage.

"Doña Isadora swore blind that after they brought Ezcurra out with legs so weak they had to carry by the armpits she found a used syringe in the bin liner which she'd changed at the start of her shift and an almost empty phial of some injectable tranquilliser or other on the steel table."

"JUST AS WELL the call from the doc got to us before news of the escape," ex-police corporal Carmen Sayago sighs with relief twenty years after the event. "The Super who'd spent the night awake at headquarters was there never seen him like that I hadn't motherfuckers he was saying you want to ruin my career you're doing this to screw me all blue in the face like inside the car screaming put the fear of God into you and Greco in that little arse-licking voice of his don't get upset Superintendent sir"—Carmen Sayago softens his voice like a woman's while quoting—"Dr Lugozzi's assured us everything's under control, and the Super was all Arielito this and Arielito that when he was in a good mood but when he flew off the handle shut it the wagons were *your* idea if he escapes you can do the explaining to the *milicos* in Rosario now and we'll see if they swallow yer poncing about had to put my hand over my mouth to stop myself laughing I swear, first time I'd seen him give Greco a piece of his mind and in front of his subordinates too I reckon that was when Greco started harbouring a grudge against me probably kicked me out the force 'cause I was a witness to his humiliation didn't he. 'Cause I never did a thing to him to make him treat me like that honest I didn't a grudge he's got all 'cause I was faithful to Superintendent Neri happens a lot that does one on his way down another on his way up and the new one gets rid of all the last guy's men so he can bring in his friends and to justify it they invent some cock-and-bull story about err you orchestrating some malicious intent and then on top of getting rid of you they build a reputation for this that and the other and nobody'll hire you for anything after that. And my old man my old man if Neri'd of been there he'd of gone and talked to him but Greco came along when my old man was retired and then all the respect he'd earned in thirty years thirty years of service like Greco gave a shit. Couldn't give a shit sir, wouldn't even've seen him he wouldn't, and me when Neri give him a dressing down I didn't laugh at all didn't even look at him but I ended up getting it in the neck just 'cause I was around, 'cause you should of seen his face white with rage he used to go a colour like candlewax, between his face and the Superintendent's made you want to crawl under the seat it did, good thing the journey was short just five blocks and we stowed the three patrol cars and marched into the little ward in a posse guns out. Dr Lugozzi put his hands up like in one of them cowboy films and yelled Don't shoot! Don't shoot! I've already subdued him! And later when we was carrying the rag doll he says to the Super Is there a reward for capturing him? And the Super goes Go to bed Doctor and pretend it was all a dream will you. Nene, 'nother shot of *caña* over here!" yells the ex-corporal, and then to me, half brash half snide, says, "If you're still buying that is Chief."

"Go ahead," I reply without returning his smile.

"Such a pleasure being amongst mates," he says and goes on. "On the way back I went in the car with Chacón and this first corporal who they said was a fucking cocksucker 'cause nobody never saw him with a bird, which ain't got nothing to do with nothing just popped into my head, where was I oh when we got there they'd already got him out the car and were shoving him along he'd take two steps and fall over 'cause of the jab the doc gave him must of been, while the sergeant went off to the wagons like I told you and gave Rodríguez the thrashing of his life, the rest of us followed the Super and the Subsuper who steered him towards the train station, the Super talking to him all the time, talking to him, saying You know why we've come to this? Eh? 'Cause you're a dickhead who can't listen when he's spoken to. How many ways did I try and warn you about what was coming? What? Thought I wouldn't dare, thought I didn't have the balls? Gave you every opportunity I did, but not him, His Lordship had to get all cocky didn't he, show everybody he's a big man here in town, an *untouchable*, the Super said into his ear, and slapped him every time he said it: Untouchable are you? See how I can touch you. Untouchable? You ask me he didn't understand a thing any more except the punches, could barely put one leg in front of the other, all wobbly like this like spastic like a flan and every time he'd fall over Neri or Greco'd pick him up by the scruff of the neck. It'd started getting light so we turned off the torches and our clothes were soaking with dew. I thought we were going to do it at the Federal Shooting Range, it looked as good a place as any, but before we went through the gate we turned right and headed for the silos, know where I mean? Down where the old mill used to be?"

"The one Ezcurra's grandfather burnt down," I nod.

"The very one and ... up for another little drinkie I am, if it's no skin off the present company's nose eh, but we never got as far as the mill, we stopped at this corrugated-iron shed, isn't there any more but in them days—"

"The Council slaughterhouse," Guido remarks.

"The very one," nods ex-corporal Sayago with an oily grin. "That was where the Super'd chosen."


"AN IDEA OF YOUR GRANDFATHER'S to sell people cheaper meat," Guido will remark as we stroll down a little track barely visible through the weeds. "They'd put a live cow in there and stick a knife between two shoulder vertebrae with everyone watching, and it would go sprawling, both eyes and all four legs wide open, without even so much as a moo. Then they'd slit its throat and stick the buckets under for the blood and start carving it up before the poor animal was dead. The butchers took the best cuts, which they'd reserved in advance, and when they were done, the second-in-line paupers'd move in. They used to pick up the last bones for a few cents, lots of families'd've starved otherwise I tell you. I saw it a couple of times, and I swear within the hour there was nothing left of the cow except a few bloodstains on the tiles. Look, here they are—he'll point to some fragments of tiles, with contrasting colours and designs like a Roman

165

mosaic, visible here and there through the undergrowth and the grass, no doubt salvaged from the remains of the various demolitions piling up in the Council yard. He never threw anything away my grandfather didn't. "The roof and walls were made of corrugated iron"—Guido presses on with his guided tour—"and over here were some gutters—look, there's one here—that drained the blood into the ditch—the rain washed it away into the lagoon. This ditch was the best place for worms for miles around. To go fishing. Remember?"

"Do I!" I reply. "Caught an eel this big once," I'd say, measuring out half a metre with my palms. "I'll never forget it."

"AND THAT WAS WHEN the shit hit the fan just before we go in. To be honest I don't know if the Super was already onto Greco or what, he was no fool but the other one was the wiliest old devil you ever seen me he didn't fool me though I saw right through him right from the start and I told that old baldy Chacón We can go next door to the kiosk now and ask him if you like I told him this one with a gob like butter wouldn't melt in his mouth he'll have us dancing to his tune when he gets promoted we watch out and start what do they say watching our arses and lo and behold wiser than me old baldy Chacón turned out to be, stuck to the Subsuper like a stamp which was how he got enough cash together to retire and set up the kiosk which is what I should of done if I'd been cleverer. But I never was any good at sucking up, chip off the old block me, and I'm no stoolie like other people whose names I could mention, where was I oh so we got there and the door stroke of bad luck the slaughterhouse door was chained and padlocked fuck me if it wasn't. And now what we going to do we can't get the mayor out of bed to ask for the key a padlock this big yer granddaddy'd put on even though there was nothing to nick inside not even mice very careful he was about everything not like the mayor nowadays who only shows up to beg us coppers for funds at election time spend longer at headquarters than in their offices mayors do ain't that the truth. No, got to be quick off the mark around here, the things I've seen in there if I squealed about everything I know not a soul in this town'd be spared right. And the Super who must of been pissed off with the whole business by now takes out his regulation gun and points it at the padlock and pow! and the padlock just sits there and again pow! pow!, and all he managed to do was wake the guy up 'cause by that stage he'd nodded off and when he heard the shots he got hold of the queer first corporal's knees and started crying like a girl, the first corporal couldn't get him off he didn't really try maybe he liked it eh? And in his fury the Super forgot the padlock and pointed the gun at Ezcurra and the first corporal goes Don't shoot Superintendent shitting himself he was I'm telling you looked to me like things was getting a bit out of hand, and when the first corporal the one as was a bit homosexual I'm telling you manages to break loose and the Super does have a clear shot he points the gun at him and I don't know if he's looked into his eyes or what, my old man who knew all the tricks used to say to me if you ever have to do it do it but don't let them look into yer eyes because you'll never get their eyes out of yer head after that, but anyroad we can all see the Super hesitate and that famous steady hand of his starts shaking."

Sayago pauses dramatically, conscious of the spell which, not his words as he believes, but the horrific events they drag behind them have cast on us. I take a last toke on a cigarette I seem to have been smoking for hours and, when I stub it out, I see all the others in the ashtray. I feel really sick and fight to turn my oncoming retch into a mere belch. Through the veil of nausea and hatred and alcohol I watch the features of the ex-police corporal as he orders another drink without waiting for my nod.

"To tell you the truth," says Sayago, downing his drink in one the moment it hits the table, "till then I had full confidence in the Super but well like, to be honest he went down a bit there. I mean a chief say sends you into a confrontation go go go with the bullets flying and watches his own arse what do the troops do then? And I tell you the moment Greco realised he was on him like a wolf on a sick lamb I'll take care of it if you like sir like that he said it to him in his little arse-licking voice but let's not kid ourselves at that moment it was the worst insult he could of come out with. And at first the Super stands there struck dumb his eyes bulging, still had his finger on the trigger, and when he gets his voice back he goes You think I can't do it. So it's *you* who's giving *me* classes now is it Sonny? What's wrong, got an itchy arse and think you can scratch it better in my chair do you? You'll sit in my chair the day the Virgin bangs her son you little dumbfuck, *you're* hurrying *me* up? What if I just don't fucking feel like it now? eh? What if I feel like waiting a bit? Got a problem with that have you? the Super yells this close to him and Greco sort of pauses and says to him in a different tone Not me Superintendent, but Colonel Carca will, and that was it, the Super couldn't of stood there stiller if he'd been hit on the head by the slaughterman's hammer. That was when the man went down in my eyes, me I knew him but he suddenly looked, how can I put it, ten years older, more … Looked like an old-age pensioner he did. Myself if he'd reacted at that moment and stood up to that Judas I'd of stood by him I swear, guns blazing if necessary but the Super he … was gone, vanished, poof, it was suddenly like he wasn't there any more. But well, no wonder right? Greco, his protégé, his man, his right-hand man, had just fessed up to him he'd been working for the military behind his back," says the ex-corporal, and for a few seconds he sits there staring into space, his mouth slack, before picking up the drooling thread of his speech. "That's what Greco was like, soon as yer back was turned he'd stick the knife in, like a woman, 'cause he didn't have it in him to do it to yer face, you need eyes where the sun don't shine with his kind, sometimes not even that's enough I mean look what happened to me and the Super," mumbles Sayago sinking deeper and deeper into the muddy bottom of self-pity. "From then on the Super may have still been giving the orders but Greco was calling the shots, blew the padlock off with one bullet he did and kicked the door open and if I'm not wrong he went in first then the Super and he says to us Greco does Surround the place he says to us and make sure nobody comes near and closes the door so we can't see."

"What about Ezcurra?" I ask.

"What *about* Ezcurra?" asks Sayago forgetting to disguise his annoyance at the interruption.

"Did they leave him outside?"

For a second Sayago narrows his grim-looking eyes even more, then they swivel back to the empty glass and decide to smile again.

"If they left him outside why would they of gone inside? To give each other some tongue? I told you, the arse bandit stayed outside."

"With you," says Licho, and realises too late that his clarification sounds like an insinuation.

"What do you mean?"

Without waiting for my order Nene Larrieu fills Sayago's glass and diverts his attention just in time. Sayago drains it before going on:

"I swear I can remember it like I was there, sun'd just come up and it was getting warmer, looked like another scorcher, no sign of the storm, blew straight past us in the end, can even remember a *chimango* on a tree branch, flew off at the shot, the metal walls made twice as much noise. People today still argue about which one pulled the trigger, for me it was the Super 'cause he had more blood on his clothes and besides he was an incredible shot, once went out partridge-hunting with him and he'd bring them down with a twenty-two, and when I counted them he'd hit them every one in the head or the neck, one shot, not one of them did I have to finish off."

"It's difficult to miss at five centimetres," remarks Guido, hating him. Sayago's too drunk to notice.

"But I can't get Greco's face out of my head. He was looking down so the Super wouldn't realise but I saw he had this grin on him from ear to ear. I reckon if it hadn't of been for him the Super wouldn't of done it. Did it 'cause Greco provoked him he did. But there you go ... Nene, I ordered another shot of *caña* for Christ's sake, are you going to take all night! You tell him not to pour me any more Don? Come on then, what you waiting for? So there they were. It was just getting light and people'd just started walking the streets, not many, it was Sunday luckily, and we hadn't brought spades or kerosene or anything. Then Sergeant Chacón got this bright idea. My brother-in-law's smallholding, he says to Greco, it's just down the road. Off the Fuguet road. We'll have everything we need there and we won't have to go through town. So that's what we did. I didn't go 'cause after we loaded him in the trunk of the first patrol car—me without looking 'cause the sight of blood makes me queasy—the Super sent us back, me and the Inspector ... Bonfanti!"

"Inspector Bonfanti?" asks Nene Larrieu, taken aback.

"No, the one from Leopardi! Told you I'd remember! His name was Bonfanti!"

"Like I give a fuck," mumbles Guido, audibly grinding his teeth.

"The inspector I can't remember what his name was, and the Super says to the inspector, his name'll come to me any second ... Bonfanti, sonofagun! errr the Super says to him I did hear that properly 'cause he was right next to me he says to him Call Rosas Paz and wish him bon appétit from me, he'll understand said the Super and after that they drove off down the highway in the other cars."

"I'm going home for a lie down Fefe," says Guido straightening up. "To get some kip before I drive you to the terminal." He says goodbye to everyone except Sayago, who, if he realises, is doing a good job of hiding it, and as he leaves the cold gusts in from the street until the door closes again.

I don't blame him. A few short blocks away the body of his lovely wife warms the bed, and here he is, reliving a horror that's none of his concern, only out of respect for the whims of his childhood friend who hasn't had the common decency to explain to him why. If I were him, I'd have left some time ago. I'm not much good at playing the faithful friend.

"Yous leaving too?" Sayago says to me, a hint of panic in his voice.

"Can't speak for the others," I say. "You all know the drinks are on me so don't worry."

"We're not staying to freeload but we do appreciate it," says Iturraspe with a smile and Licho nods. "The most urgent thing I've got on tomorrow is reading the paper, after the Sacamatas've finished with it, 'cause I can't even afford that. What about you Licho?"

"Waiting till you're through with it," he smiles.

"Well if you thought I haven't got much more to tell you Buenos Aires get a load of this," ex-corporal Sayago says to me in an altogether different tone of voice. His familiarity, which until recently had come and gone, is now systematic, even insolent. "That same day in the afternoon lo and behold Chacón's brother-in-law shows up scared witless asking to talk to him. They tell him he's gone to Rosas Paz and just then the Super walks past and sees him. What can I do for you Villalba my friend, anything wrong? And Villalba looking like he'd die there and then starts stammering and almost in tears he eventually plucks up the courage to explain that his dogs and pigs of started digging around there and ate off one of his hands and he don't know what to do, he don't want to move him without permission but if he leaves him there and the Super goes It's all right Villalba, well done, we need more citizens like you, don't worry, we'll take it from here. Before you go there's something I always meant to ask—you wouldn't have anything to do with the Villalba they say ran our founder Comandante Pedernera out of town would you? And Villalba stammering again They're just stories Superintendent sir, the Villalbas have always been law-abiding folk who respect authority, and Neri goes All right, go and put the kettle on, we'll be right over, and then from the doorway to his office so as everybody could hear Jeez, they've gone soft on me the people in this town have, where's that famous reputation for bravery? and sent for the Subsuper to discuss what to do. They needed to find a final location for him, somewhere even if people found out later they'd never get him back, somewhere safe from all the bleeding hearts, the telltales and the nosy parkers. Guessed where?"

"Yes," I say, loathing him.

"So on our way back from Villalba's place we asked the Sub what next and he goes you'll have to ask the Superintendent you've seen how much he takes this business to heart said it like he was having a laugh enjoying himself like I sometimes wonder if he didn't set the whole thing up just to bring the Super down, just like he did with me right, over the watch."

"Which watch?" asks Nene Larrieu, pricking up his ears like a gun dog every time he got wind of some new-sounding information.

"A Casio digital, gold wristband, stopwatch, lovely it was, and Subsuperintendent Greco turned round and said *I*'d pocketed it. When, say I, as yous know I wasn't alone with … for more than a few minutes and he didn't have a ring any more or even a hand and they weren't going to bury him wearing his watch and jewellery were they if only 'cause of identification right? So I really don't know what happened to that watch, 'less Villalbas pigs ate it." He chuckles at his own joke before going on. "If you ask me it was Greco himself as took it and comes along later accusing me so nobody'd suspect, You don't know well maybe you do what that man was capable of. Let's go and ask Chacón if you don't believe me I never saw that watch in my life I swear to God, but Greco was already digging a hole for me, first he got me labelled as a thief over the watch and then soon as he could—"

"So it was you," I interrupt.

"What do you mean it was me?" His eyes narrow, without actually focusing. "You calling me a liar? I told you I never touched that watch."

"No no, I know. You just helped to kidnap and kill him and … " I can't pronounce the sharp, clear words tearing my mind apart, so I just say, " … get him out … of Villalba's."

"Oh. Yeah right. Yeah. Why?"

He'd blurted it out all on his own, but he was looking at me as if I'd made him do it on purpose.

"All right, all right," I mutter through the livid strips of aggression hanging between us. "Nobody's keeping you here. You can leave when you like. We're not in headquarters here."

"Kicking me out are you?" His attempt to make his voice sound butcher rises to a cackle that makes him spin round in fury to see who's laughing at him. I keep out of the others' attempts at calming him down. Sayago knows that when he reaches the end of his tale the happy hour's over, and it occurs to me his constant digressions might be a ruse to delay the fateful moment for as long as possible. He looks more upset than Scheherazade and it takes another glass to calm him down.

"What the Super wanted was to find the right spot"—he addresses not me, but the general audience. "I've already told you Superintendent Neri liked to do things properly. Very particular he was, very well organised. So he spent the time reading some report or other he'd been sent till well into the evening."

*The genesis and evolution of Malihuel's lagoon must not be interpreted using a localist approach, for such an interpretation would, per se, be lacking the indispensable bases of its rational understanding. We must view it as the result of processes affecting our entire plain, and it is of interest to us from the point of view of Applied Geography. We believe, however, that, even extending the study to the entire Pampas, such an approach would still be one-sided, and it must therefore be seen in its precise dimensions in relation to phenomena on a continental or even planetary scale that ...*

*Viewed on a continental scale, the problem of the subsidence of one small block is minimal and would not appear to be of any great interest, but from the point of view of human facilities and the works of man, it is important. In the investigation of a plain such as ours, methods used in areas where outcrops and structures are visible cannot be applied. In the sector in question, we see an almost total lack of them, and must therefore sometimes focus exclusively on the behaviour of the surface waters and of ...*

*The observations must be megascopic in nature, as they have to cover wide areas, and the drops—almost always of several metres or*

175

*even decimetres—and the gradients, however insignificant they may seem must always be taken into consideration, as they may or may not be indicative of differential movements, the immediate consequence of which may be deviations in the courses …*

*Its broadest diameter runs W-E, its narrowest, N-S, ie not parallel to the sides of the block. Between those two isohypses (WSW, SE and NE of the basin) stretch semi-permanent floodplains and gullies from the last paleo-hydrogeological model …*

*Rising water levels are not solely due to precipitation, but also to groundwaters. The annual peaks for precipitation are reached in the storage period of monthly rainfall, aggravated by the fact that the basin is served by a single evacuator (ie evaporation), which is minimal in the months of maximum rainfall. According to official data, the highest levels recorded were those of the years 1941 and 1965, with peaks of 84.88m and 84.91m respectively, as measured by the Military Geographical Institute.*

*In terms of the influence of groundwaters, the directions of the run-off and the equipotential lines of the phreatic layer are indicated on Kreimer's hydrographical map (1968). The convergence of the former and the close-packed lines indicate heavy drainage toward the central basin.*

*According to the bathymetry conducted in 1970, the maximum depth was 6m, and this measurement has remained constant along a 3,000m trench, approximately 2.5km N of the so-called Island Beach Resort (northern peninsula).*

Elordi J & Jaimovich I  *La laguna Malihuel* in
*Estudios de geografía de la Provincia de Santa Fe*
Various Authors Santa Fe  GÆA  1973.

"HERE'LL DO, said the Super and Chacón and me thanked God and stowed the oars, we'd been rowing into a head-wind, couldn't move the day after, but the Super wouldn't use the fire brigade's rubber dinghy even if it did have an outboard motor. The moon was still up—he even made sure of that—and the sky was thick with stars, I dipped my hand in the water to wash the sweat off, it was warm I remember and if it hadn't been for the luggage I'd of fancied a swim. A couple of officers I can't remember who had spent the whole afternoon attaching bricks and bits of iron to him with wire till you could hardly pick him up, I can't explain to you what he weighed nearly give myself a whatdoyoucallit a hernia I did, I ain't saying not to take precautions but the bricks was over the top 'specially as someone else'd have to carry him afterwards ... They put some sacking over him before they tied him up, he was not a pretty sight by then, looked like a big beef roulade, and with all the heaving and shoving the boat was rocking all over the place and the Super was swear-ing at us took three attempts to get him over the side it did, the last one nearly capsized us and we both fell backwards, me I cut my hand on the rusty wire had to have two stitches and a jab case it got infected look here I still got the scar and while we're at it I'll have another shot of *caña* to oil the gun. You still paying Buenos Aires or not? You ain't telling me I let you down are you. Eh?"

My head hurts with the effort of remembering. Sunday the twenty-seventh they dumped him. I always went back to Buenos Aires at the beginning of March. But that left Monday the twenty-eighth. Was I in Malihuel that Monday? Did I have my usual last farewell dip in the lagoon? Maybe, if it rained that Monday, I can stop worrying. Any newspaper will tell me. The relief if it rained.

"Eh. What's on yer mind." Sayago's voice bursts obscenely into my thoughts. "Or are you going to skimp now I've told you what you wanted to know?"

"Give him whatever he likes Nene. The last one," I mutter through the grim cloud of my own drunken haze.

Sayago raises it enthusiastically to his lips, sipping the film that clings to the glass, his mouth a sucker filling the hole with its grey tongue meat. After hoovering up every last drop, he opens his mouth and his voice almost breaks:

"Probably reckon I been talking 'cause you stood me some fucking *cañas* eh? Been told you can have Carmen eating out of yer hand with a few shots? Eh?"

"Calm down Carmen," intervenes Licho, who can obviously see it coming.

"Get yer fucking hands off me!" Sayago shakes an arm no one's touched. "I may be called Carmen but I'm more of a man than the lot of you put together, this shitty city boy comes along and you're all running around after him kissing his arse and saying sorry! Sorry for what? Can you tell me what the crap any of this is to you? You don't fool me. I know why you're here."

I tense in my seat, while my eyes dart about looking for something I can cleave his head open with if necessary, but for now he's content just to shout.

"Think you're better than us don't you Buenos Aires. But I'm a Sayago or didn't you know? It was a Sayago as killed Musurana, the most famous bandit in the region! Now you come along asking questions but you know what? We're the

178

ones ask the questions here. I still got friends in the force. Think things have changed that much do you?"

I sit there and stare at him without answering, wondering how much longer I'm going to have to keep up a calm front. Meanwhile, Porfirio Dupuy, alerted by all the shouting, has emerged from his mysterious caverns and tells us if we're going to have a fight to have one outside, Licho suddenly remembers something very important he should have done a year ago and disappears through a side door, and Iturraspe stands a little way back from the table in case the glass starts flying.

"You're all the same," spews the not-so-ex-policeman. "When there's any trouble you run screaming to us, Police! Police! and then when we've risked our necks you spit on us. And if at some point we ice someone you raise the ceiling, but if it's one of our own you don't give a monkey's, not a monkey's! It's what you're paid for you say. What do you know? Ever had to hold a dying comrade, try to cheer him up and lie to him that everything's going to be all right when you know he's on his way out, and then go and face his folks, his wife?"

"Yes," I hiss through my teeth, but my interlocutor's so wired he doesn't realise I've answered his purely rhetorical question.

"Nobody who hasn't been through it in the flesh has the right to question us about anything," Corporal Sayago lets fly openly now, and at the expense of several more cackles manages to raise and swell his original slurring whine.

"If you want another drink just ask," I breathe without looking at him. "There's no need to shout."

179

"I'll shout all I like me! And you'll give me another glass whether you like it or not!" he gets up from his chair and grabs the table with both hands as if to flip it over, but it's really to steady himself. "You're in my town now and if I tell you to buy me another drink you'll buy me another drink get it? What's up with the rest of you? You going to let some shitty city boy walk all over us just 'cause he's got some money in his pocket! Come on, we'll show him, come on! Think we're afraid of you do you Buenos Aires? Afraid of you lot? Know what we do with puffed-up city boys here?"

He makes as if to unzip his flies, but his zipper gets stuck and, as he wrestles with it, one of the doors onto main street, the nearest one, bursts open and bounces back off the wall, and Sayago barely has time to look up before Guido's on top of him heaving him by his hair to the floor in an arc and kicking him out into the street through the door Licho has been holding open as a precaution. Relieved at the prospect of a breath of fresh air, I go outside after them and am followed by Iturraspe and Nene Larrieu. His running shoes still undone, Guido kicks Sayago in the head, who, outlined against the battery of headlights on the Fiat Uno parked at right angles to the sidewalk with both its doors wide open, writhes on the ground like a slug with salt on its back. "May I?" I say to Guido, who hasn't opened his vapour-clouded mouth except to breathe, and start laying into Sayago with my steel-capped shoes, connecting cleanly with his ribs as the cold clears my head a little, feeling the resistance of the bone yield after a few swings. Then suddenly I realise that, instead of helping me, Guido's pulling on one arm and Nene Larrieu on the other, so I stop struggling. I'd've carried on till he was dead, I say to myself and for some reason the words calm me down.

Back inside, I buy us another round—minus the *caña*—to soothe our souls, and when I breathe in, deeper and deeper, my lungs fill completely. It's a pleasant sensation. Our company—even Nene Larrieu, who, after calling Chacón to escort his ex-colleague to the little ward, breaks the habit of a lifetime and pours himself a neat gin, no ice—drink their drinks in silence.

"Good thing he never wanted to be a cop," I remark after a while.

"That's often the trouble with unbelieving converts," Iturraspe points out. Out of deference to Guido I finish my drink as fast as I can and ride back with him in the car. Next morning, after a night of nightmares more vivid than the haze I wake up to, with the winter sun already high in the sky behind the raised blinds, I remember my return ticket to Buenos Aires, which this time I've quite forgotten to change.

"I DON'T KNOW WHAT I'M DOING HERE," Clara Benoit had confessed to me with a vague sweep of the hand that might have included the freezing, empty dining room, the young eucalyptus wood outside the large windows—where one green and three blue tents have holed up till the end of the winter holidays—and the wrinkled surface of the lagoon, and beyond that who knows what vastnesses. "I mean look at this place, it's depressing, I tell Papá to close up till summer but you know what he's like, you must've got to know him well by now. Sorry," she'd added. "You asked me about the church and there I go off at a tangent. Yes, I was there that afternoon. I went to see if Father Abeledo said anything about Darío. I don't know why the others went but they did. There were a lot of people who never usually attended, I've seldom seen the church so full for an ordinary mass. What I remember most though was the silence. Pews creaking, shoes shuffling on the tiles, the occasional cough—but no one said a word. And to make matters worse the Father took longer than usual, which was quite a while. At the time I thought it was because he was preparing something special to say but apparently he was having one of his fits of depression … About Darío, of course. I don't know what I was thinking of, the father's words firing us up and afterwards all of us leaving the church arm in arm, singing, behind Father Abeledo holding the cross on high, and marching on police headquarters. When I understood what he was saying I burst out crying. I couldn't believe it of him and I couldn't stop. Papá and Mamá, who was still alive back then, looked daggers at me and kept nudging me but there was nothing I could do and in the end I had to leave in the middle of the sermon, choking back the tears and everyone turning round and staring at me and already starting to whisper, nothing new, same as usual no doubt, it was no secret that for Darío I … You'd think by that stage they'd've got bored of talking about it. I mean twenty years is rather a lot. But they're still singing the same tune aren't they."

"TRUTH BE TOLD I don't know if it was the depression or a crisis of faith as people said or just the hots he had for that girl from Fuguet let's call a spade a spade, he ended up leaving the priesthood and they must've got married I wouldn't know and they lived in Córdoba for a while which was when we all lost track of them. And there were days when there was no getting him out of bed to say mass, we'd drilled the cleaning girl but there were times not even she could work the miracle and had to go knocking at your grandparents' just next door or else at one of ours to give her a helping hand, I mean if he didn't have the vocation what did he go and become a priest for in the first place so young and handsome he was when he arrived the girls wandered around in a daze over their new little priest and he started up that whatdoyoucallit the social work and the soup kitchens and the health schemes and girls who wouldn't even speak to the darkies well maybe the maid or the gardener, and that was all, all of a sudden off visiting shacks and cooking for the darkie contingent all for a smile from Father Abeledo. But later I don't know what can have happened whether it was that little tart from Fuguet or something else but he stopped bothering and gave up and we could count ourselves lucky if he made it for mass or weddings or christenings. I remember your christening, seems like yesterday, I was carrying Leandro see he's only a wee bit younger than you are and it was dreadfully hot I had to sit down your grandmother kept everything in a little box ah the number of times we must've got it out even a cutting from the Toro Mocho paper with the news of yours she must have it with her in

Rosario I suppose but what I don't remember is whether your Mamá and Papá ... but of course not, your Papá never visited the town did he. Your grandmother wasn't one to say much and I didn't want to bring the subject up you know what it's like in-laws don't exactly get along, me and my daughter-in-law for example every time I go and visit her she makes me feel so uncomfortable me I swear if it wasn't for the children I wouldn't give her the time of day but I'll put up with anything for their sakes I've always been the tolerant sort now let me see it can't have been Father Abeledo he was too young it must've been Father Campbell I think. Isn't that right Chesi? It'll be in that cutting of your grandmother's, don't forget to ask when you see her. You are stopping off in Rosario on your way back aren't you? Weeell to tell you the truth I don't know when it could've been do you remember Chesi? Whether that sermon of Father Abeledo's was right at the time or later on? People still argue about what the Father meant, he was usually so clear, such a lovely speaker he was, and I don't know if it was because of his depression that time or what it was but nobody understood a word of what he was saying, actually, on our way out we all looked at each other and I said to Chesi I said did you understand what he was on about no did you nor did I we even asked Yori's lad who was the altar boy ... *che*, what was the father talking about and he said I don't know so there you are. Well I don't know something about arms and eyes and he started on about bacteria and viruses and my brother-in-law said he should stick to theology 'cause he hasn't a clue about medicine. Let's see, must've been that Sunday as you say 'cause if I am sure of one thing it's that Delia wasn't there, she was in Rosario, she liked going there at weekends for the cinema and the theatre and sometimes her son'd go with her and sometimes he wouldn't, I sometimes think that if he'd gone with her that weekend how much upset the town would've been spared, but anyway as I was saying as far as I know he didn't mention Delia's son some'll say he did everybody takes what they want out of it 'specially that time, kept going on about viruses and bacteria he did I can't see what it could've had to do with him unless the boy had the flu," Aunt Porota will say, sitting in her living room during the long afternoon I'll spend with her, and her sister Chesi will nod, smile and start a new row of the little waistcoat she's decided to knit for my son Guille.

"IT'S GOING A BIT FAR to ask me to remember a sermon," Iturraspe appeals to my common sense. "So take everything I say with a pinch of salt. But it doesn't need much imagination anyway. It was along the lines of the body as a model of the ideal community. In a community of men the rulers are like the head, the police the watchful eyes, the Church the soul, the workers the hands, the women the heart, the poor the arsehole—no actually that's my contribution—and if part of the body is damaged or suffers an incurable disease that threatens the health of the whole, it's better to cut it off than to allow it to ... It was clear as day he was talking about Ezcurra, that in some way he was justifying what they did. What isn't clear is why."

"Good thing he was a progressive priest," I chime in not without irony. "Imagine if he'd been your run-of-the-mill career priest."

"Exactly my point." Licho begins to insinuate one of his ineffable theories. "Greco had his eye on the little priest and that sermon saved his neck. Someone must've warned him about what was coming just in time. Quick off the blocks the father was there."

"That wasn't it no," intervenes Don León. "The only thing Father Abeledo cared about by that stage was leaving the priesthood and marrying that bit of all right from Fuguet. I met her and I don't blame him. That sermon … it was his way of burning his boats. After that he couldn't go on being a priest in his own eyes. Poor Father Abeledo, so naive, it backfired on him. His superiors were delighted. Thought they'd found someone irreplaceable, took him another six months to wriggle out."

"CAME BACK A FEW YEARS AGO, with his wife and kids. They only stayed a couple of hours, on their way to the seaside on holiday they were and decided to drop in," Leticia will tell me one night while she's getting dinner ready. "Wanted to lay some flowers on Ezcurra's grave. He looked quite astonished when he found out what he must've known all along."

"THAT SUNDAY was the last Sunday of Carnival, and everybody was there early with one ear glued to the radio for the match," says Guido, the last to arrive at the table in Los Tocayos.

"What match?" I ask innocently. From the way they look at me my question is obviously tantamount to footballing sacrilege. Grave.

"Not really a significant game in itself, though some claim—rightly if you ask me—that it was the first in a long series of victories that, just over a year later, would culminate in Argentina winning our first World Cup," says Iturraspe, affecting a pompous radio voice. "Argentina v Hungary at the Bombonera. What was the final score Nene?"

"Beat them 5-1—two from Luque, three from Bertoni."

"A thrashing with goulash," Iturraspe rounds up. "But that's not why it's a gold-star encounter in the annals of Argentinian football; it's because it was the first time a young player donned the light-blue and white, one who, despite his tender years—barely sixteen at the time—was idol-worshipped by the loyal supporters of his club, Argentinos Juniors back then."

"A minute after coming on for the forward, Luque, he slotted through a sublime pass to set up a goal for Houseman," Nene Larrieu eulogises. I confine myself to pronouncing the sacred syllables with due devotion:

"Diego Armando Maradona," I say. "Now I remember, yes. We listened to the game on the radio at your house," I say to Guido. "I'd never've guessed it was the same weekend."

"Happens to a lot of people. What between Sandro, the Carnival, the match," enumerates Iturraspe, once again taciturn, "and the relief, or the resignation—call it what you like—that the damned dog's day was finally over I don't think anyone remembered."

187

"Remembered what?" I ask.

"The day after," Iturraspe clarifies. "That Monday morning saw the return from Rosario of Señora Delia de Ezcurra, his mother."

# Interlude Three

I N TIMES OF PROSPERITY *a parish priest—who only the most elderly have any recollection of, and then only from what they'd been told by their parents—excited at the growing riches promised by modern architecture and the railway, and at the substantial donations the wealthy immigrants couldn't stop showering on the Lord, set about a task less sustained by faith than by the shared certainty of limitless progress—namely, to cover the ceiling of Malihuel's church with mosaics. The diocese authorities gave their blessing, the contributions began to pour in stimulated by the priest's enthusiasm, and Malihuel's celebrated favourite son, Aníbal Trajano—the creator in his younger days of the equestrian statue of Comandante Pedernera—was commissioned to make a preliminary sketch, which, regardless of its initial vagueness, was approved without further ado so as not to delay the start of the work. The concept couldn't fail to be to everyone's liking—from atrium to altar, the glorious epic of Malihuel's foundation and development would be detailed along the whole length of the nave, from the barbarian desert trodden only by horses' hooves to the fort founded by the viceroys, the Creole population, the arrival of the immigrants and the railways, and culminating over the altar in a vision of the future, in which the angels of divine grace and the trailblazers of progress would gaze from heaven* to earth and earth to heaven in mutual recognition and satisfaction. *Specialist workmen arrived, Italians brought in especially from Rosario along with the tesserae, and for months mass was held under a cage of scaffolding that hid the progress of the work from prying eyes. Once the first stretch was finished, the scaffolding was moved over to the centre and tongues began to wag. They were willing to accept Herculean savages with shapely torsos brandishing centaurs' spears, but not as willing to accept a host of defenceless Indian mothers trying to protect their children from the slaughter that the soldiers, sabres at the ready, were about to wreak on them. This local imitation of the* Massacre of the Innocents *was soon followed by a portrait of daily life in the fort, featuring the long-suffering figures of the ragged soldiers—one of whom was stretched out between stakes and wore the unmistakeable expression of a suffering Christ—and the tasks of the barrack whores. The proud figure that everyone had thought would represent Malihuel's founder, when the sketches had been presented in society, turned out to reproduce, in the minute geometry of the tiny ceramic squares, the mythical bandit, Musurana. No sign of angels so far, not even so much as a cross. There are already too many on the altar, came the artist's answer from on high in the scaffolding, whose fights with the deceived parish priest had reached epic proportions and, according to some, helped in no small way to speed his passage to the Glory of the Lord. And when the priest managed to conquer his proverbial fear of heights and saw with his own eyes that the work intended to celebrate the contribution of the immigrants in fact set out to depict no less than that execrable outbreak of anarchism known as the Cry of Alcorta, the rupture was inevitable. Furious, Malihuel's very own Michelangelo headed back to Rosario swearing never to return, a promise that proved none too hard to keep, since his advanced years and his health broken by all that hard work brought about his swift demise.*

*A serrated edge several metres from the holy grail of the altar was as far as the works would ever get. The townsfolk spent several months debating whether to hire another artist to rethink the remaining work and rework what had been completed to the taste of the offended parishioners (but how do you rework a mosaic?), whether they should leave it the way it was because of the artistic merit some people stubbornly saw in it, or whether, as the fanatics and the conned demanded, they should demolish the whole thing and give the ceiling a clean and democratic lick of whitewash. The years, the damp and the poor quality cement employed—supplied, it should be noted, by Don Alejandro Alvarado's general stores, the brand requested by the artist in his initial budget having been ruled out as too dear—made sure the tiny tesserae began to fall, at first sporadically and almost indiscernibly, then in hail-like profusion. Every morning before Mass, the janitor had to sweep them up off the floor and dump them on a pile, which in view of an ever-less-likely restoration, went on growing, as did the gaps, which stretched saw-tooth tentacles out across the scenes, joined with each other and went on growing, gradually morphing into shapes that were ever more obvious against the polychrome background. One of my most vivid childhood pastimes was to discover in their random and shifting outlines the insects, pirates and astronauts with which my imagination used to alleviate the tedium of the masses my grandmother forced me to attend. I wasn't the only one—several kids used to spend almost the whole of mass with their chins tilted roofwards and it was only when a tile fell in someone's eye—a girl's—and detached her retina, that the opposition to the demolitionists caved in and the trowels had the last word. Years later Don Eugenio Casarico would make off with the heap of tiles in return for a token contribution and use them to tile the first and thereafter most polychromatic swimming pool in Malihuel.*

# Chapter Four

"AND HERE IN THIS ONE are all five of us see? It was for the saint's day if I'm not wrong because we were the organising committee for the parish association. The photo must've been taken by Father Abeledo himself, or he'd be in it. This is Delia de Ezcurra, always so well dressed, and the one next to her's Clota the Superintendent's wife, you see what I was saying, she even copied her hair poor thing, never could get over what happened. And here at the other end's your grandmother, so serious, she and Delia used to be thick as thieves when they were younger but they drifted apart later in life, and they spent their time quarrelling in the association. And these two in the middle believe it or not are Chesi and I, come on own up you didn't recognise us did you. But I never had a second's doubt the moment I laid eyes on you, you were always round here playing as a boy, I used to have some felt dolls and you always asked me to get them out of the cabinet and a wooden toothpick holder shaped like a porcupine, as a matter of fact I wanted to give it to you seeing as how you liked it so much but your grandmother never let me, his parents spoil him as it is she used to say. Do you still speak English?"

My Auntie Porota passes me another sugar-laden maté and smiles. Apart from the colour television set, predictably turned down low, showing some afternoon quiz show, the chairs, which look too new, and the photo of her deceased husband on the wall, it's the same kitchen, flanked by a thin arbour of wisteria, where I used to have my milk and cookies as a boy. Almost lost in the brown imitation-leather armchair with light wood arms, Auntie Chesi flashes me the occasional smile and listens attentively to what her sister has to say, barely looking up from the once-white wool salvaged from her dead husband's favourite cardie, which, before my horrified eyes, she's knitting into a little jacket for my son, and which I'll throw out of the bus window on my way back to Buenos Aires.

"What a pity you didn't bring us any photos of your wife and your little boy, we won't forgive you you know, next time you come you have to bring them with you, if they're not comfortable at Guido's they can stay here, that Guido fancy him going to live just there, and renting, with all the properties the family owns, he only does it to irk his parents and there he is still driving the truck poor Celia, a good thing the other one turned out all right architect you know even as a boy a little darling always so obedient but Guido always raising Cain he was me I was lucky with Beba and Leandrito no complaints about either of them, each better than the other they turned out. What did you say your wife did?"

My Auntie Chesi listens to my reply, smiles, says nothing, tugs at the strand of wool to unhook it from the edge of the basket, reaches the end of a row and starts on the next. Her sister looks on sweetly, smiles at me, stretches out a photo of a gentleman with a lost expression and rather anachronistic appearance as if he'd snuck in from an older photograph, accompanying a youthful Delia de Ezcurra, and between the two of them a boy of around ten, who looks up at her, distracted from the camera the second it eternalised the scene. It's the first photo I've seen of him, I'm astonished to realise before Auntie Porota picks up the thread of her running commentary:

"She never stopped loving her husband while he was alive but what that woman felt for her son was more like adoration. Used to do herself up as young as she could and when she went to Rosario to rub shoulders with the toffs and someone took her for his wife she nearly wet herself with the excitement, no really, she had her ways about her that Delia did I can tell you … He was always bound to turn out like that, a spoilt crackpot he was, hundreds of girlfriends but always tied to his mother's apron strings, and don't think it bothered *her*, just the opposite I think, she was proud he was so much in demand, I reckon she used to keep count of his conquests, possibly more than he did. They were so close, you've rarely seen such a thing between a mother and her son, it's not that she was always breathing down his neck they led their own lives she even got let's call him a boyfriend in Rosario ooh just right after losing her husband agronomist I think he was married oh yes but her son was never jealous of her nor she of him as I said, that's why every time I remember what happened like now I get this dreadful pain right here in my chest and my only consolation is that she soon followed suit,

God didn't want to prolong that suffering and decline we all watched her falling into. Errrm I think well let me see, Delia'd gone to Rosario I think, and she came back that very Monday morning, must've been in her car, she had a Renault 12 it was wasn't it Chesi? It was her husband's and she used to lend it to her son when he was in town. Sort of beige colour it was, it looked brand new the way she looked after it, she was like that with everything. Of course she knew nothing about what had happened to her son, how could she she'd just arrived, when she got home she asked the maid who said she hadn't seen him since Friday, there was nothing odd about that at all because sometimes the lad wouldn't set foot in the house for a week at a time, he was a bit of a tearaway as no doubt you've heard if you've been asking around, but she must've spotted something in the girl's expression, especially that one who wasn't that ugly for a *chinita*, left no stone unturned he didn't Delia's son, and Delia ended up picking them for their ugliness or she'd have to send them back before their nine months were up. I don't know if it was a something in her voice or if she started crying or what but what I do think is that that was when Delia started to worry. I don't know where she went or who she talked to, what I still find strange is that she didn't come to us her friends straight away. At that stage nobody was really sure what had happened to the boy, whether he'd been taken to Rosario or was still at the headquarters, but if there's one thing I am sure of it's that when she went to see Clota she still didn't suspect anything, because she went to ask her to find out if the police knew or could find out—no song and dance—if anything had happened to her little boy. She was barking up the wrong

196

tree there, just imagine Clota, the only other person in town in the dark, because nobody'd said a thing to her, out of respect for her husband I reckon, and him least of all as you can imagine, I put myself in his shoes poor man such a difficult decision he had to take, knowing what good friends Delia and his wife were, but that's duty for you isn't it. I'll never forget the time I failed my niece in an exam and made her repeat the year, remember Chesi? Her parents wouldn't speak to me for a month after that but what was I to do, I can promise you the girl suffered less than I did. I think Clota was in seventh heaven that day, Delia'd done so much to include her in town life when they arrived, it was through her that she met us and that in a few months the whole town'd accepted her, policemen's wives often spend years here without fitting in, especially the lower ranking officers', who disappear into the Colonia where property's cheap or into the Banco Hipotecario houses I don't know if you've seen the new ones but Clota of course was the wife of the chief of police and Delia was the first one to say this one looks different it's about time we had a gentleman for once and once she'd said it everyone said it, and it may've been things like that that made the Neris decide to stay in town after he retired. So Clota how can I put it it wasn't that she was glad or anything but she felt that God was giving her an opportunity to give her friend Delia something back a few crumbs of the bounty she'd had showered on her, and she assured her that the minute her husband came back for lunch she'd ask, no, demand that he put the whole headquarters at her friend's disposal no ifs or buts. I don't know what he must've said in reply, her husband was no liar but he was no

197

blabbermouth either. The things a policeman must see every day the least he'll try and do is protect his family from them, especially seeing as they're sworn to professional secrecy just like doctors are Clota answered us whenever we tried to draw her out. What I think is that things were no longer in his hands he'd've carried out his orders and there was nothing else he could do then, but I do think he was a little slack there at least, he could've told the mother her son'd been arrested and where he was being held so she could go and see him, particularly that very afternoon when Delia had a personal appointment with him at the station, and she must've heard something else by that stage because she was really worried and Clota's husband what was his name Neri yes but his first name was … Armando that's it he assured her the police would do everything in their power and that he'd already radioed all the police stations in the area and the highway patrol and if nothing had come in in forty-eight hours they'd put out a national alert, and in the meantime some people say the boy was locked up a stone's throw away worrying about his Mamá who took the Superintendent's hands in her gratitude to kiss them and he pulled them away in time taken aback Doña Delia please I'm only doing my duty and she herself told Clota, who with tears in her eyes told Chesi and myself, I'm so fond of Delia she cried I'd do anything for her promise me both of you that we'll all stick close to her in such dire straits and we said of course of course, what else could we say? And that very night she came to see us well me because in those days Chesi and I had our own families and our own houses sometimes I tell her I can hardly believe it don't I Chesi, that's life for you in the long run we've ended up spending more time together the pair of us than with our children and husbands if you add up the years at Papá and Mamá's and our widowhoods together, and the rest of the time living next door to each other so we were never very far apart, my hubby and Dr Lugozzi were great friends as well and the children were brought up to be so close they were more like brothers than cousins, so then when Delia showed up the pair of us comforted her as best we could, and that was in spite of your Uncle Rodolfo—remember how you used to call him Uncle Rodolfo?—your Uncle Rodolfo didn't want her in the house, he was worried about the police of course we still had the kids living at home they always ask after you you know Beba had another boy not long ago I'll show you the photos later I'll be going over someday soon because I can't stand being away from them for so long. But you know I may be easy-going and can adapt to things but if I have to stand up to someone I do and I said to him then and there I said Stop it Rodolfo. Delia's a lifelong friend and I won't slam the door in her face the way the others do, think what you like about her son and she's partly to blame for the way she brought him up but the door of this house which was my parents' and so's more mine than yours will never be closed to her so it won't. We were up till goodness knows what time, Delia I remember as if it were yesterday was sitting there where you are, wringing one of those special handkerchiefs all embroidered with her initials that she had made up in a shop in Rosario all stained with her make-up it was she hadn't stopped looking after herself yet she hadn't let herself go yet the way she did later broke your heart to see her it did, she who was always the best-turned-out woman in town but as I always say the higher you are the harder you fall. Something's happened to him I'm sure my heart's telling me I've had this stabbing pain here since this afternoon it won't let me breathe she kept repeating and Chesi and I saying Come on Delia you'll see it'll be all right, look at all the times he disappeared without a word and then turned up at home with a bunch of flowers or a box of chocolates and you always forgave him, and she says No this time it's different before the minute I'd ask a friend or one of the women who always kept track of him I'd calm down but this time nobody wants to talk to me, people avoid me in the street, I've even had people hang up on me and the ones I do manage to talk to won't look me in the eye when they tell me I don't know a thing. Do you know anything? Please if something serious has happened to him don't hide it from me, I'd die if I knew he needed me and here I am doing nothing to help him desperate she was and Chesi and I you can't imagine our distress but we didn't want her to do anything stupid the way she would later she was very impulsive and was capable of doing something crazy so it would be better for her to hear it straight from her son telling her Don't worry Mamá I'm fine the sweetest voice a mother can hear now that *was* his fault, the first thing he ought to've done was call his Mamá and reassure her, the only thing I always asked of Leandro and Bebita when they went out at night was stay out as late as you like I'd tell them but please don't forget to ring, fat chance, whole nights I've spent sitting up waiting for the phone to ring you'll see soon enough your son's little now but when he grows up you'll see for yourself, they say Darío called his lawyer or one of his friends course he'll've thought they'll get me out first and then he'd tell his mother when it was all sorted out there was no need to worry her he'd ended up sleeping it off in one local police station or another on more than one occasion, never here of course for his Mamá's sake and anyway how could he know it'd be any different this time. I mean I think he was in the right if he didn't want his mother to find out, although some Jezebel or other was bound to go and tell her sooner or later you know what it's like in these towns we're never short of busybodies but not us, no, we'd never dream of it. Delia eventually ended up going home, easier I think, but she can't have slept properly because at the crack of dawn the next day she was at the parish house knocking on Father Abeledo's door who was in the throes of one of his depressions at the time I'll tell you about them in a minute and I don't know if she managed to get him out of bed I don't think so, it's so many years ago now, can you remember Chesi? No of course, if Father Abeledo'd been having one of his good days it was a joy to see him there was nothing a girl wouldn't have done for him like a ray of sunshine he was this Jewish girl even wanted to convert but her parents slapped the idea right out of her head, the Brofmans I don't know if you ever met them apart from that they're well loved and well respected in town and as I was saying Father Abeledo would have given her consolation spiritual guidance such a shame it all happened during one of his crises and then … I don't know if she'd planned it or if she had the idea there and then, the parish house is right next door to your grandparents' and our Delia went right up and rang the doorbell. But you probably know more about it than I do, you must've been told by your … Oh, see

201

what I mean, that makes two of us. You know how it is when you realise someone doesn't want to talk about something, you don't just go bringing the subject up, I never did find out where the feud between Delia and your grandmother came from, actually it was your grandmother who was the offended party, Delia used to act as if nothing was wrong always wore a smile she did Emily this and Emily that that's how she pronounced it with an English accent imagine, a crying shame it was, the only two women in town who could speak proper English and they wouldn't speak to each other, sometimes I thought Delia was doing it on purpose, she had a rather catty streak to her sometimes, and your grandmother obviously was always ready to answer her back but she knew how to restrain herself, a real lady she was, and now suddenly there she is in the wee small hours banging on her door like a mad woman, you know what people are like they don't give you so much as the time of day till they need a favour, I don't know if I'd been in your grandmother's shoes I might've slammed the door in her face oh so now that you need me we're friends are we slammm but your grandmother didn't, did the dignified thing she did and showed her in."

Again the flashes of a past that's more and more my own. Still half-asleep, barefoot on the kitchen tiles, standing in front of the door to the dinette. The sobbing that's been partly responsible for waking me, a face blurred by time and tears, and a hunched body perched on the edge of the brocade sofa, the stern expression of my grandmother, saying close the door and tell Jacinta to make your breakfast. "Don't you think?" I hear my Auntie Porota ask and I come out of my trance and say, "What?"

"I was saying she must've gone to ask your grandfather to sort it out I imagine, him being the mayor and all. I reckon that must be why she swallowed her pride and went to talk to your grandmother. She even went to see the judge, Dr Carmona, would you believe it, I don't know if you've met oh of course through Leticia then you must know they hated each other with a venom because Delia pinched her boyfriend Darío's father no less and the judge—she was still Estelita Souza in those days—never forgave her. A real catch he was Don Diego Ezcurra, Delia couldn't stop crowing when she arrived here with him on her arm one of the most sought-after bachelors in Rosario not a penny to his name but always down at the Jockey Club and anyhow with what her Papá left her Delia had money to burn whereas Estelita's all right thanks to Judge Carmona she's made a career for herself but dear me wasn't the old man ugly, and long-lasting as well!"

"CHE I SPOKE TO DR CARMONA," Leticia mentioned to me one lunchtime when she got back from work. "You were right. Neri went to see her too. They talked about the mother more than anything, Doña Delia. Neri, Dr Carmona told me, was concerned about what she might do. If I were you, I wouldn't worry Superintendent she says she told him, you don't know her the way I do. She doesn't care about anybody but herself, not even her son. Once," Dr Carmona had explained to Leticia, who repeated it to me, "the boy cut himself on some glass on top of a wall and on the way to the little ward instead of picking him up in her arms she dragged him along by the hand, crying and pouring blood, so it wouldn't stain the dress she'd just bought in Buenos Aires. The little boy was terrified and tried to hug her skirts and all she said was Don't touch me Darío, eh, don't even dream of touching me. A mother like that should have custody taken away from her at birth, the law should be changed I tell you. Of course, that isn't what I told the Superintendent," Dr Carmona had told Leticia, "I said to him Just do your job and stop worrying, there's nothing to fear from Delia de Ezcurra. And who could have imagined her," she'd told Leticia, "waiting for me at the door at seven in the morning to catch me before I went in? She never used to set foot outside her door before ten seeing how long it took her to get dressed and done up. Didn't give a hoot about him when he was alive, and all of a sudden she's playing the Virgin Mary and Mary Magdalen at the same time, should've remembered her son while there was still time she should, too late for tears dear," Leticia repeated Dr Carmona's words. "I think she was doing it to attract attention, and to piss me off of course. As if she didn't know the legal channels were a waste of time in those days, we used to use habeas corpus to turn the gas fire on, I don't know if you'll remember? Oh, that's right, I always think you go further back than you do. Well eventually she started waiting for me at the door at seven every morning to give me a hard time in front of all and sundry. In the end I had to ask the Superintendent to let me use the jailhouse gate and went in through there every day. Sheer histrionics believe you me, played the desperate mother to a tee, same with her husband, her big chance to play the role of the grand widow, I don't know if you know but she hired a funeral parlour in Rosario; Fuguet or Toro Mocho weren't good enough for her, no sir, had to be Rosario. Next thing you know it'd've been Paris. And then—you won't remember, you were too young—the widow, tarted up in a mourning dress with a plunging lace neckline. All for show, no one as far as I know saw her shed a single tear over her husband, but of course that isn't what I told the Superintendent," Dr Carmona had told Leticia. And Leticia had told me that Ezcurra's mother and Dr Carmona had been friends since they were girls and had gone through high school and started their law degrees together, and that Delia had dropped out after stealing her girlfriend's boyfriend, a lecturer at the University of Rosario and a starving lawyer, and made him drop his teaching work and brought him to Malihuel to set up in practice. The future Dr Carmona finished her degree and had a meteoric career in the province's convoluted legal system, but she never forgave her friend for her treachery and was eaten away by jealousy and envy. In Delia's eyes—the town's eyes as well—women went to university to find a husband, and whoever finished her degree had failed. "She came back here," Leticia went on, "and married the examining magistrate, old Carmona, who was already a grandfather, so there was never any question of children, I'll get even with her later Dr Carmona must have thought but the old man lasted till he was ninety-five and by then of course she was well past it wasn't she, maybe she found a way of blaming Delia for that too, you know how it is."

"WELL I THINK IT MUST'VE BEEN, was it the same day Chesi that Delia went back to see Clota's husband? It must've been mustn't it, if there was one thing Delia was no good at it was waiting. Very impulsive she was, in everything, so she went over to headquarters which is only a block away from your grandmother's and asked, or rather demanded, at the top of her voice to talk to the chief someone may also've told her her son was in there I wouldn't know and when they told her the Superintendent wasn't there she got all well you've no idea screaming and shouting she'd seen his car outside you know that space out front that fills with relatives' cars on Sundays which is visiting day well Don Armando used to leave his there so imagine the things Delia must've said to the officer on duty she didn't mince her words when she got mad and the poor fellow of course it was nothing to do with him Would you like me to file a complaint Señora and Delia tells him he can stick his complaint in well you can imagine where she told him What I want is my son you let him go right now and if you've so much as laid a finger on him I'll sue the lot of you you'll be begging on the streets if the Superintendent doesn't show his face this minute. But either they wouldn't give in to her or maybe it was true Don Armando wasn't there used to spend a lot of time going from town to town he did such a responsible man everyone around here says he was the best chief of police we've ever had or maybe he left an order not to be disturbed and Delia well imagine she wasn't going to just waltz in there because she was a friend of his wife's me the time Leandrito got beaten up by some darkies from Chabás I think they were at that nightclub of Bermejo's the times I told him not to hang around there imagine my son all covered in blood I went through the entries desk though and it was the Superintendent himself who came over and said to me Doña Poro why didn't you come straight to me so helpful he was so if he didn't want to see Delia there must've been a reason for it mustn't there really her manners dishing out orders instead of asking, like mother like son maybe if they'd been pleasanter with people it would've turned out all right in the end. And what I'm telling you mind I'm not one for repeating gossip we got it straight from the horse's mouth Chesi and I did because Clota was here she'd come to give us a hand with all the kids' things one pinafore from last year was too small, another new one was too big and had to be taken in, and she didn't have any herself because one died young on her and later she couldn't or didn't want to you know I'm not one for poking my nose in especially in painful things like that and for example when the start of classes came around I think it did her good to help, like a second mother she was to our two, they still remember their Auntie Clota today and so do Chesi and I so many years and while she was alive she never wanted to come back of course it was so hard what happened left her with a great bitterness the two of them were so happy at the prospect of staying on in town Clota never stopped talking about the new house and showing us magazines of what it would look like and in the end they were treated like dogs worse than dogs and her husband they say the upset did for him that he started drinking. To Chesi and me she was how can I put it we were like three sisters and your grandmother too of course like the elder sister you know she usually comes, every month it used to be, once a year now she's sold the house and we visit as well when we go to Rosario and well some people must just know how to make themselves loved Delia on the other hand I mean imagine we all grew up together, though she always considered herself how shall I put it a cut above the people from town let's say you know always going on about her trips and her books and her clothes, whereas Clota her husband was the chief of police but she didn't need to show off so much more like how should I say more you know like a sister, can you picture Delia darning socks for somebody else's boy never mind her own, her ladyship would never stoop so low as to pick up a thimble oh no, not her. So there we were the three of us you know with the pinafores shortly before noon it must've been because the kids weren't there yet or our husbands and Delia comes barging in, not even a hello, and Clota I swear she jabbed herself with the needle out of fright it made her bleed poor thing We're going to headquarters because your husband's trying to fob me off and I know they've told me my boy's in there let's see if he has the guts to lie to my face with you there. And Clota who was I don't know if you ever met her you know very quiet never one for raising her voice but mind you don't say a wrong word about her husband and she says putting down her sewing Delia she says all right I'll come with you but only so you see that what you've just said about my husband is slander and apologise for believing the first person you come across instead of your bosom friend, and I could see her eyes filling with tears and when Delia got like that she didn't give a hoot about the other person, Yes yes I'll apologise to you and him and the dog too in good time and she left me standing there with the gauze and the alcohol and dragged Clota off by the arm didn't even shut the door when she left. And I still wonder which one of us tipped her off don't you?"

"DARÍO'S MOTHER HAD STARTED going from house to house asking people if they knew anything about her son," Clara Benoit had told me the afternoon I went to see her at the new beach resort her father's trying to build on the ever-shifting shores of the muddy lagoon, "and when I found out I couldn't stand it any longer and went to look for her, I found her at Majul's store talking to his wife who I think wanted to tell her but Babil who's still alive never took his eyes off her to make sure she kept her mouth shut and after Delia'd said Well thanks if you hear anything I beg you please let me know straight away I went out with her. And I remember a couple of people were walking past on the sidewalk and when they realised what was going on—because anyone could tell from Delia's face—they crossed the street and disappeared. And when I'd finished Delia stood there staring at me I was crying she wasn't and she said to me You're lying. You've wanted Darío dead ever since he left you but God will punish you for this injury you're doing me she said with this faraway look in her eyes and then she turned on her heels and headed in the direction of the headquarters walking like a disjointed doll and a couple of times she almost fell over, then picked herself up and carried on again, and I ran after her and caught up with her halfway down the block and offered to go with her and she turned round and pointed to the church and said again God will punish you and I couldn't go on following her after that see?"

"ALL RIGHT if just supposing if there'd been some misfortune the best thing is to let people know as soon as possible even if it hurts, but would you believe it by now there were people in town who were saying the boy was dead imagine if the news had reached his mother's ears, people repeat the first thing they hear without caring whether it's true or not, what I reckon is that Delia she must've heard something and panicked, and maybe the person who told her even thought they were doing her a favour and actually did her a terrible injury, imagine a mother being told that about her only son, I sometimes wonder if it's thoughtlessness or just plain wickedness. Imagine the pair of us waiting for them to come out me as soon as I could I dropped all the lunch things like that and rushed off to Clota's when I see her heading over in floods of tears couldn't speak for crying and I called to Chesi and between the pair of us we made her a nice cup of tea and patted her hand There there till she was in a fit state to speak, said Delia had raised her voice to her beloved Armando and he says How dare you drag my wife into this and Delia I'll drag your wife and oh Fefe I can't repeat what she said how upset the woman must have been, I'd never have thought it possible if it hadn't been Clota that was telling me, I know Delia regretted it later and went and apologised and asked her again to help, but you know Clota she might be a very nice person but she had her dignity and never opened the door to her again, not if she comes on bended knee she told us I don't want to hear that woman's name again as long as I live."

"That isn't what happened," says Chesi.

"I'LL DRAG YOUR WIFE and that little whore you fuck at the motel and who the hell else I like into it." Don León would restore the censored sentence at the table in Los Tocayos that same afternoon for the benefit of my ears dulled by an imminent bout of flu, and Sacamata senior would add with a smile: "Now there was a woman with balls I mean the whole town knew about Neri's *chinita* except his wife, and she came out with it just like that, no anaesthetic."

"Except she said it to her at the Yacht Club," Don León would correct him, "how could I forget, I was there and so were let's see us two the pharmacist and possibly Dr Lugozzi too I don't know if you've met him. But not his wife, definitely not, that thing about the *chinita* she didn't say it in front of his wife, you're wrong there. But apart from that she didn't pull any punches. Murderer son of a bitch was the least she said to him and the Superintendent didn't know what to do to stop her see he really wasn't expecting that, had it all worked out but that's where his calculations let him down, he hadn't counted on Delia's fury. Anyway I think Delia was wrong to confront the chief of police like that, he had her son's life in his hands. She was putting him between the Devil and the deep blue sea. If she hadn't challenged him like that the lad might still be alive today."

"CHESI'S RIGHT," laughs her sister, "I think your Auntie Porota got all fuddled up. What a scream! It's just it's been so many years. What I was just telling you happened later didn't it Chesi. It was later they told Delia her son'd been killed and that it'd been Clota's husband that did it, and that

was where the last fight broke out, the parting of the ways.
That's what happened wasn't it? I've gone and got things
in such a twist I swear and now I don't know where to start
untangling them. Because Clota if you remember went to see
her one more time, and that must have been before she came
out with that thing about the *chinita* poor Clota such a nice
person I swear she was because all right what her husband
did was wrong but what did she have to do with it and she
was so very fond of Delia worshipped the ground she walked
on inconsolable she was and said to us she says to us I'll go
and see her. I'll go and see her she says to us, the three of
us were there and we offer to go with her but she says No,
thank you from the bottom of my heart she says to us but
we've got to sit down and talk this out just Delia and me,
alone, she can't go listening to the tongues wagging against
my husband because instead of asking for bribes he enforces
the law I'm sure if we can have a heart-to-heart it'll clear
up any misunderstandings, poor Clota, she knew the Delia
that went shopping or out for tea but she didn't know her
the way we did all her little ways so it came as no surprise
to us just imagine Clota broken-hearted but, Delia, I don't
understand, I beg you, in the name of our old friendship I
beg you, she told us later well you can just imagine Delia.
Old friendship? Your husband has taken my son away from
me. What the … pardon my French Fefe, I'm repeating it
word for word, What the fucking hell are you talking about,
she said to her, would you believe it, all foul-mouthed she'd
gone, you hear all sorts on the television nowadays but I don't
know from a man all right but not from a woman, but you
know what it's like, there are people who give themselves airs

and graces acting grand and if you scratch the surface a little
bit with your nail like this their loutish side comes out. So I
don't know if it was that night or one of the following nights
see that Delia went to the Yacht Club to confront Armando
who used to go there too for a hand of cards with his pals,
Chesi's husband amongst them, he was the one who told
us, so you see we're not just spouting gossip. I don't know
I don't even want to remember the things she said to him
and I'm sure because I knew him well that he didn't stoop
so low as to answer back except at one point anyway with
dignity he tells her I've already told you the Neris lost a little
one so Armando says to Delia Señora I've lost a son too but
I knew how to keep my grief to myself with dignity. And he
was right in a way wasn't he."


"YES, THAT'S EXACTLY WHAT HAPPENED," Don León
would confirm. "Neri shot himself in the foot. And Señora
Delia went sort of round the bend, but what do you expect?
He'd just told her her son was dead."


"AND RIGHT THERE to give you an idea she tells Neri
he was lying right to his face, that she knew her son was
locked up in the jailhouse and the Superintendent gives her
his word he wasn't at headquarters well you can't say that
wasn't true and that must've been when Delia said that thing
about his wife because the Superintendent got up on the spot
and told her Señora you can say whatever you like to me
but I repeat don't go dragging my family into it and listen

213

carefully would you believe Delia looks him up and down and spits out *And what right have you got to have a family?* just like that she came out with it what right have you got to have a family I mean I understand you can be blinded by hatred or pain but anyway it's not the sort of thing you say that's something I wouldn't wish on my worst enemy. Must've been later I don't know Chesi if you remember what your husband told us wasn't it that Delia sort of clicked and says to him And if he's dead where is he if my son's dead I want you to give him to me she started screaming and if someone tried to calm her down she'd turn on them, and of course nobody was going to get her out of there by force, she was still Doña Delia de Ezcurra and they weren't going to lay a finger on her so it was Armando who had to back down, and to cap it all he didn't have the car and Delia followed him down the sidewalk screaming murderer at him in front of everybody luckily Dr Lugozzi had taken his and caught up with him and gave him a lift home right Chesi? There was no stopping Delia by then she was in the grips of a kind of frenzy wanting to find out what had happened, knocking on doors and sometimes not even knocking and walking straight inside as if they were hiding her son in there or stopping someone and asking them out of the blue as if everybody knew what did people know they didn't know if he was dead or alive besides given the boy's reputation a lot of people'd think he'd seen the creditors coming and turned tail there are still people today who claim he's alive I don't know who told me they saw him somewhere in Peyrano just imagine if it's true the pointless suffering he caused his mother there are some things that just aren't done there you go you're right it was Casilda you're becoming quite an expert on the life of the … it's a book you're going to write is it? And are people over there going to be interested in something that happened so many years ago in a little town in the provinces? You know better anyway as I was telling you she covered the town from house to house asking questions or for help first from how can I put it the VIPs who ran from her like the plague by then, 'specially when the patrol car started tailing her all day so you'd open the door to her and she'd start rabbiting on at you twenty to the dozen and raising her voice besides and while the patrol car crept slowly past behind her she couldn't see it but of course you could and you were the one the policemen inside were looking at. It happened to your Uncle Rodolfo it did and he came in white as a sheet poor man and told me That woman isn't to set foot in this house again don't let me find out you've let her in when I'm not here if she wants to join her son at the bottom of the lagoon that's her business and that's what must have happened everywhere because she how can I put it started lowering her standards eventually she ended up ringing on the doorbells of the waiter at the bar, the school janitor, the butcher out in the Colonia, what do you make of it Fefe, a woman once so refined? So one day I couldn't stand it any longer and I say to her, I said to Chesi Look Chesi, if they have to kill us let them kill us but things can't go on like this. I'm going to see Delia come hell or high water and if you don't want to come I'll go on my own but I can't sit idly by with my arms folded and she I remember it clear as day put down her knitting and went to fetch a headscarf and stood there handbag in hand all ready to go, just like that without a word, like a little soldier by the door remember Chesi?" asks Auntie Porota with sisterly affection, and Chesi nods before casting on to the next row.

"She doesn't say much does she," I remark.

"Chesi? She's a bit sparing with her words."

Her sister's body shakes with laughter like a pile of bags wrapped in cloth. "But it doesn't matter, you know, your Auntie Porota does enough talking for the pair of us."

"EVERYTHING HAS A LIMIT," Don León Benoit would assure me that night. "The Ezcurrita affair let's let it go shall we, but Doña Delia was a well-loved, well-respected member of the community, Don Alejandro Alvarado's daughter no less. Never in our lives would we have agreed to let the police lay a finger on her, Superintendent Neri didn't even dare dream of it because he knew. He knew all along what the result of such a preposterous plan would be. Later on of course circumstances changed, Doña Delia was no longer the person she had been and some of the things she did might even be considered illegal. But by then Neri's opinion cut no ice here any more."

"SO WE GO AND FETCH your grandmother and she says Do you think it's wise and we say we do indeed she has great respect for you, she'll listen to you, and you know your grandmother she didn't get on with her at all but at a time like that I always say you have to put any pettiness to one side the way your grandmother did an example to us all that Delia couldn't live up to when she opens the door to us we can't believe what a mess she looks I swear it broke our hearts to see her and she looks at us with that faraway look and asks why we've come, what we're doing here. And we have trouble persuading her to let us in but we sit down and she doesn't offer us anything and her once such an attentive hostess with her fancy teas and her petits fours from Fuguet because she used to say the bakeries here in town weren't up to much and then I can see she's about to break down and I go over to her and take her by the hand and give it a pat Don't get so worked up, you're bound to get news soon you know Darío and that obviously touched something deep inside her she clung to my shoulder and began to cry inconsolably, you should've seen her it was obviously just what she needed to get it off her chest and Chesi and your grandmother came over too to comfort her there … there … and I can't remember Chesi if it was you or me who says to Delia Please this has got to stop, you can't go on like this think of your family and then she did react but not the way we expected, she stands up suddenly like this in a dressing gown I'd never seen her in before and posh shoes can you imagine what a clash I think she must have been drinking because she was unsteady on her feet and says to us What family! I haven't got a family! You lot killed them! And for the three of us it was like a slap in the face Good Lord hand on heart Delia how can you say something like that we're your friends you know you aren't in your right mind and she says First you kill him and then you come to comfort me, as if we'd been the ones responsible, so there was clearly nothing to be done about it then she wouldn't listen to reason a dreadful dreadful shame I tell you but the three of us got up to go and when we were outside on the sidewalk we turned round to say something to her but she was standing there like a statue in the doorway, and she says to us, listen because this one really takes the biscuit, she says to us The woman you came to see doesn't exist any more, so you'd better not call again. Just like that she told us didn't she Chesi. Can you imagine! She always had something ... how can I put it ... always had a flare for melodrama about her Delia did. But she went too far that time. The three of us and your grandmother had gone to see her with the best of intentions."

"She suffered a lot," I manage to say pathetically.

"Of course she did of course she did," Auntie Porota concedes magnanimously. "That's why we didn't bear her any ill will. And the next day maybe on account of our visit it backfired on us the next day she goes and plants herself outside the door to the headquarters waiting for the chief of police and after that he used to drive straight in through the jailhouse gate, then Delia went off to the courts from which she'd also been banned, she used to pester Dr Carmona in particular what sainted patience that woman had anyone else'd've had her arrested and Delia was now spending all day on the streets almost always hanging around the headquarters, there were times she'd fall asleep on a bench and the maid had to come and wake her up and take her home, they say she had to help her get bathed and dressed a saint that girl died in childbirth she did a few years later, here in the little ward in the arms of Dr Lugozzi who could do little for her, it was thanks to her poor thing that Delia wasn't wandering the streets looking like death warmed up but anyway word'd already got out I don't know who started calling her that they say it was the Superintendent himself but I don't think so he was very well spoken but because of the upset he'd already taken to the bottle and so in a moment of exasperation you can understand it he may've called her a mad hag and the name stuck. Goodness me, life's full of little surprises as I sometimes say. From being the snootiest woman in town to this, when even the kids coming out of school would go past the bench outside the headquarters and shout mad hag, mad hag, and then your grandfather, must've been at the Superintendent's request, had the bench taken away and Delia sat on the kerb, leaning against that sentry box that's always there."

"AND THIS ONE TIME it was throwing it down and I knock on the door of the Superintendent's office with some papers for him and as I don't hear anything I open the door and find him sitting at his desk with a half-empty whisky bottle and his back to the window staring into space," ex-policeman Carmen Sayago would also manage to tell us the night we broke three of his ribs, "and without looking up he goes and asks Is she still there? And I stick my head out of his office window and I can see Señora Delia sitting on her bench as usual drenched she was hair all over the place crazier than ever she looked and I go Yes Superintendent sir and he nods and doesn't say a word and I go out as I came in and take the papers to Greco."

"YOU KNOW WHO SENDS THEIR REGARDS Auntie Porota?" Taking advantage of a lull in the story, I smile and delay my answer to see if I'll get the few seconds of improbable silence the pronunciation of her dear name deserves. "Gloria. Remember Gloria?"

"Which one, Gloria Caramuto? Saw her only this morning I did. She's going gaga poor woman, can't remember a thing. The other day she went into the bakery three times running—"

"No, no," I wave my hands incompetently in the air. "Gloria who's my age, a bit older, who lived two doors down from Babil's … "

"Ahhh I know, you mean Yoli's daughter. Yes I ran into her in Buenos Aires one time I went, don't know how she found out I was there but she came to see me, with a Remember me Doña Porota? Easy game that one used to be, had a loose streak she did. Used to come in summer and go through two or three from here or the other towns and then go back to her boyfriend or boyfriends who knows in Buenos Aires, no bones broken. I always said she'd come to a bad end and that she did, what an upset for her parents, so right-minded they were, and she a guerrilla, and then she was nabbed and doesn't she end up marrying or shacking up I'm not sure with some high-ranking officer? I'm telling you she's easy that one is. No beating about the bush. And her daughters the poor things turned out retarded tell me it's genetic you can or whatever you like but you're not telling me all that sleeping around didn't have anything to do with it. And then she drops in to see me with her How are you Doña Porota, remember me? And me, Course I do my love, how could I forget?"

"We were together for two years," I remark.

"What did I tell you? Eat you for breakfast that one will."

"THE DEAD DON'T ASK FOR MUCH, they're fine with two metres of earth, a few prayers from the heart not the lips, living flowers or knick-knacks, from home, that have absorbed a lot of love. They ask so little … But then again if they're denied it they can be ruthless. The unburied dead have no peace and therefore give no respite, and Superintendent Neri must have wished he could rescue Ezcurrita's physical body from the bottom of the lagoon and give him a Christian burial. But it was too late by then and there was nothing he could do but leave town. No one can live with an apparition," Ña Agripina, the healer, explained to me the afternoon I went for tea at her smart little house in the FONAVI district. "And they wonder why the Superintendent took to the bottle. I tell you Fefe, do what you like in your life but never commit an irreparable outrage against a dead man, because that *is* the sin that Little King Jesus talked about, that's the sin that has no forgiveness. If we need to cling on to anything in this dark world it's the sleep that death will eventually bring, and to go on suffering afterwards is the greatest injustice, like life without rest. But the insomnia of the dead bears no comparison with that of the living. I don't know if you've heard about Superintendent Neri's accident, he ended up ploughing into a street light on his way back from the lagoon. They say it was the bottle but I know it was Ezcurrita who appeared to him running with water in the middle of the road, Neri himself told me the time he came to ask me for something to help

221

him sleep. Desperate he was. And it wasn't guilt that'd made him like that, he was a policeman and it wasn't the first time he'd killed a helpless man. Guilt merely comes from within, it isn't that powerful. I'm telling you these things because I can see you've spoken with the dead, more than once, so I can tell you that the tips of Superintendent Neri's fingers blazed in the dark with the evil light, blue like gas flames. And the lagoon couldn't abide what they did to it either. The drowned she sends back to shore, but poor Darío, they'd sunk him in her bosom … Water can't abide the dead. It was inevitable. You saw what the flood was like, not even the church was spared. They say it was the rains, the roads, the incline. But I know—and I'm not the only one—that the lagoon spewed up the dead man we threw into it. And we haven't had a beach resort since, except that jetty of Don León's stranded in the middle of the bare field in the droughts and in the floods you have to dive to find it. Anyway, as for me, I lost the taste for dipping in it after that. Neri, he couldn't resist the temptation to make us this parting gift—before he left he just had to spit in our lagoon. And the tormented soul of Delia's son still roams the shore, searching for who knows what. People have seen him, late at night, even people from other towns, who never heard of him. Poor Darío. Who knows, now you're here it may bring him a little peace, right? You have to take him something Fefe. It'll be good for him."

"Where," I asked in a peculiar throaty voice that came from so deep it didn't sound like my own.

"I'll tell you."

"AND BY THEN I THINK SO, she'd spend practically all day there on her bench, I don't know if anybody took her anything to eat or drink the girl did didn't she Chesi? and people didn't want to go that way any more they'd go all the way round the block but there was no other route to school and of course the schoolkids were curious and used to ask what was wrong with Doña Delia and it must have been one of the parents I reckon who not really knowing what to tell them and meaning no harm must've said Darío left town without telling his Mamá and it's broken her heart and she's gone crazy don't you ever go and do anything like that and the child must've repeated it to his schoolmates I remember hearing it at school from my students and after that some people started calling her poor Doña Delia and others the mad hag, I swear if there's one thing I pray for to God who's been so good to me just one more thing I'd ask him not to let me go downhill like that or like Gloria Caramuto who can only find her way around because the town's so small and there's always somebody to take her back her daughter's heart's constantly in her mouth it is poor thing a saint she is never a complaining word don't even dream of suggesting she should put her mother in a home they're building one here now near Majul's I don't know if you've seen it otherwise the nearest one's in Fuguet, and that's what Delia needed a son to take care of her course she only had one so as not to lose her figure so they say and look where that left her. Had it been up to me I'd've had ten but your Uncle Rodolfo wouldn't hear of it two's more than enough and of course I wasn't going to have them on my own was I. That's what Delia was short of children are a boon and a consolation they'd've stopped her with Mamá please the whole town's talking, the things she used to do, on Sunday afternoons she'd go up to the relatives of the convicts who were the only ones who'd listen to her by that stage her of all people who'd been heard to say the jailhouse ought to be moved to the outskirts of town so we wouldn't have to face that sorry spectacle every Sunday. Ah life eh? And there were some who started on about how the police ought to do something, how it was the chief's responsibility to right the wrong he'd committed, but let's face it the Superintendent wasn't up to righting wrongs any more, all he could do was leave town.

"A FAREWELL PARTY?" I'd asked in astonishment the night before, though by that stage my credulity had been strained beyond breaking point. "Didn't you say everyone condemned his actions?"

"The human memory moves in mysterious ways," quipped Iturraspe, examining the flowering tip of his toothpick, tinted faintly with a watery red.

"It was at the Yacht Club," added Licho. "I was taken on as an extra waiter, but there was no need. Half the tables were empty."

"Ten," specified Nene Larrieu. "When they went over to Neri's to explain he answered It's all right, don't worry, you should all've stayed at home. You only need yourself to leave. His breath was already strong enough to knock you flat when he got there, and he downed three more bottles of red on top of that. When it came to the farewell speeches they had to pretend they couldn't hear him chuckling to himself. Didn't know where to put herself his missus didn't."

"Speeches too?" I sighed, and, before anyone could open their mouth, "No, I know, don't say a word. My grandfather."

"He wasn't the only one"—Licho softened the blow. "He was joined by two or three others, each one more passionate than the last. Ease off boys, no need to roll out the red carpet, Nene was mouthing at them, and me I covered up the giggles with my empty tray. But Superintendent Neri—sorry, he was ex-Superintendent Neri by then—was wrong about one thing. Their warmth that night wasn't hypocritical. They were genuinely glad he was leaving."

"But he didn't miss the opportunity for one last grand gesture, did he," chirped Iturraspe, who'd set about applying the softened toothpick to his fingernails with greater precision. "Tell him Nene."

"Well for a start," began Malihuel's infallible walking database, "the local movie house had been showing the classic western *High Noon* all week in a non-stop double bill with *My Name Is Trinity*. Who's never dreamt at some point in their lives of throwing their badge into the dust, with the dignified contempt of Gary Cooper, at the feet of the cowardly townsfolk who didn't deserve a sheriff like him?"

"Course out here provincial coppers don't wear silver stars—maybe they do in Buenos Aires eh, you're way ahead of us—so rummaging drunkenly through his pockets Malihuel's ex-police chief ended up throwing down the only thing he could find—his Yacht Club membership card. While his gesture didn't lack, how can I put it, clarity, it didn't exactly bring the house down. And then that halfwit

Casarico thought he'd dropped it 'cause he was so pissed and bent down to pick it up, so, as he couldn't repeat the gesture, Neri stuffed it back in his jacket pocket and left. And he never got another opportunity after that did he. The day they actually left not even the dogs showed up to give them a send-off'"—Iturraspe rounded off the anecdote.

I had one last question.

"No Rosas Paz wasn't there," Nene Larrieu replied. "Didn't even bother replying as far as I know, and as a rule I do."


"HOW SHOULD I KNOW WHAT IT WAS LIKE," remarked Don León, shortly after joining us and ordering his first gin, "they must've loaded everything into the car and left. They'd sold most of the furniture a few weeks earlier and the house they were building never got off the ground as you know. What I do know is that a few days later their bitch appeared on the highway. Probably dumped it just after setting off, otherwise the dog'd never've been able to make it back, 'specially as it was limping on three legs by then. Well, I mean it must've been him because Doña Clota was completely devoted to the little thing, maybe he threatened to dump her too. Your pal Guido ended up adopting it, always was very dog-minded. How many's he got now? Three isn't it? counting the ones from the factory, that's what I was telling you Licho. Well I think the gesture was crystal clear. I don't know if you've heard but that bitch … Ah, course, it was your grandparents who … The gesture spoke volumes. He didn't want anything from Malihuel. Even left his *chinita* behind, though Ariel Greco used her for a while, just for kicks. Mind

you we weren't going to make it difficult for him. Just as long
as he got out here … He left us with Arielito Greco though.
Now that man was a crook, even the cows had to cough up
to get milked. He didn't leave town till the flood forced him
to and even the fleas had nothing to eat. The present one
likes to live and let live. But you know what it's like, with the
cops. In Bombal for example, which is near here but policed
by another headquarters, a little boy appeared dead, and
everyone knows who did it, a first sergeant it is and a shirt-
lifter to boot but the chiefs won't hand him over, and nor will
the judges. There've been something like six silent marches
already. It was all on TV. Didn't you see it in Buenos Aires?
The police are insisting it was a tramp, so they go out on
a raid after every march and so far the only thing all that
marching's done is to make tramps avoid Bombal like the
plague. They'll grind the marchers down in the end, they
always do. For Ezcurrita? That's a laugh. Are you serious?
The only way to get the town marching for Ezcurra would've
been to call a meeting of his creditors. We'd've filled the
square then wouldn't we," said Don León seeking the approval his fellow townsmen have been reluctant to afford him
of late. "It's like that fable … well I can't remember which
one now, the thing is Ezcurra screwed everyone and then
when he got into trouble nobody wanted to lift a finger to
help him see. 'Sides, all that marching's fairly recent as far as
I can remember. You couldn't get one over on the military,
no way, they were the only ones marching. You know what
it's like, nowadays somebody loses a poodle and the whole
town's out on the streets with candles and photos. It's the in
thing now, but in those days you could forget about it. The

military were capable of loading a whole march into the trucks. And Neri, what we heard is they headed back to the north of the province, which is where he was from, and set up a maxikiosk, can't remember where, and that they both died in a crash on the highway. And … must've been somewhere around Vera I reckon. It was only a matter of time though. I mean, if he carried on drinking the way he did."

"Brazilian truck-driver, drove one of those that look like locomotives, hit them head on like a fly-swatter. Had to peel them off the radiator like bugs," added Iturraspe graphically enough.

"SO WHAT'S THAT?" Guido'd asked a few days earlier in the cab of his truck, which he'd come to pick me up in from the Cornelio Saavedra library in Toro Mocho, when I showed him the last stamp in my collection.

"Have a look," I held out the photocopy to him.

"Oh yeah, and who's going to drive, you?"

"'Announcement,'" I read. "'We the undersigned authorities and inhabitants of the town of Malihuel, capital of Coronel González County, Santa Fe Province, Argentina, hereby express our agreement and approval for the exemplary work of General Superintendent Armando J Neri at the head of the Eighth Regional Police Unit based therein, and wish him a prosperous and well-earned rest on the occasion of his forthcoming retirement. His providential actions at moments critical not only for the region but for the country as a whole, which can finally be put behind us, the unbreakable faith of his convictions and his distinguished sense of honour and duty are all deserving of praise and emulation. With his departure from the post, the town of Malihuel loses not only one of the best chiefs of police in its long history, but also a faithful friend, and just as we regret that he has, for valid personal reasons, reversed his initial decision to remain in our midst after his retirement, we would like to assure him that his stay in Malihuel will never be forgotten and that the gates of our beloved town will always be open to him and his family.' Touching eh?" I remark after I've finished.

We'd stopped at the lights on the exit of Route Eight and Guido took the chance to grab the paper and give it a quick read, especially the signatures at the end.

"Your grandfather's there," I pointed out matter-of-factly.

"So's yours," he riposted.

I gave him my best withering smile. Guido shrugged his shoulders and pulled off.

"WHEN YOU THINK ABOUT IT we could even be proud of Doña Delia right?" Don León, who was on a rare third gin, and had evidently got hooked on the subject of marches, renewed his assault. "We ought to do something oughtn't we, I don't mean a statue but at least a plaque, a street name, I mean we've got more than enough streets to go round haven't we, 'specially in the Colonia? I don't mean for Ezcurrita see, because someone might get all het up about it, 'specially his creditors. But Doña Delia, she shouldn't offend anybody by now. We should talk to the mayor about it right? at the next Neighbourhood Committee meeting. But I don't know if there'll be a quorum. What do you think?" Don León asked and sank into expectant silence.

My sidelong glance met with a heard-it-all-before scowl from Guido, who'd just arrived. Iturraspe gazed at the floor, and only when he realised no one else intended to did Licho decide to speak up:

"Right, yes. We ought to do something," he ended up nodding after a few seconds of general silence.

"AND THAT ONE'S OUR FOUNDER, Colonel Urbano Pedernera, a hero of the Indian wars. At one time you could dismantle the statue, the rider and horse had been cast separately and once a year the people used to take Don Urbano down and parade him through the streets and down to the shore of the lagoon, where they'd scrub him and brush him and polish him till they got all the green off. My how he shone, like a trumpet in the morning sun he looked. Then they'd sit him back on his horse the wrong way round, and the next day us Council employees had to turn him the right way round again. You've no idea what he weighed! No, no, if there was anything in it, it was nothing more than a practical joke, the kind of stunt lads pull when they've had one too many, that's all, nothing political as some people claim. It's always been a peace-loving town this, people respect authority here. But there's always somebody around to quibble and carp and this is how the two of them ended up as you can see. There's the weld and the scorch marks from the blowtorch, between the colonel's legs and the saddle. Plumber's solder they used, I mean, it's a crying shame, looks so ugly. And to make matters worse he's not on straight! Weeell, let's see. Must be fifteen years ago at least, no, longer, me I started working for the Council in … "

I'd spent my first day in Malihuel on a sentimental journey around the landmarks of my childhood. I soon realised nothing much had changed, aside from the predictable, almost inevitable marks of progress that had been passively absorbed from the outside world: the once non-existent bus terminal, the TV satellite dish next to the new telephone exchange, a couple of video clubs. Otherwise there was no difference in size or appearance, only in scale: what the perspective of childhood and memory had made vast and diffuse, taking on almost the proportions of a nebulous country, my arrival had replaced with the clear, condensed and crystalline—a miniature town in a snowstorm. As if I'd been looking at Malihuel across the years through a pair of field glasses and my arrival, instead of removing them, had put them on the wrong way round. The square, on one of whose sunlit benches I'd installed myself, stiff with cold, to smoke a cigarette, sported a miniature of the same unpainted playground rides, trees that looked the same having grown, the statue of motherhood, the polished bronze of its uncovered breast shining against its general verdigris, the statue of Comandante Pedernera that I was being told about by the part-time park-keeper, a man of indefinite years dressed in a fat blue jacket and parrot-green baseball cap, who'd been sweeping the sandstone paths, wet from the recent rainfall, with a palm leaf, and had come over to my bench to ask me if I was from Rosario or Fuguet and casually, with exquisite delicacy, if I had a cigarette.

231

"What's that he's holding?" I asked him in return. "A champagne cork?"

"That? It's a thistle flower. These fields—the whole area—were thistle fields, thistles higher than a man on horseback back in the days of the Indians. Colonel Pedernera founded the farming colonies, after he wiped them out. What?"

"Who had him welded back on?"

"The mayor at the time. Don Rogelio it must've been. It was under him I started working for the Council. Later there was a plan to unweld him again, they were going to have some study or other done to see if they could get him off without ruining him, but the years passed and so did the mayors and the floods came and went and there he is. But people'd got used to him looking like that by then."

"NOW THAT'S WHERE SHE DID overstep the mark if you don't get on with people fine but with beliefs or what do you call them symbols I think you have to respect them, spitting at someone isn't the same as spitting at the cross and our founder's statue stands for all of us, like the watchtower, I always say the Tuttolomondos ought to put the watchtower on their pasta boxes it's our only export after all but you try telling them you know how stubborn they are you could suggest it seeing as you're such good friends pretend it's your own idea all right I admit I did take part as a young girl but it's like Carnival I mean just because the men dress up as women doesn't mean they're effeminate does it, nor does parading Don Urbano on the Virgin's litter which incidentally with his legs open like that and no horse

232

underneath honestly it looked like I won't say any more and of course it didn't show a lack of respect for authority, and besides I mean it was gleaming after the celebrations they say eggs and flour absorb the oxide and then washing it off in the lagoon water with all that iodine, tantamount to a purification it was, nowadays it looks so run-down, must've been twenty years since it last saw a cloth what do you expect when it's all jobs for the boys at the Council you're lucky if they bother to sweep the streets. I think that year was the first time we didn't do it I don't know why we didn't agree not to but the day of the ceremony came it was supposed to be secret before to keep outsiders away but it's ancient history now and anyway Fefe you're one of us I can tell you it was always the third Sunday of March and that year goodness knows why the third Sunday came around and not even a parrot. I think we just forgot personally. But Delia didn't. She must've been expecting us all to turn up, her of all people who'd never wanted to be part of things that were how can I put it a bit on the common side but this time she was the only one there, ah the ironies of life. And when she realised nobody'd come in sheer anger I tell you she grabbed poor Don Urbano by the foot and boom! she flipped him off his perch. The people living on the square say they heard the noise and came out to see thinking there'd been a crash. If you go and have a proper look you'll see that there's a faint line on his right arm below the elbow which is a crack he got when he fell. The strength desperation gives you I'm telling you it always took at least five men at the ceremony to get him off his horse and Delia did it on her own goodness me whenever I think how that woman must've felt," says Auntie

Porota while rolling into a tight ball the last yellowing strands of the undone cardie held by her sister's reverent hands.

"I DON'T THINK THE TIME WAS RIPE EITHER," opined Iturraspe when, taking advantage of Don León's absence to urinate, I quiz him about the fate of the statue. "We tacitly decided to put the ceremony on ice till further notice in case the military took it the wrong way, they were so fond of festivals to do with the War against the Injuns and all that. But of course, after Delia's sudden unsaddling of our founder, there was an act of redress right across the board. Well who do you expect, the mayor right? It was his duty to our beloved founder, hero of the holy war against the barbarian defeated again by his comrades in arms a hundred years later, saving the fatherland for the fifth time in its history—Professor Gagliardi and I tried to figure out his arithmetic but it just didn't add up—well anyway by the time we finished clapping two operatives from the Council team—Topo Lencina was one, I can't remember the other—whipped out their blowtorches and started welding away between Don Urbano Pedernera's pants and the saddle of his horse-faced mule. As the double jet of sparks descended his trouser leg the gallant rider took up his final position of rest, high in the saddle, which he holds to this day, though some people think he leans to the right slightly, and one time, to put an end to the eternal debate, we went to the hardware store to find Don Alberto Fischer, who fetched his level and plumb line, and confirmed the slanting hypothesis, although the uprighters didn't find the results conclusive."

"ARE YOU SURE you don't want anything else Fefe? I remember how much you liked coming here for your milk and cookies. Not even a glass of water? It's from the tap, I don't know if you've seen but we've got running water now. They found some out there by Rosas Paz. They'd been looking for it before out past your grandmother's, but it was bad. Remember what it was like before, how bitter the lagoon water was? No use not even for watering it was. You had to water delicate plants like dahlias with water from the well. What a job! So many things have changed since you used to come here, so many people that have left, your grandmother, Clota whom we miss so much, like sisters we were the three of us, you don't know how sad we were when we heard about the accident, the only consolation is that they went together, as I always say, I wouldn't wish it on anyone to be left behind. Would I Chesi. I mean it was easier for us when the little ones were here, but now, well that's why we moved in together, actually it was Chesi that moved in. I look at you now and I swear I can't believe it, so grown-up, so tall, a war hero from the Malvinas and all, makes me feel all proud … What a silly billy your Auntie Porota is, someone of my years getting all … I always get a bit emotional at this time of the afternoon, especially in winter. Chesi doesn't get like this so much, she has her knitting to keep her happy haven't you Chesi? The cardie for your little boy's nearly ready Fefe, now don't tell me it doesn't look a treat, and promise you'll take a photo of him wearing it and send it to us. Oh and make sure his Mamá's in it too, we're dying to meet her. What did you say her name was? Well, after Delia moved to Rosario we never heard another thing about her. That as well, sometimes I get this pain … I'm not saying she didn't have her reasons poor thing, she suffered a great deal over her son, but in all these years no visit, no letter, not even a phone call. A town she lived in all her life, where so many people loved her. But then she did always act as if she was doing us a favour living here didn't she, always thought she was a cut above the rest of us in town and one fine day she just upped and left. That business over her son upset her it's true, troubled her a great deal it did, and goodness knows she must've felt people here didn't help her enough. Still she didn't know how to make people help her either, first she sets the whole town against her, then she criticises it for deserting her. And anyway supposing if God forbid just thinking about it gives me a stabbing pain right here, but just supposing something had happened to my Leandrito, or to the son of forgive me Chesi it's just an example don't look at me like that, if anything'd happened to either of them do you think Delia would've lifted a finger to help us? People are no worse here than anywhere else, and I say, if you move every time you don't like something about someone you'll end up at the North Pole isn't that right Fefe. There'll always be things we don't like and as I say if you want to leave you're perfectly entitled, Argentina's a big place and Rosario has its charms, who can deny it, although you wouldn't get me out of my little town, not on your life, I've already got my little plot of Malihuel land next to Papá and Mamá, but Delia I don't know breaking off all links like that, never visiting her parents' grave again, uprooting herself out of spite and feeling not the least bit of nostalgia or curiosity. People you've known and seen almost every day of your life, not wanting to see them any more. You see Fefe the depth of that woman's resentment. I couldn't do it, I really couldn't, even if they did the worst possible thing to me, the worst thing you can imagine, and I've had things done to me here in town mind, I could write you a list, to start with … The Darío business was hard, who'll deny it, if anyone touched a hair on my Leandrito or my Beba's heads … I don't even want to think about it, worse than ten Delias I'd be so I would, but of course I brought them up to be decent and law-abiding and they never got into trouble. Because if you don't bring them up properly and they turn out to be say burglars or bandits or even terrorists and get killed in a shoot-out ah well then it's other people who are to blame. I sometimes ask myself you know especially when she was … Chesi tells me I shouldn't but I still ask myself if we mightn't've been a bit hard on Delia perhaps we didn't do enough to help her or we judged her too harshly but anyway I've already told you what happened when we tried to get close to her she went almost crazy quite unhinged she was and to be honest we reached a point where we got fed up of her. As I say we're each entitled to our own opinions, I'm very broad-minded and I respect other people's opinions so I do, but you can't say a whole town's wrong and one person's right. Because say let's say what I reckon is that it was life and when life comes into it you feel the need to blame someone and if you can find someone to blame you feel a kind of relief don't you. All right let's say somebody *did* do something wrong in that business over Darío let's say there *was* one person to blame in a way or maybe two. But it's one thing to blame one or two people isn't it and quite another Delia acting up like that because I don't think that's really the case there, you can't go pointing the finger at a whole town like that now can you Fefe."

"WHAT HAPPENED? What exactly happened?" I kept asking the table, which Batata Sacamata had joined now that Don León had stumped off in his enthusiasm to outline his proposal to the Neighbourhood Committee.

"There are several versions," Licho started again.

"I'm fed up of versions," I insisted. "Did they kill her or didn't they?"

Guido, who hadn't said anything until then, intervened.

"Yes Fefe. Greco killed her, or had her killed."

"How can you be so sure?" objected Batata Sacamata. "You there were you?"

"Come on," insisted Guido. "The whole town knows it was Greco. He didn't dare to do it here, so he waited till she moved to Rosario."

"The whole town knows, the whole town knows. You all think you know everything around here. Want to know the truth? Nobody had the faintest what was going on inside. A what do you call it a bunker the headquarters always was. Another world. Like it was in a different town," Sacamata insisted. I ignore him.

"How did he do it?" I ask my friend.

"Don't know, obviously nobody's going to admit it, but everybody knows that people from here in town went to Greco and asked him to sort out the problem with Delia.

238

'Specially after the statue episode. And Greco told them, you get her to move to Rosario and don't worry about the rest, I'll take care of it, he told them."

"So how did they do it?"

"In her younger days before she got married she used to have a boyfriend in the military, who must've risen to say colonel by then. They persuaded her to go and look him up and talk to him. Mamá told me, 'cause she bumped into Delia who'd got her hopes up again with the idea, all dressed up and made up she was and couldn't stop talking about her boyfriend and how he'd kept on calling her and writing to her and just by announcing herself she'd sort out the problem over Darío in a jiffy, that was the word she used, a jiffy. What a fool she'd been to waste her time in this little town, talking to ignorant storekeepers and policemen. They'd be bound to treat her properly in Rosario. She left in her car, a beige Renault 12, that very afternoon. No one knows if she made it to Rosario. She was never heard of again. Or her car. Just once, years later by that time, one of her brothers Eduardo showed up, who lives in Villa María in Córdoba. He came about the inheritance, to pick up some papers that were still here, and about the house."

"Which house is it?" I asked.

"You don't know? That beautiful one facing the square. The mansion with a huge front garden and the slate façade."

"Oh I know the one, sure"—I finally made the connection and then, "Did he end up with it?"

The question was addressed to everyone, but once again it was Guido who replied.

"The house? No, Greco did. He sold it after the flood. Old Widower Gius lives there now, he owns land south of the lagoon. If you want to see it we can go, he's a really nice old guy."

PREDICTABLY ENOUGH, by dinner time of the day I'd spent with Auntie Porota and Auntie Chesi, after a shower that hadn't helped to revive me, I found myself with aching bones and joints, a sore throat when I swallowed the Tuttolomondos' pasta—*Dafratti Number Thirty-Eight*—which tasted of putty with flour-paste sauce and chopped plastic, and an infinite weariness that called to mind my eminently forgettable exploits of four years ago. Leticia gave me a cup of tea with aspirin, and when my fever rose to thirty-nine she called Dr Alexander, who diagnosed flu, prescribed antibiotics which I'd refuse to take, and set out his theory about the terrorist attack on the Colonel's statue to his captive audience of one. ("A woman could never have done it on her own. Physically impossible. During the traditional festivities it took at least eight strong men to blah blah ... That woman had outside help. It's easy to guess who from. Her son's partners in crime, who were plotting vengeance on our town ... "). The following day, after getting my return ticket changed yet again—I'd lost count of the number of times—and calling home to let them know, Guido and Leticia moved me to Celia's, as they'd be out all day and wouldn't be able to look after me, and besides they'd want to go back to fucking in peace by now, they must have forgotten what it was like. I must have spent a couple of days in a constant stupor streaked with apathetic nightmares, through which stalked listless demons repeating I mean nobody any harm and I don't mean to be unkind and let's call a spade a spade. I awoke, or rather opened my eyes again to the world around me—which to the alarm of my fevered brain turned out to be the bedroom I slept in as a boy at my grandmother's, hardly any different—with Celia stroking my matted hair and the inexplicably compassionate gaze of her big dark eyes over her sad, crumpled smile. She arranges the pillows for me so I can sit up a little.

"Do you know?" I ask her, and seeing her nod, "How long?"

"Always Fefe," she answers. "I was very fond of your Mamá, and she told me … everything, I think. Ever since you arrived I wondered how long you could go without saying anything. You can't stand it any more can you Fefe."

She's right. I shake my head, incapable of speech, incapable of holding back the tears spilling from my eyes.

# Interlude Four

THE CLEARLY ABORIGINAL NAME *'Malihuel' has always had overtones of mystery and beauty in a region where all other towns bear Creole or foreign names, as if Malihuel had been the only one to emerge out of the land, rather than be imposed upon it from above. And yet the precise origin and even potential significance of this place name have given rise to the most wide-ranging disputes and conjectures without—so far—the veil of the mystery having been lifted [ … ]*

*The oldest documentary reference to the place name 'Malihuel' comes in a concession of land belonging to Gerónimo Luis Cabrera and occupied by the Choncancharagua tribe, running "inland across the Pampas as far as Malihuel" and "thence from Malihuel ten leagues north to India Vieja" [ … ]*

*The thesis regarding the Araucano origins of the toponym has been supported by most authors to have studied the topic, albeit with differing interpretations of the details.*

*a) Some have adopted the view attributed to Félix de Azara, for whom MALIHUEL may mean 'Malin's place', from the suffix 'hue', meaning a place or region, and 'Mali' or 'Malin', the name of a*

243

supposed chief who may in the remote past have established his
village hereabouts [ ... ]

b)   Another Araucanist thesis suggests that the first element of the
word might have been 'Meli', or 'four', the 'e' of which may
have switched to an 'a'—by no means a repellent idea; the
precise pronunciation of the 'a' in Araucano may have had
a sound intermediate between the two vowels, as it can have
in other languages, such as English. From this have emerged
explanations that place the geographical above the historical:
Melinhuinkul, or 'four hillocks'; Melico, or 'four watering
holes'; and even Melicohue, 'four lagoons'.[1] The four hillocks incidentally, are conspicuous by their absence from the
surrounding area; and, even in the most extreme of droughts,
there is no record that the one lagoon has ever broken into
four.

c)   In my search for a word that, by corruption in its assimilation into
the phonetics of Castilian, has lead to the elusive word 'Mali',
I came across one in the dictionary of J M de Rosas[2] that did
not figure in most of the dictionaries I had previously consulted:
namely, the word 'Malin', which properly means 'stone', 'pebble'
or 'flint'; esp. cutting- or sharp-edged, such as an arrowhead, say.
Hence MALINHUE, meaning a 'place or region of flint', from
which MALIHUEL may have derived for obvious phonetic reasons.
[ ... ]

Without the slightest spirit of scientific rigour, but merely as a wry
wink at the sometimes tortuous paths that lead to our destination by
means of chance, it is worth noting that this meaning of the original
name of the place, first revealed by myself here, Pedernal, or 'place of
flint', seems in some way to herald or prefigure the name of the man who
would become the town's founder, Colonel Urbano Pedernera. [ ... ]

*In Gagliardi, B,* MALIHUEL: etimología de un topónimo santafesino. *Cámara de Diputados de la Prov. de Santa Fe, Offprint of Homenaje al IV Centenario de la Fund. de Santa Fe, 1973.*

*1993 POSTSCRIPT:[3] Twenty years on, I am compelled to denounce my own thesis, which had met with widespread approval due perhaps more to my colleagues' intellectual sloth and negligence than to any intrinsic merit of its own. It is understandable that an 'n' may have vanished in its passage through so many mouths, but that the final 'l' should have appeared by the grace of the Holy Ghost is unacceptable from any point of view that claims scientific status. Perhaps blinded by the naive parochialism of the times, I never paid heed to the term HUELE or HUELDE, which P J Venom's dictionary of 1966 provides as meaning 'ill-fated' or 'unfortunate'. We inevitably return, then, to the idea of the prefix meli-, meaning 'four', which, coupled with 'huele' would give MELIHUELE–MELIHUEL–MALIHUEL: meaning 'four unfortunate wretches', where 'four' has a generic rather than a strictly numerical value of scarcity or poverty, as in the Spanish expressions 'four crazy cats', 'four poor devils', etc. Of all the hypotheses put forward, this one is not only the most linguistically viable, but also the only one that can be verified empirically. I am still searching for the flints of my earlier hypothesis; however, the prophetic nature of the word with which the legitimate occupants of these lands for ever branded the moral standards of those who would later usurp them brooks no reply. In conclusion, I am now in a position to state the definitive etymology of the place name, 'Malihuel': MELIHUELE–MALIHUEL: 'four crazy cats', 'four poor devils'—a paltry collection of pathetic and/or contemptible individuals.*

245

1) *P Hux Meinnado:* La Capital *newspaper. Rosario, 25/05/1970. Quoting Stieben Enrique:* Toponimia Araucana. *p. 104. La Pampa. 1966.*

2) *Rosas, Juan Manuel de:* Gramática y Diccionario de la lengua Pampa. *Suarez Caviglia & Stieben. Ediciones Albatros. 1947.*

3) *Author's note: This postscript does not feature in any of the editions of Prof. Gagliardi's noted study and, therefore, makes its appearance in printed form for the first time here. It appears in an addendum in his own handwriting at the end of the revised version, which, shortly before his regrettable passing, he was about to send to press.*

# Chapter Five

"Town of cowards, town of scoundrels," mutters Professor Gagliardi in the interview he finally granted me at his house on the outskirts of town, and within whose book-lined walls he has decided to shut himself away from life. "It's no coincidence the first settlers were Indian-butchering *milicos*. The gringos came later, when the dirty work'd been done, my great-grandfather amongst them. But all in all they were real men and women, capable of sticking to their guns and seeing their rights were respected, of standing up to authority; not like this rotten rabble toiling and crawling out there. And they ask me why I've decided to take refuge within these walls. Give them the pleasure of turning their backs on me again, giving me the cold shoulder, the way they did with your father, and your grandmother? Can you believe, dear boy, that when I was removed from my post, when that gutless Scuppa came to me with his Benjamin I implore you to understand me, in this day and age, your stay at this institution … no one, not even my colleagues, not even my neighbours, who'd all been students of mine every last one of them, or parents of my current students, stuck up for me or at least expressed their sympathy? Do you know what they used to say? He always had been a bit of a communist that Gagliardi, that's what they used to say. Because every twenty-fifth of June I used to talk about the Cry of Alcorta, because at one prize-giving ceremony I suggested the true foundation was when the entire town confronted Comandante Pedernera and paraded him through the streets naked. Do you know something dear boy?" the Professor asks me, pacing restlessly around the room as if in an imaginary classroom. "It doesn't sadden me that they've welded the Comandante's statue. He represents us a lot better than before the way he is now. What was once an authentic popular festival had all too long ago become a hollow ceremony, a self-indulgent show by farmers and shopkeepers of false nostalgia for a rebellious past that was never really theirs. It was highly appropriate that the last Malihuense to knock the Comandante off his horse was your dear grandmother. The rest of us had lost that right long ago. And I'll tell you something else. When the flood looked as if it would wipe us off the map once and for all, I was secretly glad. I'd always thought what they did to your father and your dear grandmother was quite unforgivable. I asked myself what God was waiting for to wipe this Santa Fe Sodom off the face of the pampas. Which was why I wasn't sorry when the waters came, despite the loss of some of the most prized volumes in my collection. Even so, it's still one of the most complete libraries on the history of the province, as you can see. In better times I used to travel to Rosario regularly, and to Buenos Aires, where I'd buy in bulk at auction, or rummaging through the second-hand

bookshops on the Avenida de Mayo or in the stalls in Parque
Rivadavia … Luckily, not all the schools in the area shared
the timorousness of our spineless principal, and I was able
go on teaching in other towns until I retired. I haven't much
money now to go on buying books, but instead I've found
the necessary time to read them and to write. I can dig up a
copy of my two articles about the town if you're interested,
but you'll have to be a little patient because as you can
see … " While Professor Gagliardi, with faltering hands,
rifles through the nearest pile of lever-arch files and folders,
as high as the chair back they're leaning against, I again
run my eyes over the volumes packing the shelves—running
vertically and horizontally from the water-warped parquet
to the added rows that scrape the blotchy ceiling, beyond
the last shelf. Books whose cardboard and paper time has
turned yellowish and brittle, covers once green, red or orange turned to moss, ochre and terracotta—textures that
from a distance suggest parchment, papyrus and old silk.
Editions by Claridad, Calomino, Tor, Americalee, Anteo,
Losada, Eudeba, Solar—the years of forced coexistence
making their covers uniform and possibly their contents too:
fierce polemics and oppositions undifferentiating themselves
on their way to becoming that bland and indefinable thing
some people call "period flavour". Perhaps from so much
reading Professor Gagliardi had ended up believing in history
in the same way Don Quixote believed in literature. He now
sets about another equally formidable pile, growls, talks to
himself, scolds the papers he's trying to find for refusing to
appear. "One's on the history of the fort, it was published in
the minutes of the first congress on the history of the towns

of the ... The other one, the older one, on the etymology of the name Malihuel ... I wanted to include a revision, for the time being it's in manuscript form, if I manage to get it republished ... Let me see, let me see, here it is I think ... No, it isn't here either."

"YOU KNOW WHAT SHE USED TO SAY, our Delia, when she was asked about her son's reputation? That he gave her a grandchild in every town," Auntie Porota told me the other day. "Please, Delia'd say, they're grandchildren of the ones who never taught their daughters how to get to the altar with their legs crossed. How's it the boy's fault if the young girls nowadays can't behave any better than the *chinitas*. Oh good gracious me that Delia, terrible she was, woe betide you if crossed her, with that sharp tongue of hers, and they wonder why the lad turned out the way he did, like mother like son I say, don't you agree Fefe?"

"THAT WOMAN WASN'T MY GRANDMOTHER," I'd blurt out indignantly, choking on the pasta soup—Little Stars No 16—that Celia had brought me in bed. "My grandmother's name is Emily Bullock de Echezarreta, she lives in Rosario and she welcomed me into her house—*this* house—every summer. The other one, three months of every year living three blocks away and not once, not once ... She knew who I was, and she thought it was ... amusing. Her son went from one town to the next knocking up young girls, wham bam thank you ma'am, and she thought it was funny! You heard what she used to say," I inveigh from an imaginary pulpit.

"What they say she said Fefe," Celia corrects me sweetly. "If you don't learn to listen with your heart as well as your ears in this town, you'll never understand. Darío was eighteen when he was courting with your Mamá, he was a boy. And I don't for a minute think Delia knew that you … Your grandparents kept the secret very well, and I … I know I never told a soul. And if she did know, if Darío did tell her … She'd begun to change; over those days she changed more than a lot of people do all their lives. If they'd let her live, she'd've come to love you. In you she could've regained something of the son who'd been taken from her. After everything you've been told, can't you see it couldn't be otherwise? She'd be a totally different person now. But they didn't give her time Fefe."

"WHAT YOU HAVE TO BEAR IN MIND, dear boy, if you want to get to know the mentality of the man who killed your father," Professor Gagliardi says to me, manoeuvring his open dressing gown through the piles and shelves of books that make his house a maze, "is that all his life he'd been nothing but a provincial policeman, whose experience in matters of murder went not much further than the odd working over that got out of hand, the unwitting heart patient victim who didn't tell them about his condition before getting the *picana*, the successful crook who forgets to pay their cut and remembers in the hereafter. Neri belonged to the old school of concealment—covering your tracks, cooking the files, striking pacts with judges and coming to arrangements with lawyers. He thought you should at least keep up appearances. He was too naive then, as were most of us—he thought people's natural reaction to an imminent crime would be to stop it, or report it. His need to lie paradoxically reveals his faith in people. It never entered his head that the perfect crime is precisely the one committed in the sight of everyone—because then there are no witnesses, only accomplices. His premise was correct—in a two-bit town like this you can't waste a prominent inhabitant without everyone knowing: because it only takes one person to find out for everybody to know. He mistakenly concluded that, in the face of such vigilance, impunity wasn't an option. Of course it wasn't, as certain distorters of public opinion repeat ad nauseam, because the policemen of his generation had notions of morality, honesty or honour that were later lost; no, it was simply narrow-mindedness, intellectual laziness—a eureka moment, a Copernican revolution, the Superintendent was simply too old for. All he needed to arrive at the right solution was a leap, a flip of the imagination that stood logic on its head and set the clockwork going—the realisation that you can hold your tongue while talking out loud, that town gossip can work the other way round. That silence also travels by word of mouth."

CELIA TAKES ANOTHER PHOTO from the box.

"And this must've been, let's see hold on, I bought that sundress ... Can't be long after your mother left, that summer ... Who knows maybe you're in the photo too? It doesn't bother you if I say it does it Fefe?"

In the photo are Celia and my mother, the former in a

dress blown tight against her body by a wind the photo has captured for ever in sculptural folds; the second—Mamá—in a one-piece, navy-blue bathing costume with white bows and little flounces, which she was still wearing ten years later; and in the middle Darío Ezcurra, democratically embracing them both. Celia and Darío are looking at the camera, but Mamá only has eyes for him, for the almost condescending smile, for the boastful eyes of a kid staring the future fearlessly in the face because life is definitely female, for the bronzed chest and flat stomach above the scarlet trunks—the only thing in the photo (including the sky and the water of the unmistakeable lagoon) that hasn't faded to the uniform sepia of old Kodacolors. I set it on the uneven stack forming at the side of my bed, documenting Ezcurra at his high-school graduation in an ill-cut suit that narrows his shoulders, dancing with a youthful, spellbound Clara Benoit; Ezcurra in black polo neck and brown jacket with a lean Batata Sacamata and an undyed Bermejo, posing by farming machinery and stands under construction, beneath a poster that reads *EXPOTENC*; Ezcurra blowing out the thirty—Celia specifies—candles in the reception room at the Yacht Club; Ezcurra and his Mamá, wrapped up warm for winter, having chocolate and churros at the bazaar on patron saint's day; Ezcurra in bermudas and multicoloured polo shirt with Celia and the Don Ángel of my childhood keeping an eye on the sausages on the barbecue of the house that now belongs to Mati … Celia insists I keep them and I'm still too weak to argue—a meagre haul, something to show when I'm asked "What have you been up to in that town all this time … What did you say its name was?" What else? Or did the hope of winning the ultimate prize still nestle within me, secretly, ashamed to show itself? Ezcurra's last words, before dying: "My son, my son" (yes, but which one?). A secret meeting, in Rosario, my Grandma Delia telling my Grandma Emily (perhaps in English for security's sake): "We have to discuss our grandson's future." Wasn't this what I was still hoping for, what I'd really come here to look for? Wasn't it for this hope that I'd kept putting off my return?

"I DO APOLOGISE," Professor Gagliardi says without looking at me, which he's hardly done since we began our chat. If it weren't for the additional cup and the sugar bowl, which, out of deference to my dislike of saccharine, he's brought over to the chair that serves as a makeshift table, he might be talking to himself, and answering his own questions, "for not seeing you sooner. Had I known who you were, I would have opened the doors of my humble abode to you from day one, sparing you the gruelling task of rubbing shoulders with that filthy, lying rabble in your brave quest for the truth. I understand dear boy, there's no need for you to explain, you were right to conceal your true identity, if they'd known you were Darío Ezcurra's son, every door would have been slammed in your face. What's more, this way you've been able to see for yourself that everything I've been telling you about the people of this town is true. Now, I'm glad you're here. Because twenty years is too long to bear the weight of such a secret. Many times, fearing I'd take it with me to the grave, I've been on the brink of succumbing to the temptation … But to whom? Who in this town, was or is worthy of knowing the truth?

Now, I'm glad I waited, now that you're here in front of me, and through your own, I can remember the unmistakeable features of your unfortunate father, when he died he must have been around your … See dear boy? I'm seldom wrong. That's why you came to me isn't it? So that I'll show you the key to the apparently inexplicable doings of Malihuel's chief of police, who against all logic, against the deep-seated habits of his profession, even against his own interests … I know what no one knows, because I heard it from his own lips, in the only conversation we had after those terrible events, a few days before his departure, in the name of our old relationship, Benjamín, he had the audacity to say. I didn't have the nerve to refuse. Ethics and let's call it professional curiosity were at odds in me, and curiosity won. I also needed to know, needed it for myself, how a man I'd once trusted had been capable of such a thing; I wanted to know where I'd gone wrong. We met at Los Tocayos, at the table where we used to play chess and called ours. It was no more than two weeks since we'd last met, but it was enough time to have changed him irreversibly. He was no longer fit for anything other than setting up a kiosk and dying—which is what he eventually did—for keeping order among the shelves of chocolates and biscuits; a defeated body, barely sustained from morning till night by the habit of contempt and ill feeling, and the secret hope perhaps that some hapless robber would hold up his kiosk and *force* him to use the forty-five hidden under the cigarette cartons. I don't know if you've heard of Colonel Carca, Demetrio Carca. There's no reason you should: house-plunderer, kidnapper and blackmailer, torturer, rapist, serial killer, thief of babies and corpses—nothing special; just your run of the mill career

255

soldier in those days. They were from the same town in the north, the Superintendent and he, they grew up and went to school together, and remained friends. He was the one who called the Superintendent from Rosario and demanded he indulge Rosas Paz. The Superintendent said it couldn't be done—because of the people, the neighbours; the colonel, who was an old hand in these matters, said it'd be a piece of cake. All done in a joking, matey tone of voice, you know how they talk to each other, all comrades in arms: Go on, you fat wanker, shift your arse and pick him up for me will you, and the other, You think it's as easy as that? If you're the big man here, why don't you come and do it? One thing led to another, and eventually to what the Superintendent ended up confessing to me that day."

GUIDO'S mortally offended.

"Why didn't you tell me? Don't you trust me?"

I prop myself up slightly in bed and adjust my pillows. I could murder a cigarette.

"Maybe at first. I decided not to tell anyone, and I stuck to my plan. Then it got to be the other way round. I was frightened by your loyalty. At the first bad word against Darío Ezcurra, or Delia … If you'd known who they were to me, you'd have leapt to their defence, to my defence, you'd've given me away. Guido, a drunk who raised his voice to me, you broke three of his ribs. What more can I tell you?" He grumbles but then relents. Perhaps because it's sincere my explanation seems to satisfy him.

"So when did *you* realise?" he asks.

"When Mamá died. I found a letter she'd started writing when I was going through her stuff. In her third-grade schoolgirl handwriting balanced precariously on the lines. Dear Darío, it began. I knew she'd gone on writing letters to the town, she sometimes even used to give me them to post, sealed of course—she never let me read them. Your grandmother'll get angry she used to say, and I accepted the explanation without asking; even when she spoke about God He sounded like someone you had to obey because otherwise my grandparents'd get angry. The names never varied much—Emily, Celia, Darío … She spent over thirty years writing to a man who never replied, the last twenty because he was dead of course."

Guido listens. It's my turn to do the talking now.

"It's a simple story actually. Ezcurra was banging the village idiot. An idiot and a virgin at twenty-two. Screwed her regularly he did, couldn't be easier, till he began to notice she was putting on weight around the waistline. When my grandparents noticed too they dragged her into the car and never stopped till they got to Buenos Aires, where they found her a place at Don Alberto's, a friend of the family who owed my grandfather more favours than he could pay back in a lifetime. He agreed to give me his surname, and I grew up calling him Papá. Mamá and I lived in one of the apartments down the corridor from Don Alberto's which they rented out; Don Alberto lived in the house at the front with his real children and his wife. Anyway he treated Mamá and me like his own children, and received the money my grandparents sent for our expenses. Mamá was banned from ever going back to town in case she let the cat out of the bag, and me

257

every summer when I arrived they briefed me about what I was supposed to say. And when I got back Mamá'd drive me crazy, asking me to tell her about everyone, every detail of what had changed, what was the same. I can't say it was bad, growing up with her, but it was strange. She was more like a sister than a mother. An idiot sister. She liked to read *Mafalda* but didn't get most of the jokes. I'd watch her, concentrating, scanning the bubbles, following the words with her finger and moulding them letter by letter with her lips. When she realised I was there she'd look up and smile and ask me will you explain for me Fefe? After Felipe, her favourite character was Guille. I've only just realised, it's my son's name too. It's a pity, she couldn't enjoy him more—she'd've made a great grandmother. They were difficult the last few months, because she didn't understand. It hurts Fefe! My belly hurts! She'd clutch it and weep like a little girl—it was the cancer that killed her. A few weeks after the funeral, when I found the letter, I decided I'd gone long enough without knowing. My first attempt failed, as you know—the night before I left I couldn't get a wink of sleep and by the morning I was running a temperature of nearly forty. My second attempt was a success—I went to Rosario and put my grandmother between the letter and the deep blue sea for starters. I hadn't seen much of her over the last few years—after I got back from the Malvinas my life was erratic to say the least—and the woman I remembered as being impenetrable as a closed convent wall had become a doddery little old lady, all smiles, and I didn't have to twist her arm to get her to come clean. I can see clearly now that my grandparents'd never been that formidable, except in Mamá's and my impressionable imaginations. They'd had her late in life, and when they realised she'd turned out … The only daughter of a couple of tired old folk choking on the anger of not being able to show their hatred of Ezcurra publicly—and Ezcurra, aware of this, revelled in it all the more—no room left in their hearts for any other feeling for the man who was after all … She's one of those who thinks Ezcurra isn't dead my grandmother—she needs him alive the better to indulge her anger and grief. For her the crafty devil's living in Brazil with a black woman and coffee-coloured kids—any day now, she assured me again at the terminal in Rosario when I went to take the coach that brought me here, he'll be back in town to visit, with Garotos for everyone, end of story.

"IT WAS A BET," says the Professor.

"A what?" I ask.

"A bet between the Superintendent and the colonel. According to the Superintendent, it was the other's idea and he accepted because he was certain of winning. They both promised not to cheat, gave their words of honour— the Superintendent to carry out his duty if, as the colonel contended, it turned out to be a piece of cake; the colonel to shelve the whole affair if the Superintendent found that the town's inhabitants refused to cooperate. And his subordinate, Greco—although the Superintendent had no idea—was to be the secret referee and make sure *fair play* was observed. So the terms of the contest were formalised. I don't need to tell you how it turned out," says Professor Gagliardi, as the afternoon light dissolves amongst the books in his room. "That's why the Superintendent was so dejected at our last meeting. The town had failed him, we'd made him lose the bet. He'd had faith in this town, with its stories of struggle and resistance—and we'd let him down. We hadn't lived up to our own legend. Worse still, we'd made him look bad. His friend, the colonel, took the mickey on the phone now. That's why he'd decided to leave he told me. He spoke softly, staring into space. As if he'd lost his faith not just in Malihuel but humanity. The Superintendent, I realised that day, had survived his whole life on a strange kind of faith—the faith that others, people, were better than he was. A convenient kind of faith that exempted him from any personal responsibility. You should all've stopped me was his way of answering the reproach. The Superintendent was an idealist at heart, and there's no more desperate cynicism than that of a failed idealist. It was an odd situation, no doubt about it. For a while Malihuel became the theatre of a curious human experiment conducted rather cack-handedly by its chief of police. But the results are plain to see. You can make the equation as complex as you like, all imaginable variants can be included, but the result will always be the same—Ezcurra dead at the bottom of the lagoon." The professor, a greying shadow in the half light, approaches the lamp, which he switches on with sharp tug on the thin chain of tiny bronze globes. The entire room spins and folds in on itself, then organises itself around the new centre of the gleaming lampshade. My feet have frozen inside my shoes with the immobility and the cold, which the quartz heater is incapable of keeping at bay. "He was a contemptible man the Superintendent, in the most precise meaning of the word. He approached people for what was worst in them, and he always found what he'd gone looking for. The dead part of the heart, where all the meanness, baseness, laid down by the years is stored, that's what he spoke to—and of course his words always found a sympathetic ear."

"Not everyone gave their consent," I object.

"That's true," the professor concedes. "In a way the Superintendent cheated. Himself. He didn't ask at random, his probing was selective. He didn't ask the mother. He didn't ask me. He didn't ask people who could … stop him."

"But you knew," I say. "You were in the know, like everyone. Why didn't *you* go and see *him*?"

"I wanted him to come to me," he answers unhesitatingly. My incisive question has dissipated the thin veil of equanimity behind which the professor's prolix indignation had momentarily concealed itself, and again his chin trembles and his eyes harden over. "To see if he had it in him. Had *I* gone to see *him*, it would've been a sign of weakness."

He stands there staring at me, his lower jaw jutting slightly and open, fists clenched, neck tense. I ought to go on with my half-hearted inquisition but I can't, because I'm already far away—in the window seat I've booked on the 4.50 La Verde coach to Rosario, staring at my own reflection in the glass against the black of the invisible fields; on the 7.15 Chevallier to Buenos Aires, the sun still floating like a balloon just above the rectilinear horizon of the pampas and shining high above the Retiro coach terminal when I'm reunited with my wife and son. I'm not here any more, I've finished, I'm on my way back, I think, cupping my hands over my closed eyelids. I light a cigarette and look at the professor.

"What did you play?" I ask him.

TIME TO GET MOVING. Since I told Guido, with tacit permission to broadcast it, the News has already been round town several times. At first Celia did what she could to hold back the rising tide of visitors, adducing my delicate state of health; but as my health improved and my excuse weakened, at the risk of sounding rude and coming in for criticism, she was forced to give in. Auntie Porota and Auntie Chesi, Vicente and Vicentito, Alfredo Sacamata senior, Don Eugenio Casarico, the loathsome pharmacist Mendonca, who furiously I refuse to see, and many others I don't know or only by sight introduce themselves, I worked for Señora Delia, she helped me, she gave me, I was so sorry to hear about your … My visitors insist on referring to "your father", your "dear grandmother", and suddenly their faces, once perfectly camouflaged in mine, shine brightly through my features; people's eyes overflow with tears, their hands with presents and their mouths with stories that display an alarming tendency to morph into cloned versions of the heroic struggle of a town to wrest from the despicable clutches of the police two heroic inhabitants, whose praises they sing for the benefit of their no-less-heroic descendant. I entreat Celia with my eyes to chuck them out as soon as possible and pretend to be asleep but it only makes matters worse; when word gets out that I've woken up, they flock in in droves. What a good thing I concealed it from the outset—I tell myself, my hacker's instinct didn't let me down. I'm not a sponge, I can't absorb so much remorse. They can settle any pending accounts of conscience with the priest, I didn't come this far to be a catalyst for collective catharsis. Collective but not mass catharsis, I note a few days later when I step out into the street. Dr Alexander crosses the road to avoid me, a young man driving a dazzling four-by-four I've never seen before eyes me grimly and turns out to be one of Rosas Paz's grandchildren, Batata Sacamata has vanished from the table at Los Tocayos, whose other members Guido has kept away from my sickbed with the promise that I'd drop in as soon as I was better. Nene Larrieu comes and goes, filling the constantly emptying glasses and emptying the constantly filling ashtrays.

"I'm not saying what you did was wrong," Don León insists. "But in a way you did abuse our good faith. I reckon if you'd've been open about it from the start, without hiding anything from us … "

"Ezcurra never said anything," murmurs Iturraspe still in the grips of delayed shock. "In all the years we … The best-kept secret in Malihuel. We didn't know he had a son then. If we'd known, that you … you were, or rather that he, and you … Your Papá. If we'd known you then, and … But we didn't know," he concludes eventually.

"Nor did I," is the only thing I seem to be able to reply.

"There's something I need to tell you … "—Licho joins in the conversation—" … you know how it is, someone or other says I saw Ezcurra in such-and-such a place and the story catches on and gets passed on by word of mouth and you try persuading people otherwise then, you know how stories get better and better with the telling and they get to a point where they're perfect and nobody can add anything to them and they repeat it word for word, even the one who started the ball rolling," he blurts out in one breath and slumps backs in defeat.

263

"Anyway"—Don León goes on the offensive again and everyone out of habit goes quiet to listen to him—"you have to be from hereabouts to understand these things. It's easy for someone from outside … "

Out of the corner of my eye I see the colour rising in Guido's face and race to head him off.

"Both my parents and all four grandparents are from Malihuel. I was conceived here and baptised here. I spent every summer of my childhood here, with the best friends I've ever had. My father died here and is buried here—or submerged if you prefer—and my grandmother's heart was broken here with grief. Malihuel made me and Malihuel unmade me. What outside are you talking about?"

"Yes but what I'm saying's different. Coming here to visit isn't the same as … Besides, it's not as if those two actually were your father and grandmother. You yourself said that … "

This time I don't get there in time.

"Why don't you shut up?" Guido spits at him. A spectral silence falls over the bar. Even the hands on the clock seem to be waiting.

"What did you say?" Don León stares at him in disbelief.

"Why—Don't—You—Shut—Up?" Guido articulates with offensive clarity. "Do you think we're going to sit here straight-faced all our lives listening to you spouting garbage? Don't you think we might be fed up of always having to listen to the same old bloody shite? Eh?"

Don León looks at all of us. Blank, impassive faces that give his potential indignation no purchase whatsoever. His chin trembles slightly as he answers:

"All right, Guido. Apologies. No offense intended."

"And you wanted me to tell you from the start," I rib him later on, when he gives me a lift to his Mamá's. He smiles in profile, without saying a word. He's glad, but not just for me. The table in Los Tocayos has just changed hands.

"BEFORE YOU GO DEAR BOY"—Professor Gagliardi intercepts me—"I have something for you. I've been working on it for twenty years. I began when I realised that everyone in town knew what happened and bore their share of the responsibility. But to claim they were all guilty like that, across the board, is almost like saying no one was, which is why I set out to establish, as far as I could, how and how far each of Malihuel's inhabitants played a part in this tragedy, what they did or didn't do, what they said, and how they acted before, during and after the events. This is the result," he says advancing towards me, with a bulky, black-and-white marbled folder in hand. "I'd feel honoured if you'd accept it. It will tell you everything you want to know about the people who killed your father and grandmother, and many other things besides. All the basenesses committed in the last decades of the life of our town, including those the law would punish were it applied, and the petty daily crimes that fall outside its scope are recorded in them. If you really intend to put it all down in a book, I daresay you'll find them to be of great help, perhaps indispensible."

I open it. The title page reads: *A Record of Iniquities in Malihuel*. Then came the dossiers in alphabetical order, by inhabitant. One of the first was Dr Alexander's, running to page after page, covered from margin to margin in handwriting tiny and tight at first, but becoming progressively more expansive over the years, with its anarchic variations of ink type and colour. I start reading, taking advantage of the professor excusing himself to go to the bathroom.

*Alexander, Albino. Self-styled doctor, though, to my knowledge, no one has ever examined his original certificate. Visits town sporadically until 1964, when his predecessor, Dr Arturo Rocamora, decides to retire and sells him the practice and telephone line. The first measure Malihuel's brand-new principal medic introduces is to remove the two afternoons of free care that Dr Rocamora had instituted for the less-well-off members of our community; "I don't want to take customers away from my esteemed colleague, Dr Lugozzi," he has been heard to comment cynically on the matter in the Yacht Club bar. He also puts up the percentage that specialists will have to pay for the use of his surgery from twenty per cent to thirty per cent, driving several of them to discontinue their visits and forcing the townspeople to travel to neighbouring towns for care. In collusion with the pharmacist, Mauro Mendonca, for a percentage cut, he devotes himself to overmedicating and/or always prescribing the most expensive medication in the vade mecum, a procedure known in medical and pharmacological circles as "ana-ana", or "fifty-fifty"; the samples he receives from medical reps also end up on Mendonca's shelves, after the "free-sample" stamp has been erased (see File No 1,002—Mendonca, Mauro). Subsequent disagreements over the actual amounts owed eventually bring about the breakdown of the incipient partnership and lead to the current situation, in which the pharmacist diagnoses and prescribes independently and Dr Alexander almost exclusively prescribes drugs that are only available in Toro Mocho or Fuguet. In the first decade of his practice, he is directly or indirectly responsible for the following cases of malpractice: 1965—Don Timoteo Fernandes, deceased as a result of the administration of corticosteroids for the treatment of what at the second autopsy (conducted in Rosario at the family's request) was diagnosed as herpes zoster (shingles) of the trigeminal nerve, an ailment that our local healer, Doña Agripina Morales, is in the habit of curing by the simple application of Chinese ink on a brush. Don Timoteo's family chose, on completion of the due process, to come to an out-of-court settlement, reached on 15/3/66, making them moral accessories to any deaths or disabilities suffered by Dr Alexander's patients after that date (see Files Nos 782 & 783—Fernandes, Diego Hermes; and Fernandes, Dora Zalaberry de). 1966—Don César Enciso Vera, total loss of vision in left eye and partial loss in right, due to the administration of free samples of insulin with adulterated expiry dates; 1967 …*

*In 1974, upon Dr Armendáriz's resignation (apparently after threats made by a purported parapolice group relating to his ruling on the case of some so-called guerrillas gunned down by the police; the absence of any such groups in the area around that date leads us to the conjecture that the calls were made by Dr Alexander himself, or at least at his instigation) he takes over as police doctor; years later he does likewise with the judiciary (a marriage of convenience that does little to favour the transparency of trials). Dr Alexander's methods in his dual role are characterised by his unusual consistency—in twenty-two years not one of his reports has ever even partially questioned the official version of events. It goes without saying that Dr Alexander has always tailored his reports to the needs of the police or the judicial authorities (a procedure with a whiff of scandal about it during Superintendent Major Ariel Greco's infamous leadership—1977-1983—who directly dictated to Dr Alexander the contents of autopsies that were never even performed), or to the litigant*

267

*favoured by them, eg the trial over the death of two farm workers in a collapsed silo on the La Primera Argentina Estancia in the vicinity of Elordi—his 'providential' discovery of traces of alcohol in their blood deprived the families of due compensation.*

*Kidnapping and subsequent death and disappearance of Darío Z Ezcurra—On 25th February 1977, in circumstances known to all—and I mean all—in this town of Malihuel, the abduction of the young journalist and respected inhabitant took place (see Files Nos 271 & 272, Ezcurra, Darío Z; and Ezcurra, Delia Alvarado de). From the start of the 'general inquiry' by chief of police Armando J Neri, Dr Alexander proved to be one of the most enthusiastic …*

*Illegal abortions—During the 1980s he practised illegal abortions on the following young ladies (and ladies) of Malihuel: 1) Valle, Ana Obregón; a maid in the household and commercial establishment of the Sacamata family, any male members of said family being held responsible; operation paid for with money from said family, later deducted monthly from wages of said maid (see Sacamata, Alfredo senior and Sacamata, Alfredo junior; Files Nos 2017 & 2018 respectively; and Valle, Ana Obregón, File No 2126); 2) Anunciata, Herminia; high-school student …*

*Its being midnight 27th April … glaucoma … refusing to tend Gervasio Lafalla, temporary farmhand (see File No …) … clearly unnecessary Caesarean section … septicaemia … reuse of disposable material … refusal to tend a patient contaminated with the virus … premature birth … chronic medicamentosa … difference in the calibre of the bullet … alleged indecent assault case dismissed … amphetamines … diuretics … antidepressants …*

I snap the folder shut when I hear him coming back.

"THAT ONE, the one in the window," Nene Larrieu had pointed out on one of my first evenings. "That's where they'd play their famous games of chess. Used to spend the time talking actually, and when they remembered, one of them would move a piece now and again."

"That's what I mean," Batata Sacamata had rudely interrupted. "I don't know what the professor's playing at, 'cause Neri and him they was always thick as thieves."

"Sometimes when they put the board away they hadn't moved a piece"—ignoring him, the waiter of Los Tocayos had gone on. "Someone once suggested they should be in the Guinness Book of Records as the world's slowest players."

"That'd've been you," Iturraspe had cheerfully peached on him.

"The games could last for weeks. Tuesdays and Fridays, they'd get together. Religiously. Unless the Superintendent couldn't make it. That Friday—the dog's day as they call it—the professor waited in vain, with the board open and the pieces the way they'd left them at their last meeting. He said something to me but I can't remember what. I wasn't paying much attention 'cause it was only a few minutes since Ezcurrita'd left—they almost ran into each other. He confided to me that in three moves, four at most, he'd have the Superintendent in checkmate. But they never got to finish the game."

"He could never forgive himself for that friendship," Iturraspe'd said.

"I'M TIRED OF IT," the professor says to me when I look up. "I don't want to go on. It's extraordinary what something like this can take out of you. I'd rather you have it and keep no copy myself, I don't want to be tempted. You'll be taking a weight off me if you take it with you, and at the same time you'll make me feel that all that effort was worth something. There's only one file that I'm afraid you'll search for in vain—your grandfather's. I hope you'll understand."

I thanked him for both gestures—the gift and the sleight of hand—with a shallow nod. Right then I planned to throw the monstrous mausoleum of moral misery out of the coach window, wrapped in the little jacket Auntie Chesi had knitted for my son with her dead husband's wool. But my determination wilted and I ended up keeping it. I told myself it might be of use in the event of legal problems, that I'd keep it in the trunk room at home, in a double-seal bag (you only had to glance at the cover to sink into a profound depression for the rest of your day) and would give it to my lawyer as a keepsake; but to be honest, in the end it was a kind of reverence that stopped me getting rid of it. The extraordinary folder documented not only the dark side of the multiple existences batting about without rhyme or reason in this patch of the gringo pampas that's so like any other it reminds you of the samples carried by travelling fabric salesmen; but also something more precious—the sterile sacrifice of a life that, rather than moving somewhere, had chosen to bury itself in this place in order to hate it the more. Professor Gagliardi's soul had given itself to the most insidious and perhaps illicit of the passions known to man—cringing embarrassment at others (which is not to say he neglected

270

his own; I'd be lying by omission if I forgot to mention File No 827, corresponding to Gagliardi, Benjamín F). This hefty tome, this promiscuous cohabitation of police dossier and small-town gossip, was also the melancholy testament to a life devoted to moral mortification.

"A COUPLE OF KILOMETRES out of town down the Fuguet road there's a place on your left with the branches of a ceiba sticking out of a little patch of young willows. That's the best place to stop because the hard shoulder's wider, then you walk a few metres till you see a little footpath branching off that's been worn by people walking through the weeds. Follow it till you come to a wire fence," Ña Agripina the healer had told me, and following her instructions I find the place easily. There's a girl there, kneeling, and she barely raises her head to glance at me over her shoulder before bowing it again. On the other side of the wire fence stretches a garbage dump, whose muddy ground is shared peacefully by some pigs and numerous mud-bellied gulls, and, at the far end of it, a shack shaded by Persian lilacs, where generations of Villalbas have been returning their legendary past drop by drop to the common anonymity of the poor. There Ezcurra's body at least found a brief respite in the earth, a siesta rather than a sleep, his temporary grave. Beneath that mud he slept, until he was unearthed by the parents and grandparents (I don't know how to measure the generations of pigs) of the ones now nosing around the garbage tip.

On the near side, by the wire fence, partly serving as a framework and support, stands a mixed conglomeration, which I can't find a simple word for. At the centre of the group stands a stick cross, bound with strips of black inner tube, which also hold two bunches of anonymous dried flowers in an X that divides the cross into eight acute angles. Intertwined at this intersection hangs a rosary of little red balls, its plastic cross resting on one of the lower legs of the X of flowers. Most of the ones surrounding the base are plastic, opaque and brittle from years of exposure to the elements, peeping out of little baskets, the cloth or crêpe paper ones faded to watery green, pale pink and light blue. The natural flowers droop and dissolve into a vegetal impasto—making it impossible to tell them apart—over vases of topless mineral-water bottles: and here and there, strewn across the ground, small succulents have managed to take root and grow in the artificial shade of the others. Emerging from the neck of a half-litre Coca-Cola bottle half-full of clear water wave the heads of a bunch of yellow daisies, upright in the wind, rear-ranged now and then by my current companion. From the wires taut with the cold, hang the most varied assortment of ornaments, as if from a little Christmas tree: purple-flowered air plants, plenty of them; two plastic babies, one with no arms, the other with no legs; a light-blue baby's dummy, a knotted silk handkerchief, which would fall apart like ash when touched; charms representing hearts, legs and arms; a key on its key ring; a burnt-out light bulb. Due to the pro-verbial absence of pebbles or flint in the region, the candles are mounted on improvised supports, some still recognisable as bits of tile or brick, rust-eaten tin cans, jars, a beer bottle embedded in concrete; others invisible beneath successive layers of different-coloured wax.

The image is nailed onto the larger stick of the cross and wrapped in cellophane, which has protected it to an extent from the rain, but not from the ravages of the sun. It's a reproduction of an old master, with every look of having been torn out of a calendar, showing a young woman, seated, covered by an old pink dress and ample blue drapery over her knees; she wears her hair loose and her big Spanish eyes stare straight out at the observer. The naked child standing on her lap must be at least one, and stares out with the same dark eyes; a barely perceptible luminescence surrounds his curls, which are the same chestnut-brown as his mother's, who holds him with one hand—her left—under his buttocks, her right hand steadying him just above his navel. The left hand of the child, who has no need to hold on, rests on her right arm; his right seems to reach instinctively for his mother's breast. There's nothing else in the picture; in the dark background you can just make out the edge of a relief on which she's sitting.

The girl gets up and, glancing at me as if to say your turn, gets ready to leave.

"Why are you here?" I ask her.

"I flunked six subjects at school señor and came to ask them for help in my exams coming up."

"Why them?"

"They're very miraculous," she answers me.

I stay there for a while, sitting on the grass in the sunshine, but can't think of anything to ask them for. I get up to go, leaving no other offering than a butt stubbed out in one of the puddles of melted wax.

"YOUR FATHER WAS A BRAVE MAN," Professor Gagliardi comes out with at one point, I don't remember the context. "He fought for what he believed to be just, for a better society, for the rights of the least fortunate, at the expense of his own interests and the risk of his life, which he eventually laid down. He fought against mediocrity and hypocrisy, and they never forgave him for it. When I realised there was another young man amongst us willing to move heaven and earth for the sake of the truth, I knew in my heart it could only be his son. Seeing you confirmed it. You're as brave as he was. Your father would be proud of you."

I thank him for his words—or at least the intention they reveal—because I feel incapable of saying what I really think—that none of it's true. The professor's cloistered idealism was trying to make a hero out of an involuntary martyr, but the truth is that, in those days, in identical or worse circumstances, thousands and thousands of people had shown more bravery or dignity than this father of mine. And I, his worthy son, had sat at the table with those who betrayed him, concealing my identity and his, denying him, as he denied me, until the cock crowed itself hoarse; disguising with growing obstinacy my relationship with the man in the scarlet swimming trunks, so that, in a lost town I may never return to in my life, people whose opinion I care little about wouldn't feel uncomfortable when they spoke to me about him.

The professor does so now. But he seems different. For the first time there's something that looks like a smile on his face, perhaps the first beneficial effect of ridding himself of the fearsome marbled folder. He has another one in his lap—large, lined with faded spiderweb paper, open. It's a photo album, from Malihuel High School, and the picture in question is of a far more erect and hirsute Professor Gagliardi, who's now smiling openly, and under his insistently tapping index finger is the roguish gaze and rebellious quiff of a lad looking astonishingly like photos of me as a teenager, *pace* that ineffable period flavour. Towards the lower right corner a little girl, whose features leave me blank, holds a slate with white plastic letters, saying *Eva Perón Fiscal School No 16. Malihuel. First Grade, 1955.*

"It's the first one I have of him," Professor Gagliardi's voice says behind me. "There are two more, up to ninth grade; then they expelled him and he had to finish school in Fuguet. He always was a restless boy, never one to respect authority. Oddly enough, they're the ones you most remember over the years. I have other pictures of course, of later on, when he was grown-up. Look at him here, dressed up as a condom for the annual ceremony of the Comandante's statue. The bearded cabaret dancer peering out behind him is me. And here we are the two of us at the annual school-leavers dinner, must be around, erm let me think, the summer of … "

I don't need any more details. I remember that summer too, I must have been ten or eleven. I remember it especially for the unmistakeable yellow bow tie and blue shirt which the photo brings back to my memory, I remember the man wearing them, who one afternoon calls me over in the street, squats to examine my face and with a smile asks: You're Don Julián's grandson aren't you? Poli's son. Say hello to your Mamá from me. You know who I am don't you? before stroking my rebellious quiff, once, and breezing off down the sunny side of the street, whistling. Was this the memory

I'd ultimately come here to find? Was this the paltry fruit, the end product of so many days and nights that I'd lost count, the crowning of all my efforts, these alms? Or was I just imagining it, to leave a little less empty-handed, another delusion? In a way there's no difference, I told myself. Fantasy or memory, if I hadn't come, I'd never have found it.

Professor Gagliardi enthusiastically agrees to give me the photo.

THE RIGHT SIDE of Widower Gius's body became paralysed a few months after his wife died, which must have been why what in others is just a stage, a painful transition, was in him an essence that became part of his name for all time. But it didn't stop him living on—as if the death wish had been sucked in by his paralysed side, his other side had a ramp built in his house, widened a couple of doorframes, which the electric wheelchair he'd had sent over from Buenos Aires couldn't negotiate, and had the car fitted out so that he could drive around town or visit his estates whenever the reclusion started to get to him. He has to let go of the wheel to change gear and in any big city he'd be banned from driving. But in the jurisdiction of Malihuel the police turn a blind eye, on the strict condition that he goes no higher than third, or further than the neighbouring towns. Twice a day he stops at the corner of Los Tocayos—mornings to have breakfast over the newspaper, and evenings for a beer, or a vermouth and nibbles. Nene Larrieu serves it to him through the car window, like a drive-in movie, and anyone who comes over to chat sits in the passenger seat and sometimes orders something too—the Ford Falcon is his living room. My first afternoons at the bar I spent looking on at the ceremony without making any sense of it—I got to thinking Widower Gius was Malihuel's dealer (I wish) but the mixed bag of his companions' faces didn't quite fit. My problem was one of point of view—in the parked car, his good side faced the sidewalk, concealing the other half of the story, the one I needed to fill in the gaps. To help him at every turn he has a maid at home, who sleeps in (in his own bed, as evil tongues are quick to point out; the good ones adding that it's only to warm up his dead side, which gets horribly cold at night). Her name's Dorita, and she's the one who opens the door in the slate facade for me now, the morning I finally summon up the strength to visit.

My pupils closed to the white sun on the square can't adapt to the half-light of close-shuttered rooms—I can barely make out the outlines of furniture and ornaments on our way from the front door to the kitchen and out into the garden. Widower Gius is waiting for me in his wheelchair, his legs warmed by a light poncho and the rest of his body by the sun. His dead side isn't so shocking; it looks more asleep than dead. His speech is almost normal, just a touch of the card sharp with a fag in his mouth. He holds out his left hand and, ready, I take it in mine, he then offers me a maté, which he insists on brewing himself.

"We can look around the house after if you like, although except for the walls and the doors there are no reminders of the days your father and grandmother lived here. What the flood didn't ruin Chief of Police Greco took with him. Even had to have the wiring replaced my dear wife and I,

I reckon he left the doors because they were so swollen he couldn't get them out of the frames. We signed and paid for everything in good faith, but I understand you now wish to make a fair claim … "

I reassure him. I'm not here to discuss the ownership of the house, the thief was Greco and I'd get round to him later. Widower Gius's body visibly relaxes in his chair, and the look that accompanies his half-smile of relief softens. Sitting on a recently painted white bench, I look around the garden. An imposing lemon tree, its branches heavy with gleaming fruit, stands to my right in a round brick bed; further back a monumental wisteria forms a grotto in the angle of the wall, and between the two a double row of gnarled rose bushes, pruned for the winter. Behind me rises a jungle wall of plantains, somewhat frost-burnt, and a thick palm tree. On the other side of the path of yellow, grey and red flags grow plum and apple trees, and just the odd brick in the low party wall can be glimpsed between the lush branches of a redvein abutilon, a star jasmine and a Chinese hibiscus with crimson-red flowers; great kiskadees and green parakeets call to each other noisily from the highest branches; mockingbirds and thrushes sometimes come down to the grass and run around amongst the trees.

"Señora Delia had green fingers," Widower Gius speaks. "She planted almost everything you can see. Some my wife and I had to add because of the salt in the flood waters and all those years of neglect. I can't see the chief of police even putting in a geranium; but if I knew he'd planted anything, I'd have it pulled out."

I return his smile. I feel very good in this garden, much better than I probably would have felt inside the house, surrounded by objects preserved in the aspic of time—the plants have kept on growing. Dorita, who was waiting attentively by the kitchen door, obeying an invisible gesture from her boss, takes the maté away to change the yerba and when she comes back she's carrying a laced-up shoebox, which she hands to me. Intrigued I untie the string and lift the lid—it's overflowing with letters, in envelopes of different shapes and sizes, some yellowed with time, with stamps from a few years back; all unopened, addressed to Darío Ezcurra and to this house. The handwriting is familiar, the first I ever learnt to recognise.

"They started arriving the day we moved in," explains Widower Gius, "and they went on arriving regularly, all those years, till one day they stopped. Shortly after that I heard about the passing of your dear Mamá and I understood. They were probably arriving before too, but that fiend Greco must've destroyed them. I decided to keep them, supposing that someday someone might want them. I'm glad I wasn't wrong. I haven't opened any of them," he adds unnecessarily.

I do so at random. *Monday, August 1987*, Mamá had annotated on the upper line in her laboured schoolgirl hand, and beneath:

*Dearest Dario,*

*Dario im riting to tell you the latest news Don Albertos been down with a cold all winter but luckily hes getting better now me and Seniora Amelia insistid he stopt smoking but ive alredy told you how pigheded that man is worse than Mama over the bisines about our wedding he is see but i think hell change his mind in the long run me for my part i havent lost hope nor has Seniora Amelia luckily it wont be long before springs here i can picture the town now with the flowers and the new leaves coming out and the lagoon in the summer theres no beech neer here and the one there is is dirty and a long way away weve been sometimes but i didnt like it and i remember when we use to go to the Yacht Club with Mama and Papa makes me want to come back it does but they say i cant well Mama does coz Papa died a few years ago like i told you i dont know if people in town know cos it happened in Rosario and there was the funeral me i sometimes get scared the same will happen to Don Alberto me i dont tell them anything about you so Mama wont get mad she wont let me talk to anyone about you but i rite in secret and i dont tell anyone coz it make me so happy to be able to tell you Dario i think of all the things well have to tell when we see each other me every lovely thing i see or that happens to me i keep for you its so lovely for example when i dream im in Malihuel and were in the square having an icecream there at Don Braulios say hello to him for me when you see him and to your Mama Doña Delia as well it cant be long before her birthday can it Señora Amelia helped me to embroider some cushions and i was thinking about sending you both some only without the stuffing but i dont know coz of Mama Dario i miss our games at nite and i miss not having a foto of you too coz if i had one id hide it and not show it to anyone but at nite i can take it out and look at it but i dont know what to do if somebody from town comes maybe you can send it Auntie Porota used to come sometimes but its been a long time since she did i had reely bad toothache the other day and Seniora Amelia took me to the dentists i started crying coz i was scared but it stopped hurting afterwards*

*and our sons doing fine thank goodness i dont see him much coz he
has this important job and sometimes when i call him a machine
answers and i get all flustered like and hang up you should see how
lovely he is people say hes got my eyes or my mouth but to be honest
he looks more and more like you every day hes a very good boy youll
love him lots and youll feel proud of him i promise you well Dario i
cant think of anything else to tell you so ill say goodbye with kissis
i miss you my love ill rite soon.*

*Signed—Nora Julia Echezarreta*

"Didn't they ever tell her?" Widower Gius asks me once I've
finished, folded and put it back in its envelope and its box
with the others.

"She died without knowing," I say.

"WHAT NOW?" asks Guido. My zipped bag lies by his front
door, next to the box of Tuttolomondo pasta I'm taking with
me as a present, just as I used to every end of summer. I've
come over from Celia's because Guido's insisted on taking
me to the bus, which leaves in the small hours.

"I'm ready to go."

"Aren't you coming back?"

"Yeah, course I am. But in summer, on holiday, with my
family. To be continued ... but not here."

"How does it go on?"

"Greco. I'm going to report him and get his name on
all the lists of dirty war criminals. I'll contact HIJOS in
Buenos Aires and Rosario. Maybe we can organise a rally
against him. And that's just for starters. If I can get him

on some legal loophole or other I'll put my lawyer on it. I've got plenty of information now. I'd do the same with Neri and Rosas Paz, but the sons of bitches are dead. Whatever. I'll learn as I go along. It's not easy at my age, finding out you're the son of a *desaparecido*. That's stuff you go through when you're twenty. Then there's the business about filiation. You know Delia had a brother, who lives in Córdoba. I spoke to him to explain the situation and he sounded sort of cagey about it, so just to mindfuck him I asked him if he'd be willing to give blood for a DNA test. He told me he wasn't. So I offered to go over there and get it from him personally and he reconsidered and said yes. But I don't know if I'm going to get into all that. I guess not."

"What about the novel?"

"Eh?"

"At the start you said it was all for a novel. Was that just a cover story?"

"I guess so. I couldn't come up with anything better. I've got this friend who's a writer and has already written one about the things I told him, and he's already included a few pages about the town. He was the one who came up with the name Malihuel. And he called you Guido. Maybe he'll want to write this story too."


"THERE'S ONE THING I always forget to ask you," Iturraspe had remarked at one point during my farewell afternoon at Los Tocayos. "Why does everybody call you Fefe? Your name isn't Federico is it?"

"It's what Mamá used to call me, then my grandparents and everyone here. From my name and surname, Fe for Felipe—which Mamá later claimed was from Felipe in Mafalda, even though I was born before—and Fe for Félix—not Felix the Cat as some people think—but from my godfather Don Alberto Félix, who gave me his surname. That's my name. I'm Felipe Félix."

# Epilogue

A T THE END *of every summer my grandmother and sometimes my friends—Guido, Mati, Vicentito—would take it in turns to carry my suitcase as far as the corner of the Los Tocayos Hotel-Bar, where the Chevallier bus to Rosario, with a connection to Buenos Aires, used to stop in the evenings. At the end of every side street was the ever-present horizon and over it a half-disc of sun would still be hanging. But by that time the entire town had poured out onto the streets, which still smouldered like embers from the fire of the afternoon. To me, the image of that last walk at twilight through the living streets best captures the peculiar, faltering happiness of those years. That must be why the images of Malihuel are fused in my memory into one quintessential one, identical to all yet to none of them—me walking through the streets of a town that comes to life in summer and catches fire at sundown.*

*If dawn—when the cool air and lemon-coloured light bring out the outlines and differences between one thing and another, and infuse the town's early risers with energy—comes in answer to the dark dream of night, evening is a celebration of the end of the red-hot day, when life had to take refuge inside the houses, and the sun and the heat were the sole masters of the deserted streets. At siesta time everything hardens to withstand the sun—the buildings and the trees and even the flowers in the gardens seem to turn to stone, and grin and bear it. The town clenches like a fist, and waits.*

*Evening is the relaxation of all that pent-up tension. The doors and windows that were sealed against the light and heat are flung wide, releasing the breath held within; and the entire town spills unhurriedly out of its houses, softly, like a hand opening, to walk the sidewalks and streets, ride their bicycles, put their chairs out on the sidewalk, gather on every street corner, in shops and bars, to chat with neighbours. No one stays indoors at that time of day—all the life of Malihuel is out on the streets. As day recedes, the street lights catch fire—dimly, save in the two streets with mercury lamps—and the light of the houses spills yellow out of the open windows and doors, guiding passers-by from one to the other, like Chinese lanterns in a purple dusk. The town lights up as the surrounding fields darken, and it is never more beautiful or more fragile than the moment it seems to ripple over the plain, soft and evanescent like an alcohol flame in a half-lit room. Then, everything is fire—the houses are blue flames and the streets long flaming wicks, the trees torches, the vehicles embers, the people candles that move by themselves as if carried, and even the omnipresent dust, whipped up by the wind from the endless fields, becomes a smoky incense and softens the outlines, perfumed by successive passes of the sprinkler truck. Everything seems momentarily redeemed and justified by the grace of the light—as in Millet's* Angelus, *the world is one. It's nothing but an illusion of course—a hybrid of the magic of the light and the sentimentalism of the observer, who watches it now from the top of the coach that pulls inexorably away, and who could be forgiven for thinking, for a moment while the illusion lasts, that there is no better place on earth to live.*